MW00476912

The Duke's Masquerade

IMPROPER LORDS
BOOK ONE

BY MAGGI ANDERSEN

DRAGONBLADE
PUBLISHING, INC.

© Copyright 2023 by Maggi Andersen
Text by Maggi Andersen
Cover by Dar Albert

Dragonblade Publishing, Inc. is an imprint of Kathryn Le Veque Novels, Inc.
P.O. Box 23
Moreno Valley, CA 92556
ceo@dragonbladepublishing.com

Produced in the United States of America

First Edition April 2023
Trade Paperback Edition

Reproduction of any kind except where it pertains to short quotes in relation to advertising or promotion is strictly prohibited.

All Rights Reserved.

The characters and events portrayed in this book are fictitious. Any similarity to real persons, living or dead, is purely coincidental and not intended by the author.

ARE YOU SIGNED UP FOR DRAGONBLADE'S BLOG?

You'll get the latest news and information on exclusive giveaways, exclusive excerpts, coming releases, sales, free books, cover reveals and more.

Check out our complete list of authors, too!

No spam, no junk. That's a promise!

Sign Up Here

www.dragonbladepublishing.com

Dearest Reader;

Thank you for your support of a small press. At Dragonblade Publishing, we strive to bring you the highest quality Historical Romance from some of the best authors in the business. Without your support, there is no 'us', so we sincerely hope you adore these stories and find some new favorite authors along the way.

Happy Reading!

CEO, Dragonblade Publishing

ADDITIONAL DRAGONBLADE BOOKS BY AUTHOR MAGGI ANDERSEN

Improper Lords Series
The Duke's Masquerade

The Never Series
Never Doubt a Duke
Never Dance with a Marquess
Never Trust an Earl
Never Keep a Secret at Christmas (Novella)
Bella's Christmas Wish (Novella)
The Duke's Brown-Eyed Lady (Novella)

Dangerous Lords Series
The Baron's Betrothal
Seducing the Earl
The Viscount's Widowed Lady
Governess to the Duke's Heir
Eleanor Fitzherbert's Christmas Miracle (A Novella)

Once a Wallflower Series
Presenting Miss Letitia
Introducing Miss Joanna
Announcing Miss Theodosia

The Lyon's Den Series
The Scandalous Lyon

Pirates of Britannia Series
Seduced by the Pirate

Also from Maggi Andersen
The Marquess Meets His Match
Beth
White Lady Lost

"Doubt thou the stars are fire; Doubt that the sun doth move; Doubt truth to be a liar; But never doubt I love."

Hamlet by William Shakespeare

DEDICATION

This book is for my husband, David, who listens tirelessly when I talk (endlessly) about my stories, and whose support means so much.

Prologue

Cloudhill, Ashford, Kent
February, 1815

As Tate entered the hall from the stables, the butler, Knox, approached him. "The duke has arrived from London, my lord. He wishes to see you in the library."

Tate glanced at his dishevelment in the long gilt-edged mirror. He considered whether to change out of his riding clothes then decided against it. This must be important. "Thank you, Knox."

When Tate entered the library, the duke rose from his seat behind the desk. Shocked, Tate noticed the deep creases on his father's face. His skin was alarmingly gray.

Feeling apprehensive, Tate crossed the carpet. "You wished to see me, sir?"

"I have a grave matter to discuss with you, son."

"Yes, of course." His father had never called him son. As the spare, Tate had never been his father's favorite, but Edward was dead.

The duke staggered toward Tate and his knees buckled. He slumped to the floor.

"Papa!" Tate ran to kneel beside him. His father's breathing sounded raspy. Tate rose and ran to pull the bell cord for the

1

butler, then returned to ease the cravat away from his father's throat. "Papa, I've rung for Knox. He'll send for a doctor."

"No time." His father groaned, his face crumpled in agony. "You must be brave, Tate. And wise beyond your years. I rely on you. You won't let us down."

His head fell back.

Through eyes blurred with tears, Tate saw his father was dead.

Chapter One

Six weeks later

IN THE LIBRARY, His Grace Tarleton Fanshawe, Duke of Lindsey, gloomily stirred the flames to life with a poker. The enormous fireplaces ate up coal, and the lofty rooms remained chilly throughout the coldest months. Or, at least, that was how it felt to Tate today. With his father's body resting in the family vault, all the concerns of keeping this family afloat lay heavily on his shoulders. And there was the question of his father's will, which offered scant clue as to the disaster that had befallen them. His father had passed away before he could explain what caused this calamity. The only thing Tate knew was that his father expected him to resolve it.

"I think I make good sense, Tate," his Uncle Clive, Earl of Butte, said from where he sat in the burgundy leather winged armchair. "Marrying Ianthe Granville hardly condemns you to a life of purgatory." He put his brandy glass on the occasional table and rose to stalk the deep maroon and cream Aubusson carpet, his thumbs tucked into his waistcoat pockets, stretching black silk over his wide girth. "She's a delightful young woman. And no surprises. You've known each other since you were children."

There seemed no way to distract his uncle from his favorite subject. Tate's marriage. He gritted his teeth. It was like a stab to the heart every time he referred to it. "We have a friendship of long standing." He wasn't about to confess his feelings for Ianthe. He wouldn't ruin her future happiness by bringing her family down.

"An excellent foundation for marriage," his uncle continued, warming to his theme. "Friendship, as well as the joining of two noble families. These modern love-matches don't wear nearly as well."

"Ianthe deserves better." Tate refused to think about his own needs. That no longer mattered. Far more important issues had wiped out any chance of his marrying for years.

Clive's graying eyebrows snapped together. "She'd be marrying a duke. Few women would turn their noses up at that."

Tate lit a cheroot and inhaled deeply. "Dashed if I'll marry Ianthe or any lady whose fortune far exceeds mine. There are names for such men."

"You are too sensitive. We accept unions of this type among noble families as a matter of course."

No longer the joining of two great estates, though, Tate refrained from pointing out. "You wish me to go cap in hand to the earl and explain to him I wish to marry his daughter, despite being little more than a pauper?"

His uncle huffed. "It's regrettable that the Lindsey holdings are mortgaged against Cloudhill. They shall have to be re-financed. You are not in Dun Street, but you must employ strict changes while you rely on the money from those leases to keep things afloat. Hopefully, in a year or two, the financial situation will improve, but without the million pounds invested in Cloudhill…" He hit the arm of the chair with his fist as distress and anger contorted his usually benign features.

"Not good enough, is it?" Tate said bitterly. "I no longer have what Ianthe's father would expect."

He felt so cast down, so damnably tired. And he must dredge some energy from somewhere to fight this confusing and alarming state of affairs.

Ianthe. He wasn't sure how she felt about him. Although he'd always sensed…but nothing had ever been expressed between them. Knowing her as he did, she would expect a marriage filled with excitement and passion. Unpalatable as Tate had little to offer her apart from himself, burdened with financial troubles and the concerns of his mother and sisters. He would make a very poor bargain. And he very much doubted the earl, a canny man, would accept his suit, as things stood. Tate needed time. Time to discover what had caused his father to sign over Cloudhill, which had been the Lindseys' country seat for centuries, to a gambling hell owner named Donovan.

Tate tightened his jaw. No, dash it all, he wouldn't give up on his dream to one day marry Ianthe if she'd have him. But he wasn't about to tell his uncle that, for it would only add fuel to the fire.

He slouched in the chair, a cheroot burning in his fingers, a half glass of brandy on a table at his elbow. How was he to go about seeking information to help him? He could hardly go poking about like a Bow Street Runner, or even employ one, without it appearing in the gossip sheets. It would spread all over London in no time. There was no alternative. He must somehow get inside Donovan's club. His uncle would object to this plan, of course, and his mother, devastated to lose his father, would be utterly horrified. His sister, Emily, soon to turn eighteen, expected to make her come-out next spring, and he refused to see her become the subject of unsavory gossip. How would the elder of his two sisters, delicate Clara, handle this news? She'd become seriously ill during her London debut last year and was convalescing with their Aunt Mary, who lived in a village near Oxford. News of her condition was not encouraging. His mother had made the journey to Kennington several times to see her, and came home looking ill herself.

Tate regarded his uncle, who stood ramrod straight before a portrait of Tate's father, tall and handsome in his ducal robes of scarlet wool with a collar of white miniver fur, worn on a ceremonial occasion in the House of Lords.

"How *could* Richard have done such a thing?" Uncle Clive asked again. He turned and stalked the carpet. "Naturally, he suffered financial pressures, a few disappointing investments which have yet to prosper, but nothing that would warrant such an action. Must have gone raving mad." His troubled gaze rested on Tate. "I'm trying not to think too badly of the brother I've always been fond of, or upset your mother and sisters who are unutterably sad, but it's a blasted mystery."

Tate stood and flicked his cheroot into the fireplace. A hand resting on the mantel, he watched the flames turn it to ash. "Papa wasn't a gambler."

"Richard preferred conversation to gambling at social engagements. He enjoyed the odd hand of faro at Whites, but nothing extreme. At home, he preferred chess to whist. The only gambles he took were taking a chance on some share or other on the 'Change, and even then, not without the assurances of his broker."

"This betting slip, or vowel as they are called, bearing my father's signature, must be a forgery," Tate said bitterly.

"Why did he not declare it so?"

"I wish I knew. But I suspect my father was about to tell me when he died."

"To confess? He was seen at the Lexicon club. There's a witness."

"Witnesses can be bribed." Tate tossed back the last of his brandy. It traveled in a slow burn down his throat but failed to warm him. "Papa didn't have time to deal with it. He knew he was going to die and looked to me to fix this."

"Eh? That's all very well. But I don't see how you can. It's done, Tate. Once the contract is drawn up, we will be obliged to sign it, and the family has a few months before you must all vacate Cloudhill. In the meantime, there's much to be done. You'll need to employ a secretary. Your father let Cedric Lynch go over some disagreement. The thoroughbreds will have to be put up for auction at Tattersalls, most of the staff let go, and then your mother and Emily must come to us in Butte Court until matters are settled. Your mother has expressed little desire to stay in London, not while in mourning."

Tate drew in a sharp breath. "Then I'd best get cracking. I'll leave for London tomorrow morning."

"To do what exactly?"

"To see this Bernard Donovan for a start."

His uncle's eyebrows peaked. "Donovan is a gangster. Would you venture into London's seedier gambling houses and tackle a gang of thugs? The men who run those places for Donovan are cutthroats." His expression turned stricken. "You have barely reached your majority. Must we also lose you?" He sadly shook his head. "And it would do no good."

"I shall take the greatest care." Tate sounded so purposeful to his ears, while he was hardly confident of success. Somehow, he must infiltrate Donovan's Lexicon Club and discover what caused his father to become indebted to this Irishman. But he admitted it was fraught with problems. If he was spotted gambling at the Lexicon Club, it would be all around London in an instant. Difficult then to delay the news about the loss of Cloudhill. Once that reached the *ton,* it would be on everyone's lips for a year. Many would suspect why Tate visited the Lexicon, including Donovan. The man owned two gambling hells, and now, although Tate could barely countenance it, Cloudhill.

"Better surely, to propose to Ianthe," Clive said. "You shall have to find a wealthy bride."

Tate could consider marrying no one but Ianthe. "I will go today to see her, but I'm not about to commit myself."

"Foolish of you," his uncle growled.

Trouble was he quite saw his uncle's point. Right now, the family's future looked bleak indeed. "I beg you to be patient, uncle."

With a groan, his uncle shook his head. "I see I shall have to be. I'll put it about that you are mourning your father and will not attend to business matters for several weeks. That might keep some creditors from the door. But I don't imagine it will last long. Sentiment is seldom found in business."

Tate laid a hand on his uncle's shoulder. "I am very grateful for your support, Uncle Clive."

His uncle patted his arm then made for the door. "I'll pay my respects to your mother. Bellows tells me she's in the conservatory potting begonias. Says it calms her nerves. Probably does. Uninspiring plants." He turned, his hand on the door latch. "I shan't ask for details concerning this plan of yours, Tate. I doubt my heart could stand it."

"Nothing dangerous, I assure you," Tate hastened to say, although that might not be the case. "Please don't worry."

"Promise me you'll be careful, boy." Clive stared at him for a moment and then left the room.

By road, the Earl of Granville's estate was twelve miles distant, but Tate shortened the journey by riding across country. In the woods, nesting birds flocked noisily in the trees. Emerging into the sunlight, Tate jumped his gelding Bayard over a fence and galloped across the meadows, scattering sheep.

While leading his chestnut by the rein over the grass, he spotted Ianthe by the brook, a lock of golden hair falling forward over her shoulder as she peered into the water.

She looked up and saw him approach. "Tate!" The satin lining of her straw bonnet graced her blue eyes with violet depths. "Well, this is a pleasant surprise."

His heart constricted as he released Bayard to tear at the grass. He sank down beside her, searching the bubbling stream. "What is of such interest in the water?"

"Nothing, really." Her fair-skinned cheeks flushed. "The brook reminds me of a poem."

"One you have penned?"

"No. Samuel Taylor Coleridge's sonnet, *To the River Otter*."

"And you hoped to find an otter here?" he asked, smiling.

She huffed. "I knew you'd tease me. I shan't tell you more.

You've no interest in poetry. So don't pretend to."

He shrugged sheepishly and stood. "Sorry, Ianthe, if you care to recite the poem, I promise to listen."

She climbed to her feet and arranged the skirts of her yellow muslin gown. "I have no intention of boring you."

"You never could." Keeping hold of Bayard's reins, he offered her his free hand to climb the bank.

When Ianthe put her small hand in his, the touch of her soft skin made his breath hitch.

She flushed as if she felt it, too. "I shan't scold you. Losing your father so suddenly has shocked and saddened us all. Mama and Papa have lost a good friend. The duke was always kind to me. I shall remember him in my prayers."

A lump threatened to block his throat as he murmured his thanks. He desperately wanted to hold her, to talk of a future together. But it was impossible. Past events had caused him to keep his feelings secret. His brother, Edward's, unexpected death from influenza a year ago, which plunged the family into mourning, and Ianthe's father's decree she could not marry before her sister, Cecily. And now, his father's death and the upheaval that brought.

There had been no mention of romance between them. While he hoped Ianthe cared for him, he wasn't sure. Tate hadn't forgotten the game they had played at a house party a year ago when it was required for them to kiss. He realized in that moment he loved her. His heart swelled and his lighthearted mood deepened to desire. Afraid he'd give too much away, he had stepped away before his lips touched hers.

What if he had kissed her? It was unhelpful to dwell on it now. He smiled as Ianthe chatted about her London Season and how horrid her gown for her presentation in the queen's drawing room was. "I look like a silk balloon in it," she said with a grimace.

Ianthe would look lovely in a turnip sack. "I remember Clara saying something similar about her presentation gown." *Clara.*

His shoulders tensed. Was his sister well enough to withstand this debacle they found themselves in?

"Will you come to the house to see Stephen?" Ianthe asked. "He's down from Oxford for a week and is working on some paper in the library."

The prospect of seeing her brother, a good friend, eased an icy knot in his stomach. "I shall indeed."

They walked across the greensward toward the stable yard.

"Mama tells me we are invited to a masquerade next month. Shall we see you there?"

"Yes, in evening clothes. I draw the line at dressing as a court jester or Henry VIII."

"I'm a fairy princess. My costume is blue with sparkles. And I'm to wear Mama's tiara."

He smiled, imagining how lovely she would look. All the men would surround her like wolves, he thought with a sad pull at his heart. "Then I certainly will come. Save the waltz for me?"

"I will. Dancing with a duke shall make me the envy of all debutantes and set tongues wagging."

He supposed it would until some other man claimed her.

She darted a glance at him. "When you went up to London last year, you told me you disliked balls."

"I don't dislike them. I just didn't particularly warm to them. Ballrooms are crowded and overheated, and the ladies peer at a fellow and gossip behind their fans." It would be even worse now, Tate thought.

"Then I expect we shan't see you at Almack's either. Mama has procured vouchers from Lady Jersey."

He shook his head. His bachelor friends avoided the place like the plague. "Not this year."

They walked on in silence, and then with a carefree lilt in her voice, Ianthe said, "Countess Lieven has introduced the waltz this year."

Aware he disappointed her, he said, "Almack's is a marriage mart." Ianthe was the only partner he wished for the waltz. But what good would it do to tell her the whole truth and have her desperately sorry for him when she should enjoy her first time in London?

She eyed him carefully. "And you don't wish to marry."

"My mother will expect me to be discreet and observe a period of mourning, although I shall be in London to engage a secretary. There's a pile of correspondence awaiting me."

She bit her lip and turned to him, her eyes wide. "Oh, I am sorry, Tate. That was thoughtless of me. You have so much to worry you."

He smiled. "I wish I could be in London. I look forward to our waltz."

Ianthe ducked her head. "You know, since Cecily married, there was some talk about you and me..." Her voice fell away and she flushed.

Did she care for him? Tate's spirits soared and then plummeted, leaving him crushed. He'd longed for a sign she wanted him, but not now, not when it wasn't fair to ensnare her. It was so painful he feared she would see it. He turned his attention to his horse, who was investigating a clump of nettles. The last thing he wanted was to embroil her in the mess which was now his life, and he shoved away the urge to hold her, although he needed to desperately. The news that they'd lost their estate had yet to reach London, although Cloudhill's uncertain future had spread among his servants. They would soon have to be told the worst.

"Good thing you don't want a prosaic fellow like me," he said.

Ianthe nervously touched her tongue to her bottom lip, drawing his gaze there.

Tate steeled himself. "I know the sort of husband you would like. A charming fellow," he said, forcing lightness into his voice. "Someone who will spend every Season in London and escort you uncomplainingly to every function."

Her gaze grew fiery. "I want no man to dance attention on me, but yes, he must adore me. Foolish of them to think we might marry when you've always been more like one of my brothers. But I hope we can always be friends, Tate."

The hurt in her voice twisted his stomach. "You don't make a man feel at all brotherly," he said, refusing to allow her to think that of him. "I'm not blind, Ianthe. You are a beguiling woman." She'd always caused a fuss among the men at the Assembly dances, and would do so in London. He struggled to conquer the jealousy eating at him.

"Pish. You are good at offering compliments to a lady. When you know you are safe."

His laugh strained, he pulled off his hat and swiped back his hair. Was it foolish to hope for a miracle? "I daresay I shall have to marry, eventually," he conceded.

Her sad gaze searched his. "A duke will need an heir."

He could not ask her to wait. Although the words hovered on his tongue. "Certainly, I hope to in the future."

Ianthe's pale forehead creased. She wanted him to tell her what had happened. Why everything had turned on its head and changed him. Had he hurt her? He refused to cry poor, and bemoan the disaster that had befallen his family. As things stood, he wouldn't be able to offer her a good life with him for several years. Unless he uncovered something to put a stop to this mad claim. For now, he must accept the bitter reality. While Ianthe was about to make her debut where there would be suitors to please her father, Tate's dreary future threatened to plunge him into financial turmoil. Impossible to imagine Cloudhill lost to them.

She shook her head and was about to speak when Bayard chose that moment to nudge Tate's shoulder with his head. Tate grinned and stroked the white star on the horse's forehead. "He wishes to visit your mare, Freckles."

Ianthe patted the horse's glossy neck. "Leave Bayard with the groom. Warren will take care of him." She picked up her skirts and hurried over the grass. "You will take tea with us? Cook heard you were planning to visit and made your favorite Queen cakes."

"Excellent. The ride has given me an appetite." He smiled, admiring her slim body in butter yellow like a willowy flower, and for a moment, enjoyed that warm rush he always felt in her company. The man who married her would be a lucky sod. Bayard pulled at the rein as they neared the paddocks where horses thrust their heads over the fence to watch them.

He left Bayard with the groom, and they walked to the handsome redbrick mansion with long windows and towering roof. Tate remembered his uncle saying the earl was a smart man. He'd invested wisely. Besides the Granvilles' two daughters, there were five boys: Stephen was the eldest, Colin, two years younger, also at Oxford. William and Frederick both attended Eton, while Bertie was tutored at home. Tate had always enjoyed coming here, but today he felt as if he'd stepped out of his skin. He would hate to be viewed as a needy suitor with pockets to let.

At twenty-three, Stephen was two years younger than Tate. He had chosen a career in academia. Tate found him bent over the library desk. He raised his blond head from his books, and his blue eyes behind his glasses brightened. Pushing back his chair, he came to offer Tate his hand.

Tate gave it a hearty shake. "Always with your nose in some ancient tome. Can't be good for a fellow," he teased. "I haven't forgotten my promise to drag you off to London to get up to mischief. It might be a while before we do, though."

Stephen sympathetically eyed his black armband. "I'm sorry I missed the funeral. Dashed awful, Tate. How are you all faring?"

"My mother finds it difficult, of course. Uncle Clive is looking after them as I'm off to London tomorrow. I need to see the barrister I've been clerking for. I shan't continue with the law."

"What a shame. You'll have a lot to take on now, I expect," Stephen said. "I wish you well with all of it, Tate."

"Thank you," Tate said grimly. "As I'm invited to tea with your mother and sisters, I should join them."

"I'll come with you. Could do with a break from trying to

decipher an obscure passage of ancient Greek." Stephen settled his glasses over his nose and glanced at Tate hopefully. "I don't suppose you could help?"

"No sense in asking me," Tate said with a firm shake of his head. "I put all that behind me with some eagerness."

Stephen headed for the door. "But you broke some records in athletics and excelled at rowing. Some still talk of it."

"Had some great times there," Tate admitted. It seemed a long time ago when he expected a rosy future lay ahead of him. "I made some good friends." And he had enjoyed mathematics and history.

In the morning room, three decorative ladies and a boy sat around the tea table. A small terrier and a gray cat lay side by side before the hearth. The dog bounced to his feet, annoying the cat, and rushed over, tail wildly wagging.

"Good to see you, fellow." Tate bent to pat him.

"You would greet Tate before me?" Stephen said in mock annoyance. "Shame on you, Felix."

"He sees you every day," Tate said with a laugh. "I'm a novelty."

Lady Granville sat beside Cecily on the sofa. Ianthe in a chintz chair. Her mother held out her hands to him. "Tate! Come and give me a kiss, you poor boy."

Crushed against a large bosom, Tate was engulfed in a waft of scented powder. Then he turned to greet Bertie while Cecily smiled sadly.

Gerald, Cecily's husband, entered the room and strode over to shake Tate's hand and ask him how he fared.

The maids brought in trays, and tea was served. Tate sat back as their sympathy for his father's death washed over him. While he appreciated it more than he could say, he needed to be strong for what awaited him in London. When he left here, the period of life he'd enjoyed as a feckless younger son, and a friend and neighbor of this wonderful family, might well be at an end. For who knew where he would be? His heart heavy, he turned to

Bertie, who could be relied upon for an enlivening, if unpredictable, conversation.

※》》《《

CECILY CURLED UP in Ianthe's bedchamber chair, holding up her wedding band and engagement ring to the sunlight. "I hoped Tate would propose, especially now that Gerald and I are married."

"Well, he didn't." Seated before the mirror, Ianthe gave a careless shrug as she removed the pins from her hair. She met her sister's gaze in the glass, a little envious of her happiness.

"He has to marry someone now he's the duke. He'll need an heir." Cecily giggled. "Gerald says he wants a spare, too."

Ianthe seized her brush and stroked it through her tangled, curly locks. She still wasn't sure of Tate's feelings. There was that time at the Frobisher's house party when the game required them to kiss. As he bent his head toward hers, kissing Tate, when she'd thought of nothing else for months, made her suddenly shy. He had drawn away with a laugh. Had it been her fault? Or did he just not think about her that way?

Cecily taunted their ginger cat with the tassels on a cushion. "Mama will be very disappointed."

"Poor Mama. Her hopes are dashed. She's fond of Tate, and hoped I would one day live at Cloudhill."

"But you want to marry him? Why don't you tell him how you feel?"

"And make him feel obliged to ask for my hand?" The thought horrified her. Ianthe put down the brush and swiveled on the stool. "Tate has just lost his father. He has much to deal with." She smoothed an errant curl and gave a puff of annoyance when it defied her ministrations. "And, anyway, I want a man who cannot live without me. Who loves me desperately." Tate didn't want her enough, whatever difficulties he faced. He was prepared to stand by and see her become betrothed to another man. And her father would certainly urge her to do so. She turned from the mirror. "No matter how much I might hope Tate wished to marry me, I must accept that he doesn't." Although she still believed he cared for her. She remembered how his hands lingered when he lifted her down from the horse, how he looked at her, really looked at her, as if they shared a secret, and especially when he teased her and made her laugh. Could she have been so wrong and so foolish to believe it was love?

"Seems a terrible shame, though," Cecily said, eyeing her sadly. "When you always seemed so perfect for each other."

"Nothing like that was ever said between us. You were always confident about Gerald's love, weren't you? Tate and I could make each other very unhappy." She wished she could believe that; it might help. Her tight throat made it hard to hide her distress. She forced a bright smile on her lips. "I shall go to London next month and dance with every gentleman who asks me." She picked up her brush again as her vision blurred in the mirror. "And have a wonderful time!"

Chapter Two

ON THE WAY to London, Tate's coach was forced to stop at Tenterden after a horse threw a shoe. Tate, tense, and burdened by the inexplicable problems he now must deal with, left the blacksmith's and strolled along the wide village High Street to stretch his legs. He arrived at the Ship Inn, a neat establishment of white painted brick with walls covered in ivy, and stepped inside for a mug of ale.

In the busy taproom smelling of warm bodies, smoke, and hops, he gazed around for a spare seat. Every table was taken. In a corner, a gentleman sat alone, his head bowed over the tankard in his hand. Tate put a hand on the spare chair. "Mind if I sit here?"

"Certainly." The man waved him into the seat. He raised his head.

"Dear God." Tate sank down because he wasn't sure his legs would hold him. It was like staring into a mirror.

Startled, familiar green eyes observed him. "Exactly," the man said in a croak. "Who are you, sir?"

"Tarleton Fanshawe, Duke of Lindsey," he said as his ale arrived. He took a deep sip and wiped the froth from his lips. "And you are?"

"Bret Kilbridge, Your Grace."

Tate shook his head, bewildered. "Are you my long-lost twin brother?"

"I don't believe so. Do you have one?"

Tate sat back and studied him intently, noting the olive tones of his lean face and high cheekbones. "Confound it, man, not that I know of. Where are you from?"

"This village, Your Grace. My father, Adrian Kilbridge, was the vicar here. I'm on my way to take up a position as tutor to Mr. Baillieu's son in Clare."

"Call me Tate. We could be distantly related. The resemblance is remarkable, although I've never heard your family name mentioned."

"You wouldn't. But my grandfather was Sir Edward Bainstoke. The family turned their back on my mother when she married my father."

"Don't know him." Tate finished his ale and turned in his chair to signal to the servant. "Allow me to get you another."

"Thank you. I could use it."

"Have you any brothers or sisters?" Tate asked.

"No. Just me. My father hoped I'd follow him into the church, but it wasn't something I wanted to do."

"The vocation isn't for everyone."

"No. I would have preferred the army, but that wasn't to be."

"Your hair is several shades lighter than mine," Tate observed.

Bret nodded. He leaned forward. "Your nose, if you pardon my saying so, has a slight bump."

"Broke it playing football at Oxford."

"You were at Oxford? I always wanted to go."

"Did you? Tough luck."

"I was fortunate. My father, an educated man, taught me the classics."

"Then you are probably more familiar with them than me. I was an indifferent scholar. Prefer being outdoors." Tate eyed Bret's tall physique. "We aren't so very different in build. How tall are you?"

Bret shrugged. "Over six feet."

A plan began to take shape. But would Bret agree? Tate pushed back his chair. Bret rose, and they stood back-to-back before a smoky mirror hanging on the wall. "You're about a half inch taller than me."

"You are broader in the shoulders," Bret said, raising his voice above a loud argument which had erupted at the next table. Something about whose bull would bring the better price at market.

They sat again. "Keep your voice down," Tate said to Bret.

Bret's eyebrows rose. "Why?"

Tate leaned forward to study him closely, still caught by the uncanny resemblance. Having dealt with the shock, his mind was busy enlarging on his idea. At least, in theory, it looked like a perfect way to free him up to take on Donovan. But there was much to work through, not least Bret's participation, and if he could play the part. "With a touch of hair dye, those who don't know me well would never suspect you."

"Suspect me of what?" Bret looked alarmed. "Dye my hair? And why should I do that?"

The potboy placed two tankards on the table.

"Drink up," Tate said, making a snap decision. "I'll explain more while we travel. My coach is at the stables down the road."

"Traveling? Where? I'm about to catch the stage for Sudbury and make my way to Clare."

"I have a proposition to put to you. But my carriage will take you to Clare if you prefer it. Do you have your heart set on teaching some reluctant young man his letters in a drab village? Or would you like to engage in an adventure?"

Bret looked wary. "I shall need to know more, Your Grace."

"Take my place in London society. A month at the most. You'll be well compensated, and I'm happy to find you a new position, should you wish it."

"Become you?" Bret gasped. "But that's absurd. I don't know how to behave like a duke."

"As I have only just inherited the title, I doubt much will be expected of me. Or you, for that matter. If you accept my proposal, that is."

Bret eyed the black armband. "May I offer my condolences? But still…"

"I shall instruct you. I imagine, as the vicar's son, you have mixed a good deal in society? Visited the big houses in the district? Attended the assembly dances?"

"Yes, but that's hardly managing a large estate, and knowing how to address the *ton*, let alone the ladies." His eyes, more hazel than green, widened. "What if the Prince regent wishes to meet me?"

"According to the newspapers, the regent is caught up with celebrating the Duke of Wellington's success in the war at Waterloo."

"Still hard to believe the long war is over at last."

"Yes, Napoleon finally beat," Tate said. "And London awash with visitors enjoying the festivities. I've never met the regent, but he knew my father."

Bret's eyebrows shot up. "That is precisely why I cannot do it."

"Should he engage you in conversation, talk about art, sculpture, or books; he's an aesthete."

"I know little about paintings. I didn't make the grand tour," he said with a hint of irony. "Anyone else I should avoid?"

"I don't believe so. A friend of mine, the viscount, Hartley Montford, will be in London. I'll write to Hart and ask him to make himself known to you. As I'm in mourning, you need only appear at the odd affair and slip away before anyone engages you in conversation. A black armband will deter strangers from approaching you. That will be enough for people to see I'm in London. I don't want people questioning where I am. It would get back to my family and they have enough to deal with. I'll furnish you with a list of those who might approach you."

Panic widened Bret's eyes. "A list?"

"Not a long list. I don't expect any of my friends to be in the city. And if they are, it's highly unlikely they'd attend a ball. Don't worry. We'll spend a few weeks at my hunting box before London. I'll school you well."

Bret studied him. "Why do you want to do this?"

"There's something...covert I must do. You'll understand more when I clarify it. As I've explained, your presence in society is to prevent questions about my whereabouts."

"If I don't make an appalling hash of it. Is this thing you're about to embark on dangerous? What if you get killed?"

"I don't intend to; my family depends on me." Tate shrugged. "But one never knows."

Alarmed, Bret said, "And you *will* tell me what this is all about?"

Would he agree to the scheme? "I promise to fill you in on everything you need to know. Once we reach the hunting box."

Tate hoped he could persuade Bret, but knew he asked a lot of him. But he had not said no. Strange, that after feeling as if heavy weight bowed him down, a restless energy made him keen to carry out his plan. It would be intriguing to become someone else for a while. Someone who didn't have to answer to anyone. This was just what he needed, to be free to pursue the course of action he'd set for himself. But could Bret pull it off? He was obviously intelligent, an educated man. And was Tate mad to try it? He gritted his teeth, considering his only other option. To accept Cloudhill was lost to them, and this he would not do. "Can't keep my horses waiting," he said. "Sorry to rush you, but you must say yea or nay."

For a long minute, Bret stared at him, and then slowly nodded. "I was bitterly disappointed not to join the army and fight for my country, but my father was ill, and I had to remain at home to help with parish duties. Father passed away a few months ago. My home is no longer mine now that a new vicar has been appointed."

"That would have been hard. So, what do you think?"

"When I rose from my bed this morning, I never expected to

embark on an escapade. My life was laid out for me, steady, reliable, if a little dull. I must admit, this has a certain appeal." He shrugged. "Who knows where it might lead?"

"That's the spirit," Tate said, clapping him on the back, relieved that Bret had responded to the call of adventure. They were not so different, it seemed.

They left the inn and walked along the street toward the stables.

Bret turned to Tate. "I have a horrible suspicion I'll come to regret this."

"You can still refuse if you wish. We can discuss it further on the way. Pull up your collar and draw your beaver brim down over your face. No sense in alarming my staff until I've explained."

They approached the lacquered blue and gold coach, the gray horses standing in the traces. The liveried footman, John, put down the steps while Charlie, the groom, sat on the box with the coachman. They stared with surprise at Bret.

"Milson, I've changed my mind about London," Tate said. "We go to the hunting lodge in Epping Forest. The caretaker, Mr. Moody, and his wife will take good care of us."

His father's coachman was too well schooled to question the order. Despite hunting being out of season, and the prospect of few staff in residence, he nodded pleasantly.

"While I don't want you to drive the horses too hard, I hope to get there before dark."

"Shouldn't be a problem, Your Grace."

John took Bret's luggage and strapped it to the back of the coach.

Bret followed Tate into the interior and sank onto the soft butter yellow leather squab as the footman closed the door. The coach drew out onto the road.

Bret looked around. "This certainly beats the stage."

"There's one other thing I should have mentioned," Tate said. "You are likely to meet Ianthe. You must invite her to dance.

I promised her a waltz."

"Ianthe?"

"Lady Ianthe Granville. My neighbor's daughter."

"How will I recognize her?"

"She's a blonde Venus and will eclipse most of the women there."

"Is she your young lady? Do you have an understanding?"

"No," Tate said bluntly. "Merely a good friend."

Bret removed his hat and smoothed back his hair. "If she knows you so well, she'll see through my disguise immediately."

"With half the male population at her feet, I doubt it." But Tate wasn't entirely sure. Ianthe was observant. "I said I'd dance with her at the masquerade. You will be disguised, which will help. Please pay your respects to her mother."

"A masquerade?"

"Many wear costumes, but I said I would wear evening attire. You shall need a mask. There's always an unmasking at midnight; best leave the ball before then. You won't find a problem at Lindsey Court, my house in Mayfair. I'll write to my butler, Knox, who you'll find is discreet. He'll attend to anything you require. My valet is away visiting his family."

"Won't Lady Ianthe guess?" Bret asked with a worried frown.

Tate wasn't sure Bret would pass muster with Ianthe, but he didn't want to dissuade him. "Not if we do something with your hair and you keep most of your face hidden."

"There could be several attractive blonde women there that evening. How will I avoid approaching the wrong one?"

"She will be in blue. Dressed as a fairy princess."

"But there may be more than one fairy princess."

"It's possible, but none are as lovely as Ianthe. Her eyes are bright blue, her hair is the color of butter, and she has three golden freckles on her nose."

Bret eyed him, looking skeptical. "Not your girl, eh?" he said wryly.

"No. We are neighbors."

"As many people in England have blue eyes, will I have to peer at her nose to identify her?" Bret leaned back against the soft squab and folded his arms. "I feel better already," he added in a dry tone.

Tate pictured her long legs in his mind's eye and smiled. "Ianthe's quite tall." He noted Bret's use of hair wax. "You'll need a haircut. The popular style is a more casual, unruly look."

"Unruly?" Bret studied Tate's hair and narrowed his eyes. "You aren't a dashed fop, are you? Pardon, Your Grace, but I refuse to become one."

"Lord, no." Tate pushed a careless hand through his hair. "I'm not known for adopting the latest fashions. Have little interest in it. But you will have to dress well. As the new duke, you're on display." He stroked his chin. "I shall have to send for my tailor. I can give you some of my clothes, but you'll need evening attire. Shoes and riding boots too," he said, eyeing Bret's feet. "You might receive an invitation to ride in Rotten Row." He glanced at Bret. "You can ride?"

"What, brought up in the country and not ride?" Bret grinned, obviously pleased to find something not to feel inadequate about.

"Yes, of course. Beg pardon," Tate said. "Now I'll give you a quick summation of what to expect…"

As the thoroughbreds made quick work of the miles, Tate watched Bret for signs he might renege.

"I might have lost my mind," Bret said finally. "I suspect the study of ancient languages will prove far easier than becoming a faux duke."

Some hours later, tired and hungry, they arrived at the hunting lodge. Dusk had turned to night, the moon shining through the dense forest. Mr. Moody and his wife hurried out to greet them. Moody held a lantern up, and after managing an awkward bow, said how good it was to see Tate, and how distressed they'd been to hear the news of the old duke's death. After a deep curtsey, Mrs. Moody ushered them inside, assuring them they would not go hungry as she'd send the stable boy to the local farmer for a loin of pork and a couple of chickens tomorrow. She ordered the maid upstairs to put fresh sheets on the beds and hurried into the kitchen to prepare supper.

After a welcome meal of mushroom soup, ham, bread, and cheese, they retired to the comfortably furnished parlor to drink a glass of port.

Tate prodded the fire with a poker while wondering if he'd completely lost his mind.

He joined Bret, taking the chair opposite. Stretching his legs toward the heat, he sipped the smooth liquor. "My father loved to come here during the hunting season," he said, gazing around the familiar room. "He and Edward were keen hunters."

"Edward?"

"My elder brother. He died from an illness last year."

"You've had your fair share of heartache," Bret observed.

Bret's compassion touched Tate. He seemed a decent fellow. Tate had judged him so from the outset, and he was seldom wrong. Perhaps this madcap scheme might just work?

During the following weeks, Tate's confidence in Bret grew, especially when his tailor, well-compensated and sworn to secrecy, arrived to create suitable outfits for them both, and remarked on their incredible likeness. He brought an array of fabrics and accessories, and after he took out his tape measure, he and his two assistants busied themselves at the dining table, cutting cloth.

After close to a month, Bret's transformation was complete. It was uncanny how like Tate he'd become in his appearance and mannerisms. He even modulated his voice to sound like him.

"You could always seek a career on the stage," Tate said, impressed.

"I have no desire to tread the boards," Bret said with a laugh.

"You could kill me and become me, and few would know," Tate observed, as they stood side by side before the mirror in their new clothes.

Bret chuckled. "What makes you think I'd want to?"

"My uncle would see you hung," Tate said with a laugh. Then he sobered. "And you wouldn't want to, as things stand." He got down to business. "Once you reach the city, you'll stay at Lindsey Court, as I've explained. If word arrives of my mother's intention to come to London, you must leave. You wouldn't fool her. But I doubt she will. She and my younger sister, Emily, are to remain in the country while in mourning."

"I am not confident of fooling Lady Ianthe either," Bret said. "I'll give her a wide berth."

"You must waltz with her. Ianthe expects it." Tate's disappointment at not fulfilling his promise himself sunk him low. "But be vigilant. She is quite observant." Eyeing the man who stood before him, he said, "You can waltz?"

Bret shrugged. "I have had little practice, but I'm adequate."

"I am not about to have my dancing besmirched," Tate said with a grin. "We'd best polish your technique."

"What?" Bret huffed out a laugh.

"Come on. I'll hum a waltz."

Bret joined him on the rug. With a groan, he clutched Tate's hand. Keeping as far away from each other as was possible, they danced twice around the room, then collapsed onto the sofa, laughing.

"You have a natural style," Tate admitted.

"What does that mean?"

"You don't have two left feet."

"Well, well," Bret said with a grunt. "And my table manners are up to snuff?"

Tate laughed. "We should discuss etiquette and wine. A gentleman is an excellent judge of the grape. I shall get Moody to procure a bottle or two. We keep a good supply in the cellar."

"So we are to be in our cups?" Bret asked with a lift of his eyebrows.

"Not a bad notion, but no. I shan't add an aching head to my troubles."

There was puzzlement in Bret's eyes. "Are you ready to tell me why you're doing this, Tate?"

"I am, but I'll need a glass of wine to dull the pain beforehand." Tate went to ring the bell.

Over a glass of claret before the fire, he explained how Bernard Donovan, the owner of two gaming houses, had by some nefarious means got his hands on Cloudhill. Putting it in words made it even more baffling. Never a careless gambler, Tate refused to believe his father wagered their future on a game of cards. He was a fair-minded father and loving husband. His family and Cloudhill meant everything to him.

Bret, expressing outrage, asked how Tate planned to get it back.

"I need to get close to the man, and I can only do that by becoming a professional gambler. Donovan has connections with a criminal gang, so it won't be easy."

"Sounds dangerous. Why not consult lawyers?"

"These criminals operate outside the law, but according to my father's solicitors, this vowel is a legal document. After he died, my uncle sought their advice and was informed there was nothing to be done, as my father failed to contest it. It's a mystery. My father would never have signed away Cloudhill on a vowel, even with a gun held to his head. He must have agreed to it under duress. I have to find out what they held over him. A life and death matter, surely. There must be more to it. My father was not a coward. The first thing I must do is examine his signature on the vowel."

"Pardon my ignorance, but what is a vowel exactly?"

"It's written proof of a wager," Tate replied.

"And you believe it to be forged?"

"The solicitors didn't raise that possibility. But there's a small but important detail my father shared with me about his signature they might have missed." He sighed. "If it is absent, it might be enough to contest it. At least it will delay the proceedings and give me time to investigate further." He leaned his head back against his chair and gazed into the flames. "Trouble is I don't know if the vowel still exists, as Donovan kept possession of it." It had to exist. Everything hinged on it. There was no way he would let this end without a fight.

"What about the contract for the sale of Cloudhill? Didn't your father sign it?"

Tate shook his head. "My father died suddenly before it was drawn up." His father had died before he could explain, but if he had, would it make a difference to the outcome?

"But he made no move to stop the sale going ahead?"

"No. It's impossible to say what he intended."

Tate struggled to rise above that confusing fact and think ahead.

London, three weeks later...

IANTHE GAZED OUT the window at the busy Mayfair Street. Visitors crowded the London thoroughfares and parks to celebrate Wellington's glorious victory. The metropolis was festive with banners strung up and parades in Hyde Park. A Victory ball was to be held, and the Prince of Wales would attend.

Ianthe's debut had been delayed after Frederick broke his arm playing cricket. Sent home from Eton to recover, Mama refused to leave him. They finally departed for Mayfair several weeks into the Season, but Ianthe wasn't about to let that hold her back. She would make the most of every minute. But she did not intend to find a husband. She seemed unable to give up her dream of marrying Tate, although she wouldn't tell her mother that. But a suitor who would make Tate sit up and take notice might be welcome. She frowned. Tate would come to the masquerade and waltz with her because he'd promised, and he always kept his promises. But she allowed herself no illusions. She might dress as a princess in a storybook for the masked ball, but life was no fairytale. She drew her bottom lip through her teeth and sighed.

Ianthe turned from the window. She was woolgathering, and wished she would just stop. While Tate was in mourning, he would not be in London often, so her silly plan to make him jealous couldn't work, or anything else she might think of. With a deep pang inside, she admitted Tate was farther away from her than ever.

Chapter Three

A FTER A MONTH spent at the hunting lodge, Tate arrived in London alone, on the stage. He took a room at an inn near Covent Garden and made a cursory check for bedbugs, then unlatched his portmanteau and spread his few belongings over the coverlet. He had left his monogrammed luggage with Bret, along with the luxuries he'd enjoyed all his life. It was a novel experience. A sense of excitement and purpose outweighed any discomforts. He donned the new clothes, fashioned with haste and some reluctance by his tailor, in the cupboard and arranged his shaving gear, cologne, toothbrush, and hairbrush beside the basin and jug on the dresser. He would begin life tomorrow as a flashy cove that lived by his wits. He peered into the stained mirror at his hair, in the style of the Caesar, brushed forward over his forehead with longer sideburns. The decision to alter his appearance seemed wise and far less intrusive than Bret's. Mrs. Moody's ministrations to his hair involved a mixture made from a plant extract and nut ashes. The couple got into the spirit of the deception without asking awkward questions. They kept him and Bret well-fed while Tate went over everything endlessly, explaining anything important for Bret to know while pleased his protégé was quick to learn it.

Bret would have arrived in Lindsey Court to spend his first night in London. Tate hoped it would prove relatively uneventful as he shrugged on his coat and left the inn.

Dusk had fallen and the lamps were being lit in the busy streets surrounding Covent Garden. A few ladies of the night gave him the eye while hawkers plied their trade and shifty pickpockets hugged the shadows. Tate ate a savory pie. It pleased and surprised him to find it so tasty.

He would spend a long, boring night in his room. Close to midnight, the *ton* would emerge on Covent Garden, departing the opera, the theater, or seeking the brothels and seedier pleasures on offer. He would put his disguise to the test at the Lexicon Club, where he doubted he'd see anyone he knew. His friends weren't serious gamblers, and to his knowledge, none would frequent a gambling hell.

Back in his chamber, Tate lay on the narrow bed staring at a damp mark on the ceiling. He wasn't to waltz with Ianthe. He sighed. If it wasn't for Bret, he would have allowed himself that much. While he divorced himself from the past, it felt as if she belonged to a different world. But even when he returned to being a duke, he would face an uncertain future with his estate gone.

He'd had some success at Hazard. While he didn't expect to win back what his father had lost either by fair means or foul, Tate wished to become a regular visitor at Donovan's gambling hell. It was the way to meet the man behind his father's ruin and, apparently, many others.

His wandering of Covent Garden at midnight the previous evening had proved uneventful. A few young blades in their cups accosted him for the price of a ride home, but none recognized him. Ladies alighting from carriages nary glanced at him.

It was fortunate that he did not physically resemble his father, he thought, as he prepared for his first night at the Lexicon. He dressed in his new clothes: a waist-length, tight green silk jacket, an orange-and-cream striped waistcoat, and thigh-hugging cream pantaloons. His hair slicked down with pomade, he gazed at himself, half amused, half horrified at the garish colors. Tweaking the extravagantly arranged cravat which would send his valet into hysterics, he added a large gold pin and a fob to the waistcoat. Satisfied that he looked the part, he went out to hail a hackney for Donovan's hell in a narrow lane off St. James' Street.

The clock in St. Paul's southwest tower chimed ten o'clock as the jarvey drove Tate to Donovan's club. Watching the passing pavements lit by arcs of lamplight, Tate reflected on what a friend had told him about the owner of the gambling hell. An Irishman, Bernard Donovan had risen from poverty to amass wealth by establishing several gaming houses which appealed to young nobles. Donovan had researched their family histories and used the knowledge to entice them into his web with disastrous results for the families involved. Young Lord Frank gambled his recently inherited estate away and cast his family into the poor house while playing vingt-et-un. Now the war had ended, Tate feared there would be an influx of bored young men retiring from the army and navy looking for excitement. Those without the funds to be accepted, who wished to enjoy what was free on offer, were permitted entry if they agreed to introduce others to the club. Many had barely reached their majority and were termed pigeons.

Tate would not take Donovan lightly. He came to London poor as a church mouse and as an Irishman; his rise to riches would have been a steep climb. Helped by his connection to the underworld. And that was enough to make Tate wary of him.

He and Bret were to meet beside the Serpentine Lake in Hyde Park on Saturday week, at the unfashionable hour of seven o'clock in the morning, to exchange news. By then, he hoped to have something to impart.

Bret would be attending the masked ball. Tate hoped he managed it well without mishap. Fooling Ianthe would not be easy. If she saw through his disguise, she would insist he tell her the truth. Tate refused to have her mixed up in this unsavory business. As he could not declare himself, he could not protect her from any harm which might arise from criminals searching for a means to hurt him.

How enchanting she must look in her princess costume, wearing a bewitching mask. Would she enjoy being in Bret's arms? He ran a finger along his bottom lip and frowned. Jealousy and bitter disappointment soured his stomach. He leaned forward as the hackney pulled up outside a tall building, the windows ablaze with candles. A stout fellow stood in the doorway greeting patrons, refusing entry to some while giving the nod to others. Tate was confident they would admit him. All young men with a few coins to rub together were welcomed. Most would lose at the tables before the night was over. He did not intend to be one of them. If he did well tonight, he would gain Donovan's attention.

He alighted. With a nod to the tough-looking individual whose tailored coat sat uneasily on his beefy shoulders, Tate passed him into the wide hall. Another equally hard-faced servant directed him up the stairs.

Raised voices reached him first, then an unpleasant blend of candle smoke and nervous sweat from men crammed together enveloped him when he entered through the door. He straightened his back and looked around.

Beneath twin chandeliers, gentlemen in evening dress stood around the tables while some strolled about. Dedicated gamblers hunched over their cards at the many gaming tables. No one hailed him. A thin fellow with an outlandish puce coat and a neck cloth tied uncomfortably high beneath his chin was the only one to eye him speculatively. Tate turned to the waiter, hovering with a tray of champagne flutes. He nodded, took a glass, and then moved through the pack to the French Hazard table. Men stood two deep around it, watching the dice fall.

Tate eased his way through. One player was losing heavily. Sweat gathered on his brow and desperation filled his eyes.

"You wish to play, sir?" the croupier asked.

"Not yet." First, he wished to study the play.

>>><<<

IANTHE HAD DANCED every dance, and her feet hurt. Beneath her chair, she surreptitiously slipped off a shoe and wriggled her toes. There was no sign of Tate, and the unmasking would take place at midnight. She searched for a tall, dark-haired gentleman among the crowd of chimney-sweeps and foreign potentates, dancing with queens, shepherdesses, dairy maids, and exotic gypsies.

The waltz would soon be announced. Ianthe hoped to avoid any gentlemen who looked as if he would approach her for the dance, as they had in numbers all evening. But if Tate didn't come soon, her mother would insist she stand up with the first man to ask her.

She prayed he would suddenly appear. He was always kind and wouldn't deliberately disappoint her. He'd never laughed at her like Stephen when she'd escaped her governess and demanded they let her ride with them. And when she left the schoolroom and nervously dressed in her new habit, Tate had invited her along before she'd even had to ask. She'd felt so grown up and very much aware of him atop his big chestnut stallion, controlling the animal easily with powerful hands and thighs. So handsome it made her sigh. And she'd said to herself, *one day I shall marry you*.

She held up her fan to hide her disappointment from her mother. If only she could forget him. Her mind might consider they would never be together, but her heart wasn't listening.

"His Grace Duke of Lindsey," the butler announced in a loud, important voice.

"Tate is here," her mother said. "I didn't expect to see him in London."

Ianthe sat forward in her chair as she looked toward the doorway. She spied a dark head above the crowd of well-wishers surrounding him with a shiver of anticipation.

Tate emerged from the crush dressed in black and white, and a striking black and gold mask. At first, she thought he would miss her, as annoyingly, his gaze flicked over the row of debutantes. But then he saw her and nodded. She quickly slipped her foot into her shoe.

He crossed the floor to her, smiling, his teeth white beneath his mask. This would be his first ball as the Duke of Lindsey. Already there was something different about his walk and the way he carried his shoulders. The responsibility would change him from the carefree man she was accustomed to. She wasn't sure what she felt about that. She had seen so little of life. Would he seek a more sophisticated woman for his duchess?

He bowed over her mother's hand and then held hers, while through the slits in his mask his green eyes studied her, as if taking in every feature. As if he'd never seen her before. Her toes curled in her shoes. Did he approve of her costume? She thought it flattering and had chosen it with him in mind.

"You make a delightful fairy queen, Lady Ianthe. Will you grant me the pleasure of the next dance?"

How formal he was. Not like Tate at all. Ianthe missed his mischievous smile, which held the implication that she could never pull the wool over his eyes because he'd always see through her.

Trembling a little, she rose. She had always wanted this. To dance with Tate at a ball. The debutantes still seated looked on. They must be envious. As Ianthe rested a hand on his arm, she reminded herself not to forget that he did not belong to her. And was unlikely to now. Confused and hurt, she lifted her chin, wishing she could see more of his face.

The musicians struck up. "I wasn't sure you'd come," she said as he led her through the steps. She felt jittery in his arms, not that soaring delight she'd expected. It was as if he wasn't Tate at all. How silly. What was wrong with her? Had she put too much store on this one dance?

"I almost didn't come," he confessed. "An urgent matter threated to send me back to the estate."

"Surely your staff can deal with it?"

"I've left it with my steward."

"But you'd rather be there than dancing with debutantes?" It was a leading question. She blushed. How transparent and pathetic she was.

He smiled. "There's a bevy of beauty here tonight. And you, Lady Ianthe, are the lovely Queen Mab."

She laughed, surprised. "Do you liken me to the mischievous Mab in Shakespeare's *Romeo and Juliet?*"

"No, I refer to Spencer's poem. Queen Mab, who is virtuous, beautiful, and fair."

She widened her eyes and forgot her nervousness. "When did you become a devotee of poetry?"

He coughed and raised a dark eyebrow. "I have long enjoyed reading poetry."

"It's the first I've learned of it."

"I fear my knowledge is poor compared to yours. I dared not mention it."

She grinned. "What frippery!"

He bowed his head. "You wound me deeply."

"Pish. Will you stay for the unmasking?"

"Unfortunately, I have another engagement."

Was it a woman? She firmed her lips to hide her disappointment. "Shall we see you again in London, or will you return to Cloudhill?"

"I hope to stay awhile, but I'm not sure."

Urgent business resulting from the duke's sudden death, she supposed. As it would be insensitive of her to ask what it was, she had to be content with that.

The music ended, and he escorted her back to her mother, where he bowed and left her. Ianthe looked after him, dismayed. He had not stayed to talk to her!

It was true, she hadn't felt that rush of excitement she always had in his company. Ianthe gazed after him. He wore his familiar cologne, but he didn't seem like the man she had known since childhood. She lamented the absence of that curious thread which she'd sensed always bound them, even if apart. Was Tate moving out of her life? She hurriedly swallowed her tears before her mother asked her what was wrong. Would she see him again this Season?

A gentleman of medium height with fair hair approached to invite her to dance. He was in evening clothes and wore a rather dashing scarlet domino with a black mask. He introduced himself as Lord Ormond and charmed her mother, leaving her smiling. On the dance floor, he leaned close to Ianthe. "I plan to see more of you this Season."

How audacious! She stared at him, unable to see much of his face. Only his hazel eyes through the slits in his mask and his sharp chin. "We have only just met."

"I confess your beauty has me in thrall."

"You put me to the blush, sir."

He smiled enigmatically. Here would be the perfect gentleman to make Tate jealous, Ianthe thought. Then chided herself. Such a plan was beneath her. And she doubted Tate would even see them. Was he still at the ball? She searched for him, failing to find him among the swirl of dancers or those wandering about the room.

"In time, you will only have eyes for me," Lord Ormond said when the dance ended.

Ianthe dismissed this outlandish statement with a slight smile. Surely he didn't mean it? Was this the rakish talk she'd been warned about?

"You will, Lady Ianthe. I am determined."

She found the bold statement presumptuous. And curiously lacking in emotion. But perhaps she misjudged him.

The following Saturday evening in the Picard's ballroom, a smaller affair, Ianthe settled the gold bracelet over her gloved wrist. She had not expected to see Tate at Almack's Wednesday dance, and nor had she. Nor did he appear at the card party on Friday. It hurt her to think she wouldn't see him again in town. The Season she had so looked forward to appeared diminished by his absence.

Mama leaned over and alerted Ianthe to the gentleman approaching. Stirred from her thoughts, Ianthe smiled and rose for the quadrille.

Tate danced past her, partnering Millicent Tyndale. He nodded to Ianthe. Upset at his casual attitude, she watched him surreptitiously as he moved through the set with Millicent, who flirted for all she was worth.

Was he avoiding Ianthe to prevent gossip? He certainly behaved strangely and not like himself at all. She'd always admired his easy grace and manner, but here he seemed a little stiff. Or had Millicent's flirtatiousness unsettled him? Ianthe's curiosity was roused.

A devilish idea entered her mind. As soon as her mother was engaged in conversation, Ianthe would slip away and speak to him. It wasn't unreasonable to want to know how he fared, was it? She supposed it was a jolt to suddenly find himself the Duke of Lindsey. Ianthe had to admit that Millicent was lovely. Most men would think so. Refusing to give in to jealousy, she shook her head, which provoked an inquiry as to her wellbeing from her partner.

Her chance came a half-hour later when a friend of her mother's drew her into a discussion on recipes for capons. The lady's chef had apparently created a masterpiece. Her mother obviously felt the need to defend Gibbons, who had been their cook for many years.

Across the ballroom, Tate left a circle of men. He looked oddly nervous and tugged at his cravat. He appeared to be making his way to the door.

Trying not to draw attention to herself by hurrying, Ianthe pushed through the crowd to halt him before he reached it.

"Surely you aren't leaving without coming to see me?" she said to his back.

He turned and smiled at her. "You seemed to be otherwise engaged. I would have had to fight my way through a long line of suitors."

It wasn't true and a poor excuse, unworthy of him. "Which would be a terrible waste of your time," she fired at him. She stepped closer. "Oh, Tate, how can you say such a thing?" Her gaze rested on him. The first thing she noticed was his eyes, and then his features. Shock flooded through her. Tonight, without the mask with the candlelight blazing, she could not believe what she was seeing. She felt dizzy. "You are not Tate," she said, a hand at her breast, suddenly short of breath. "What...have you done with him?"

The man's greenish eyes widened. He took her elbow. "We'd best talk, Lady Ianthe. But I warn you, Tate will not be happy."

"Not happy?" She gasped. "Where is he?"

"I don't have the slightest idea." He glanced toward her mother, who, thankfully, was still involved in a stirring conversation. He steered Ianthe toward the doors leading to the balcony.

A few guests had ventured out and stood huddled at the far end away from a cool breeze. Wishing she'd brought her shawl, Ianthe shivered, struck by a sense of foreboding. "Who are you? I demand you tell me," she hissed.

"My name is Bret Kilbridge."

"But...but you look like Tate, although I see now... You must be a relation of his."

"Maybe. I don't know. We met at an inn when Tate was en route to London. He devised a plan for me to show myself in London in his place. He has something important he must do."

Ianthe stared at him, her heart galloping. "That is extraordinary. What is the thing he must do?" She narrowed her eyes. "Or have you hurt him and taken his place?"

"I could hardly get away with that for long, now could I? I couldn't fool you, let alone his family."

She scowled at him. "Still..."

"I am to meet Tate Saturday week. I'll know more then."

"Where is this meeting place?"

"The Serpentine Lake before the park gets too busy."

Struggling to believe him, she wondered whether she should trust him. But she adopted a politer tone. "Will you please tell me what this is about?"

He looked stricken. "I cannot. Tate suspected I wouldn't fool you, and swore me to secrecy."

That was the first thing he'd said she was inclined to believe. "Well, it is different now."

"I don't see that it is. I promised."

"You men and your honor! Wait until I see him!" She glanced through the French doors. Her mother was on her feet, looking around for her.

Bret eyed her cautiously. "You won't give me away? I'd have a devil of a time explaining myself. They'll probably throw me into Newgate."

"Not yet," she said, still unsure of him. "What is the name of Tate's coachman?"

"Milson. And Mr. and Mrs. Moody are caretakers at the hunting lodge where we've been staying."

She nodded, a little relieved, but still desperately in need of more. What had happened for Tate to do this? "How long must I wait until I can reassure myself Tate is alive and well?"

"I'll get word to you after Saturday week, as I have said, my lady. I certainly hope to find him well," he added, causing her to gasp. What could this be about? Now that she thought about it, Tate had acted strangely the last time she had seen him.

She grasped the man's coat. "Is Tate in danger?"

"Lady Ianthe, please. We must not draw attention to ourselves." He carefully removed her fingers and smoothed the cloth. "In all honesty, I don't know. But I suspect His Grace can take good care of himself."

"Well...yes. That is true," she admitted, thinking of how strong and active he was. "But I shall worry most dreadfully until I see him."

"See him? When?" he asked, cocking an eyebrow.

"I shall join you on Saturday week in the park, of course."

Bret groaned. "I'm for it then. He'll be as mad as hell. Please pardon the expression, my lady," he added hastily.

"Well!" She put her hands on her hips. "Let him be. Now quickly, tell me more about yourself."

After a lengthy explanation in a strained voice, he fell silent.

"A tutor? This must be strange for you. I suppose I shall have to help you." She decided to believe him. This was just too outlandish for him to make it up. "I wish we might speak again, but I'm promised for the next two dances. We can talk further at another function. It will lend you credibility to be seen in my company."

"I would appreciate your help," he admitted. "I was considering leaving when I heard the regent might make an appearance tonight. It's a devilish hard thing Tate has asked me to do."

"Why did you agree to it? Is he to pay you?"

"To be honest, I'm not entirely sure why I agreed."

"Tate can be very persuasive," she said sympathetically. "We'd best go inside." Her mother had seen her and looked cross.

They entered through the doors into the smoky warmth and the infectious laughter of the gossiping *ton*. "You are remarkably like him," she said. "It's a mystery, isn't it?"

"Indeed, it is." His hand went to his cravat. "And right now, I'd much rather be tutoring Mr. Baillieu's son in Clare."

She raised her eyebrows. "Are you sure?"

"Well." He glanced around. "Perhaps I might warm to the role."

"I don't think my mother should see you close up. She knows Tate well. I'll be at the Browns' soiree on Friday evening. You have received an invitation?"

"I think so, but..."

"I will see you there."

She hurried away before he could give a definite answer. A decent man, she decided. But he had none of Tate's... She failed to find a word for exactly what it was Tate had, but it made him much more attractive.

What was Tate up to? When she visited his mother at Cloudhill, she had noticed the servants whispering. It was very odd and decidedly unnerving. She would not sleep until she saw him and convinced herself he was all right. Struggling to calm herself, Ianthe joined her mother.

"Wasn't that Tate you were talking to?"

"Yes, Mama," Ianthe said, hating to lie. She had never lied to her mother in all her life, but now she must.

"I prefer you not to favor him with your attentions, Ianthe. Most suitors will step aside for him. Much as we are fond of him, your father would not countenance a marriage between you now."

"Why has Papa's view changed about him?" Ianthe asked, wanting to defend him.

"There are serious financial problems. But that is not our concern. I'm disappointed too. I had hoped..." Mama waved her fan before her pink face. "But we must rely on your father's wisdom in these matters," she said firmly.

"Yes, Mama," Ianthe whispered. She desperately needed to know more. Perhaps she could persuade Bret to tell her all he knew when they met again.

Chapter Four

AFTER HIS THIRD successful night gambling at Donovan's, Tate counted his winnings. A good evening, but close to dawn, he feared he'd lose his edge after hours of intense concentration. It was time to retire. As he made for the door, a lackey approached him. "Mr. Donovan would like to speak to you, Mr. Bradley."

By his manner, Tate suspected it wasn't an invitation. If he refused, he might have his mind changed for him. "Very well."

He followed the man across the half-empty room to a door. The lackey opened it and ushered Tate through.

Tate glanced around the elegantly furnished room with interest. His gaze alighted on a large cupboard. The open doors revealed stacked files. Would they keep the information he sought there?

A red-haired man somewhere in his late forties sat behind an ornate French desk. He looked up from writing in a ledger and put down his quill. Lit by a large candelabrum, his face was all sharp angles, as if chiseled from stone.

Shrewd brown eyes flickered over Tate's clothes then rose to study his face. He gestured to the ornate chair opposite the desk. "You have some skill with the dice, sir."

Tate sat. "And a degree of luck."

"We have not seen you here before."

"I've recently returned to London. Been living on the Continent for several years."

"Are you a relative of the Duke of Lindsey, previous owner of Cloudhill? There is a distinct resemblance."

"So I've been told. We Bradleys hail from the poor side of the family, too distant to be of note. Perhaps I should pursue the connection?"

"They will not have much to offer you soon," Donovan sneered.

Tate fought not to coil his fingers into a fist and punch the man in his smug face. He shrugged. "I prefer to make my own way in life without handouts."

"My philosophy exactly. A professional gambler such as you can do well. Too well, perhaps, to gamble in any establishment of mine."

Tate tensed. "Sadly, a couple of good nights don't necessarily spell a long run of luck, although I should welcome it. With the expense of relocating myself to London, my digs are less than fashionable."

"Mm. Perhaps you should try your hand at vingt-et-un. Fortunes have been won at that table."

And many lost. Tate needed a losing night, or they'd show him the door. "Not a favorite of mine, but I appreciate the opportunity."

"Then you are welcome. But as you will have noticed, many of my clientele hail from the best families. Your connection to the duke's family, no matter how remote, is in your favor. If you know of anyone who might like to try their hand here, they are welcome to accompany you. Should you bring one or two, it will assure your entry in the future."

Especially a plump pigeon. Tate had no intention of obliging him. "I have yet to reconnect with old friends, but I shall certainly ask around."

"Excellent." Donovan picked up his quill and drew his ledger toward him.

Tate rose, the interview at an end.

He left the club and took a hackney back to the inn. The horse's hooves echoed on the cobbles. Dawn light peeked above the rooftops in the east, the streets all but deserted. Covent Garden was livelier, with carriages picking up the last of the evening's revelers. Hawkers were already setting up their wares. Soon, the markets would open and there'd be a rush of activity, the streets clogged with carts.

Tate dragged off his clothes, and lamenting the absence of his valet, arranged them over the chair. He washed, brushed his teeth, and then fell onto the creaking bed. An arm over his eyes to shield them from the dawn light creeping in through the thin curtains, he went over the evening in his mind. Balance. It would require skill to win enough, and lose enough, to satisfy Donovan's watchful eye. But the more he played, the better his eye had been at picking up trends. And the better his skill at throwing the dice. But now, he must play vingt-et-un, a far different game and even more challenging.

He slumped back in the bed, exhausted and confoundedly lonely. Apart from Bret, only his closest friend, Hart, knew the truth about his circumstances. Tate had taken him into his confidence about his scheme to save Cloudhill. Hart, fearing for Tate's safety, had tried to dissuade him, but seeing how desperate the situation was, finally agreed. He would become Tate's eyes and keep him informed how Bret was faring, and be there should Bret need an ally. They were to meet for breakfast in a tavern at ten o'clock.

Tate groaned. If he *could* save Cloudhill. He had to move fast. He would not see his mother and sisters suffer. And lose Ianthe. An image of his love swam before him as his eyelids grew heavy: her laugh, and the fiery emotion in her blue eyes, which belied her insistence they were more like brother and sister. He longed to laugh with her and draw her into his arms. To reassure her that his feelings had not changed. To love her and make her his own. They were meant to be together, him and Ianthe. But he'd been careful not to reveal his true feelings while hating that it confused and hurt her. Not everything in life was certain. It was a hard lesson to learn. He must accept she may never be his. Her father would already be considering prospective suitors. Ianthe would have little sway in the decision her father made for her. Tate had lost the support of Lady Granville, too, who had always favored him, and rightly so, as any mother would want her daughter to have a secure future.

On that depressing note, sleep blessedly claimed him.

Later in the morning, he sat at the table in the noisy Red Lion opposite Hart. In the warm air, redolent with the smell of bacon grease and hops, they tucked into their ham and eggs.

His friend yawned and rubbed a bloodshot blue eye. "The things I do for you, Tate. You know I never rise before noon during the Season." He shook his head. "Can't get used to your altered appearance either. The thought of this new undertaking of yours fair chills my blood."

Tate guiltily studied his friend for signs of recently tumbling out of bed. Hart gave every appearance of taking time to dress. His dark hair carefully styled, his cravat neatly tied, his coat of marine blue matching his concerned blue eyes. Tate still hated to have to worry him with his concerns. "You were always a lazy fellow. Couldn't get you out of bed at Eton. The lengths we went to in order to save you from getting into trouble from old Falkner."

Hart gave a half-hearted smile. "I have grown up since then," he grumbled.

"But old habits die hard." Tate pushed away his plate. "What you need is a nursery filled with your progeny."

His friend shuddered then chuckled. "You sound like my father. No! Not for years."

"Have you anything to tell me?"

"I saw Kilbridge at the Browns' soiree last night. Thought he looked as if he'd like to be somewhere else. Fortunately, few engaged him in conversation as they remain sympathetic to your loss."

"He didn't blunder?"

"Saw no evidence of it. Lady Ianthe spent some time with him." Hart smiled. "Until her mother came and drew her away."

Tightness gripped his chest. "So Ianthe hasn't realized he isn't me?"

"I cannot say. They talked for some time. I introduced myself to him when we had a chance for a discreet conversation. He expressed relief to have met me. Said things were not going according to plan. Then a lady and her daughter approached and drew him into conversation, and we didn't get another chance to talk."

Tate leaned forward. "Not according to plan? What the devil did he mean?"

The people at the table next to them turned to view them.

"I wish I could tell you." Hart spoke in an undertone. "The worst of it is, I have to leave immediately for Tunbridge Wells and will be gone for a week or more. The marquess demands I visit him at Pembury. He has become difficult since his rheumatism prevents him from enjoying his favorite activities. All his attention now rests on me. No doubt I'm in for a lecture about my rakish ways."

"Please give him my best wishes."

"I will," Hart said. "Oh, there's one thing. The lady who insinuated herself into Kilbridge's company is the widow, Mrs. Forth. Her husband made his fortune in some business at Spitalfields and then, somewhat conveniently, some say, passed away. She's determined to marry her daughter to a title. A duke, preferably. The girl would be damnably pretty if she smiled, but looks thoroughly miserable."

"Should I be worried about Bret?" Tate asked.

"Although one wouldn't expect Mrs. Forth to look as high as a duke, she seems audacious enough. I wouldn't put it past her to corner Kilbridge and force him into an indiscretion with her daughter. And the fellow is plainly out of his depth."

"Could it possibly get worse?" Tate grabbed his tankard and took a hearty swig of ale.

"Mm. I suspect it might." Hart looked at him doubtfully. "Do you still feel there's a chance of pulling this off?"

"I won't know until Donovan leaves for his club in Soho and I can search his office."

"I'm sorry I can't offer more support to Bret. He doesn't stay long at functions, and rarely dances, which is understandable, but so far appears not to have put a foot wrong. I've not heard anything to the contrary."

"Bret's proved to be a wily fellow. I can be thankful for small mercies," Tate said. So much could go amiss. If Donovan banned him, his time at the club might be over before he could find the vowel and put his plan into action.

>>>><<<<

IN HYDE PARK, Ianthe greeted Bret as she shook the raindrops from her umbrella. "Thank you for meeting me, Lady Ianthe." Bret joined her, tucking his long legs beneath the park bench. "Am I making mistakes? I value your opinion."

Ianthe glanced around at the deserted paths. Gray skies hovered low overhead, the air damp with the smell of wet greenery from an early shower. "You have exceptional manners and appear to be at ease in society. I cannot say more, as I am not privy to your conversations. When his brother was alive, Tate spent most of his time in the country. He is not well known among the *ton*."

She studied the man next to her. In daylight, his resemblance to Tate was not so marked, his mouth softer, his chin more rounded. A man who liked poetry. She couldn't imagine him as a member of the Whip Club, in a curricle race or taking part in boxing bouts like Tate was fond of doing. Odd that she'd always wanted Tate to appreciate poetry, and now she didn't care. Poetry seemed unimportant when one's life was held in the balance. She dragged in a breath. She just wanted him safely back in Cloudhill. For everything to be as it was. She was foolish enough to hope it would all come right in the end. She would marry Tate if he hadn't a penny should he ask her, but knew he wouldn't. "I noticed you spent a lot of time with Mrs. Forth and her daughter, Lily, at the Browns' soiree."

"I felt sorry for the young woman," Bret said. "Her mother is a veritable dragon. When we had a moment alone, Lily told me of her circumstances. I don't much know how this marriage mart works, but it horrified me to learn that Mrs. Forth cares little for Lily. She is merely a means to move the family up in the world."

"Nevertheless, you cannot become involved, Bret."

He sighed. "No. I suppose not. She is the sweetest girl. Quite simple in her tastes. I believe she grew up in the country before her father made his fortune."

Ianthe grew alarmed. "You must not allow the *ton* to think you are interested. It will not look good for Tate."

"I shall be careful." He gazed at her anxiously. "Apart from that, I'm doing well?"

"Very well," she said in an encouraging tone. "I doubt anyone suspects you are not Tate."

"Viscount Montford made himself known to me."

She glanced at him with a worried frown. "He's a good friend of Tate's."

"Tate has told him everything."

"Did you mention me to Viscount Montford?"

Bret shook his head. "I wasn't sure how you would feel about it. Tate has instructed Lord Montford to assist me should I need it, but the viscount is going into the country to visit his father."

"Oh, that is unfortunate."

A group of horse riders cantered past along Rotten Row. Although she saw no one she recognized, Ianthe picked up her reticule and umbrella. Her mother would come down soon. "Attend the Rothes' rout on Friday," she said, rising. "We can talk in the garden without being overheard."

Bret stood. "I am very grateful, Lady Ianthe. You have been a tremendous help."

"There is not much I can do. We must be careful when we meet that we don't cause gossip."

He smiled. "That cannot be such a bad thing."

"It would anger my father. Papa is considering a gentleman's suit." She fiddled with her umbrella, fighting to compose herself.

Bret nodded, but said nothing.

"I've yet to know much about him," she said cautiously, wondering whether Bret would relay this to Tate. While a part of her wished he would, the better part of her nature didn't want Tate to worry about her.

She said goodbye and hurried away. Even if she could avoid an engagement to the widower, Lord Ormond, who was showing particular attention to her, it would not change Tate's mind. Unless whatever he was up to bore fruit, and it restored his finances. Even at her lowest ebb, awareness that he loved her came from somewhere deep inside. She wasn't that silly girl mooning about over a crush her father accused her of. But was Papa right? Lord Ormond seemed quite presentable. Attractive, with a pleasing manner. His father was a marquess. Many would be delighted to accept him.

She hurried to meet her maid, Aggy, who waited for her at the park gate. Ianthe refused to cry. She'd cried enough. But she would never stop loving Tate. Never! Would that be fair to Lord Ormond or any other man she married?

Chapter Five

THE NEXT TWO nights at the club, Tate lost most of his winnings while Donovan strolled around the room, showing no inclination to visit his other gambling club. He had glanced at Tate more than once, but so far, they permitted him to play.

On the third evening, Donovan left the club with two of his men. When a fellow playing Hazard caused a ruckus, accusing another of cheating, the man Donovan left in charge escorted him to the door and unceremoniously threw him out. Tate took his chance. He walked to the office door, turned the handle, and slipped inside, away from the smoke and noise.

A candelabrum lit the room. He hurried to the desk and searched the drawers. Nothing. Opening the cupboard doors, he hastily scanned the files for his family name.

Several minutes passed. His search unsuccessful, Tate looked around the room. Could Donovan have a safe hidden behind one of the large oil paintings decorating the walls? He circled the room, glancing behind each one, finding only red and gold flocked wallpaper. A large gilt-framed Hogarth hung above the fireplace, but he would need something to stand on and he had been away too long. Someone would soon notice his absence and come to find him.

Frustrated, he strode to the door and opened it a crack. Donovan's employee now talked to a waiter carrying a tray of champagne flutes. Tate stepped out and closed the door behind him. A man at the nearest table raised his eyebrows. "Looking for the convenience," Tate said.

"In the next room behind a screen." The player turned back to his cards.

Tate recouped some of his losses before he went home. Just enough to make it seem plausible. Weary to his bones, he climbed the inn's stairs to his room, wondering if he was wrong about Donovan. He considered him the arrogant sort who would keep the evidence of his clever swindle to gloat over.

How long could Bret carry on with this deception? What if one of Tate's friends from the Whip club turned up in London? They knew him well. Henry Sinclair lived at his country estate, where his wife had recently given him an heir. But it wouldn't keep Henry from the bright lights of London for long. It would place Bret in a devil of a spot if he turned up, especially without Hart to back him up. That worrying thought kept Tate awake for hours.

The next evening at the club, several courtesans arrived, and the atmosphere changed. Champagne flowed, and all but the most hardened gamblers laughed and flirted. A few paired up and slipped away upstairs.

Donovan spent most of the evening moving around the tables. There was no chance for Tate to get inside the office. He sipped his champagne as he studied his cards, annoyed with himself. He would have to wait for another chance to check for a safe. And if he failed to find it, he would need to visit Donovan's other club, and even his home if need be.

In the morning, he dragged himself out of bed after two hours' sleep and dressed to meet Bret. Hyde Park was quiet in contrast to the busy streets Tate had passed through around Covent Garden, where carts of produce were already being unloaded. The cool early morning breeze rippled across the tall grasses. In the distance, cows grazed.

Tate spied Bret standing beneath the massive aged oak over-looking the chilly gray waters of the lake. Bret looked different. Better dressed, but more upright with his shoulders back, unlike his usual scholarly stance. As Tate hailed him, he wondered if the experience had changed him.

"I'm relieved to see you, Tate," Bret said after they sat on a nearby bench.

Tate glanced around, but there was only a man in a rowing boat that was too far away to overhear them. "Call me Bradley if anyone's around. Has anything happened?"

"Well, you might say that." Bret's eyes widened. "Lady Ianthe…"

Tate gazed at him with a sense of dread. "What about Lady Ianthe?"

"Lady Ianthe is here," came the sweet voice behind him he knew so well.

Tate swung around. She stood on the path wearing a sky-blue pelisse and a bonnet the color of her eyes. He jumped to his feet. "I might have known Bret wouldn't fool you." He stifled a groan as she approached him.

"Of course he didn't. Although, he's made a splendid job of taking your place. It is fortunate, however, that he's avoided my mother, and others who might know you well." She frowned. "But that could happen at any function, and would not go well for him, I imagine."

He took her arm and drew her to the seat Bret had vacated. "I'm aware of it. But why have you come?" He frowned. "And alone?"

Her concerned eyes met his. "You must tell me what this is about, Tate." Her gaze took him in. "Why are you wearing that horrid-colored coat? I have never seen you dressed this way. You look foppish, like my brother's friend, Grantly Somersby." She rushed on. "Never mind. I am so pleased to see you."

"You must leave me to deal with this, Ianthe." His gaze scanned her lovely face, delighted to see her despite his misgiv-

53

ings. Then, with a deep breath, he shored up his resolve. "It is risky for you to be here. I have no intention of involving you."

Her eyes implored him. "But I can help."

"You already have, Lady Ianthe," Bret said from his position, leaning against the oak's trunk. "I've been most grateful for your help."

They both turned toward Bret. For a moment, Tate had forgotten him. Ianthe's intense blue eyes and flowery perfume had blinded him to everything. The harsh reality of his predicament hit him hard, tightening his chest. He faced the truth of his situation. Ianthe could not become involved in this. He must not offer her an ounce of encouragement. "Thank you for supporting Bret. It would have been a dreadful shock to you. I'm sorry, Ianthe." He drew in a sharp breath and steeled himself to remain firm. "I appreciate you want to help, but there is nothing you can do. I would like you to go home now before your mother finds you gone."

Ianthe's anguished expression went straight to his heart like an arrow. Her lips trembled. "How will I know if you are all right?"

With every unsteady breath, he fought not to reach for her, while fearing he would never get the chance again. "Bret will advise you. Enjoy your time in London. Dance at balls in your prettiest gowns." Life was unbearably cruel. It should be he who held her in his arms. He who should marry her, and make love to her. But he must stay firm to his conviction that this was best for her.

She flushed. "You make me sound so...trivial."

"Never that, Ianthe. I'm touched and grateful. But I must do this alone."

She frowned. "Do what?"

"Try to right a wrong," he said evasively.

"Why won't you tell me what it is? I fear it is dangerous."

Relieved Bret hadn't told her of his intentions, he said more gently, "Hardly that."

She scowled. "I am not stupid, Tate."

"You mustn't worry. I will send word to you through Bret."

"Do you promise?"

"I do." He turned and glanced around to put a stop to her questions. "The park will fill up soon. Where is your maid?"

She stood and briskly settled her bonnet over her hair. "Aggy is waiting for me at the park gates."

"Then I shall escort you to her."

"There is no need. I came here alone and shall return the same way." She glanced back at him. "A gentleman wishes permission to ask for my hand. Papa is considering it."

Tate went cold. "Who is he?"

"A widower, Lord Ormond. He is heir to a marquessate."

"I don't know him. How old is he?"

"Thirty."

"Young to lose his wife." *And the wrong man for you,* Tate thought heatedly.

She nodded. "It was tragic."

"You like him?" he asked, forcing a lightness into his voice.

"He is personable and has exquisite manners." She bit the words off, and with a nod of farewell, turned to Bret. "Goodbye, Bret. I'm sure we will meet again soon."

"It seems likely, Lady Ianthe," Bret said with a half bow.

Drawing her pelisse about her slender body as if she had suddenly grown cold, she walked away down the path.

Tate hurried to join her. As there was nothing further to say, they walked in silence. He watched her until she reached her maid. She glanced back at him once, her expression indecipherable. He remained until they walked out of sight up Brook Street. Feeling sick, he returned to Bret.

Bret sat on the bench, his hands resting between his knees. "I'm sorry, Tate."

Tate shook his head and stared over the water, rippled by the breeze which carried the busy water birds' cacophony. "I didn't really believe she'd fall for it."

"No. A lady knows the man she loves."

Tate swung around. "Ianthe cares about me, certainly. We have been friends for many years."

"Every man should have such a friend," Bret said with a lift of his lips. "If you'll excuse me for saying so."

"Our friendship will end when she marries Ormond." He swallowed the bitterness.

Bret frowned and fell silent.

"Now," Tate said more briskly than he felt. "Tell me who you have met."

Bret filled him in. "I have been fortunate to avoid meeting the regent." He paused. "But there is the matter of a young lady."

"Oh? Who is she?"

"I realize, of course, I must be discreet. But Lily's mother is an awful woman."

Uneasy at Bret's use of her Christian name, Tate said, "Who is her mother?"

"The widow, Mrs. Forth." Bret held up a hand. "Don't worry. Lady Ianthe warned me not to become too familiar with Lily, and I shall take heed of her advice. But I worry about her. Lily told me her mother has a new gentleman she plans to marry who seems to have exerted control over her. He urges her mother to marry Lily to the highest bidder. Lily is an exceptionally pretty girl, you see."

Tate saw only too clearly. "Be careful, Bret. The woman might target you."

"Apparently, they've squandered most of the fortune Forth left and seek a suitor of great wealth. They have Lord Bolton in their sights."

"Bolton? I remember meeting him once. He must be sixty."

"Yes, and looking for his third wife. They don't care about his age or questionable history. He's a wealthy baron."

"It's best to avoid this family. And the young lady, Bret. It wouldn't do to become too fond of her."

As Donovan didn't move in social circles, the news that Tate had lost Cloudhill had not yet raised a whisper in town. But it would once the contract was signed. Tate's unease grew. How little time he had.

"I wish I were able to rescue Lily," Bret said. "I know this is not the life she wants. But you're right; I have little to offer her. Her mother would never agree to our marriage."

They walked back across the park. Tate adjusted his hat to shield his face. "I will leave you here. We can meet again a week from today. I hope to have news which will set us both free." He turned to the man he'd come to know and like. "But as I've said, if you wish to stop this and return to your former life, you must do so. You can put it about that you are returning to the country. That will give me time to continue my search."

Bret shook his head. "I find I'm not ready to leave this fascinating city just yet."

"Perhaps your life as a country tutor will prove a little dull?"

He grinned. "I fear it might, Tate. It's a fine thing you've done to me."

"I will make amends, Bret, once Cloudhill is safe. And then you might snatch your Lily away."

"Perhaps both ladies will no longer be free to choose."

Tate wished Bret wasn't so insightful. He nodded soberly and left, returning to his miserable existence.

THE FEAR THAT what Tate was involved in was dangerous stayed with her, and Ianthe fought anguish and frustration as she hurried home. She entered her bedchamber, having successfully avoided exposure, and sat before the mirror to order her locks before going down to breakfast. Mindlessly tidying herself, she dwelled on the hopelessness of her situation. Never again would she embarrass herself by laying her feelings bare before Tate. It would serve no purpose. But she hadn't missed the misery in his eyes, and how his gaze lingered on hers. How his chest had risen sharply in a deep, despairing breath. Nothing had changed, the pull of attraction between them as strong as ever. But she must face the truth. He had not asked for her hand after Cecily and Gerald married. And he certainly would not do so now. She moaned. Telling him about Ormond did not have the effect she hoped for. There was nothing more she could do.

The door opened and her mother hurried in, still in her dressing gown. "Ah, you are up, my love. We have a busy morning ahead. I require a new bonnet from Bond Street and dancing slippers for you, silver, to go with your new ball gown and Lord Osmond has invited us to dine with him. Such a nice man, is he not? So very polite and agreeable..." As her mother prattled on, Ianthe tried to ease her panicked breathing. Her future appeared to unfold before her eyes in a way she had never wished for. And worse, she seemed helpless to change it.

Chapter Six

A FEW NIGHTS later, another opportunity presented itself to search Donovan's office when the Irishman left the club again. "Where has he gone?" Tate asked a man playing beside him.

"His club in Soho." The man raised his voice to make himself heard over a boisterous group of young men loudly cheering someone's success. "Apparently, there's been some trouble at Fortune House."

"Trouble?"

"Some fellow burst in and shot up the place."

"Why would he do such a thing?"

"Suffered losses at Hazard, apparently. With the promise he would return, he escaped them and vanished into the night. You should have heard Donovan's roar of rage when he learned of it. Had his staff scattering in all directions."

"They haven't found the fellow?"

"Avoided them so far." The gambler studied him. "Why so interested?"

"No particular reason. Some people are poor losers. Shouldn't play if they aren't prepared to lose their money."

"Sir Eric Walmer was the shooter. But it was his son, Henry. He lost a small fortune and then jumped from Westminster Bridge. They fished him out of the Thames stone-cold."

Tate bit down on a curse. He had never met Henry, but Walmer's younger son, Michael, had been a year behind Tate at university. "Tragic business."

"Indeed."

Tate placed the ace of hearts on the table beside the nine of clubs.

A moment later, the player leaned over to Tate and said in an undertone, "I wouldn't want to be Walmer. Donovan has underworld connections, and I doubt he'd accept an apology even should one be offered."

"No. But if I lost my son that way..." While he spoke, Tate kept an eye on the office door, and the position of Donovan's remaining staff.

"Yes, quite." The gambler eyed his hand then tossed down his cards with a grunt. "Well, I'm out." He nodded to Tate, pushed back his chair, and walked to the door.

Tate swung around. Donovan's men were involved at several tables. Could he make it to the office without being seen? He tossed in his hand and left the table, then wandered about for a few minutes watching play. Someone else had a good win and men scrambled to view it. Tate walked to the office door, opened it, and stepped inside, closing it quietly behind him. Dragging a chair over to the fireplace, he climbed on it and reached up to ease the painting's frame away from the wall. There was nothing behind it. With a soft curse, he jumped down and returned the chair to its original position. He opened the door a crack. Seeing it was safe to leave, he walked out the door and left the club. It was unlikely Donovan would be at Fortune House again tomorrow night. But Tate would be.

When at last he rested his head on his pillow, thoughts of Ianthe returned to keep him awake. He'd made her unhappy. He wanted desperately to tell her the truth, and take her into his confidence. *Impossible.* It was safer that she didn't know, even though she would think badly of him.

Where was she tonight? Searching his memory, he recalled an

invitation to the Montgomeries' soiree. Would Bret be there too? He'd stated his intention to avoid soirees because he felt too exposed. Bret may not bring news of Ianthe when Tate saw him again. He wouldn't know whether she'd accepted Ormond. He gasped at the pain that possibility caused him. It was so soon. It had been rash of him to think he'd have a few months up his sleeve before a serious suitor appeared. That he'd have time to restore Cloudhill. He should have known. Ianthe was a diamond. Before long, he'd have to deal with an invitation to her wedding. With a curse, he forced his mind on to Donovan's Soho club.

They spoke of Fortune House as an elegant establishment where ladies were permitted to gamble at the tables. If searching Donovan's office proved impossible, Tate would break into the building after the club had closed.

He yawned, too exhausted and worried to sleep. Poor Walmer, his heart must have broken to act so rashly and stir the ire of men such as these. Tate felt deeply sorry for him and very, very angry.

When Tate arrived in Soho that evening, he found the gambling club door barred. He spent a long, aimless evening at a nearby hotel, cradling a tankard of ale. In the taproom, he learned much from the surrounding chatter. Some renovation had been necessary to replace damaged mirrors, tables, and a smashed chandelier.

He wondered if Walmer still escaped Donovan's thugs. He hoped he'd left London. Otherwise, he would probably end up in some alley with his throat cut.

At two in the morning, Tate returned to Soho intending to break in, but Walmer's actions had caused them to place a guard on the door. Tate could do nothing but return home burning with impatience at the time lost.

The following evening, he returned to gamble at his usual haunt while wondering when the Soho club would reopen. Tate prayed it wouldn't be long. He was fast becoming a fixture at the Lexicon, appearing every night to play vingt-et-un. Not his favorite game. He'd lost more than he won this last week, and his funds grew short. If it continued in a downward spiral, that meant a trip to the bank, which he was reluctant to do. Dressing as himself, the risk of exposure increased, making him and Bret vulnerable.

On a dreary and unusually chilly Saturday morning, he and Bret met at the oak tree. Bret handed him the post. There was a letter from his mother, which Tate would read later. Bret had little to tell him, apart from describing in painful detail how Ianthe danced twice with Ormond. "Gossip has it they are about to announce their engagement."

Tate's chest became so tight he felt strangled. "Did...she seem happy to you?"

Bret eyed him carefully. "Quite subdued, but that might not mean much."

"No. Etiquette requires a young lady to act in a modest, restrained manner." Tate didn't believe it, though. Ianthe had never felt the need to be anything but herself. It was one of the many things he admired about her. She was never missish.

He stared into the distance where a flock of birds filled the branches of an enormous chestnut tree. Did Ianthe believe he didn't care for her? Why would she think otherwise when he'd been so careful not to reveal his true feelings? He should be relieved if she had transferred her affections to another man. But he couldn't bear to think it might be true.

"What's your next step?" Bret asked, drawing him out of his thoughts.

Tate explained about the Soho club. "I'll visit it when it reopens," he said. "When Donovan returns to the Lexicon, I'll attempt to search for the vowel." He glanced at Bret. "How are you? Any problems?"

"No. But when the regent arrives back in London from Brighton, there will be." He gestured at the letters Tate had tucked into his coat pocket. "There's an invitation for a dinner party at Carlton House from the regent among those. I fear urgent matters require me to depart London before then."

"I agree. After I search Fortune House, there's nothing more I can do. It's my hope there will be nothing more I need to do. As soon as you choose to leave, I'll return to Lindsey Court." Bret would no longer need to appear on Tate's behalf. Bret's presence had worked brilliantly to allay curiosity or concern regarding Tate's wellbeing following the death of his father. And he kept Tate informed about Ianthe. And right now, he selfishly thirsted for news of her.

"I'm to attend the Kendalls' spring ball tonight," Bret said.

"Because of Lily?" Tate asked, making a shrewd guess.

Bret colored. "Yes. Another engagement soon to be announced, I fear. If Bolton decides a lovely young girl like Lily is worth him marrying beneath him."

"You sound bitter. Is it a *fait accompli*?"

"It looks likely. I'm more worried than bitter. Her mother's new husband controls them. The despicable wretch has his eye on the prize. Lily could soon be married to a man of extremely dubious character unless I can prevent it. We have managed to snatch a few moments together. Our whispered conversations tell me enough to want to help her."

"Help her or marry her?"

"It amounts to the same. And both are impossible."

Tate felt deeply sorry for him. "I wish there was something I could do to assist you."

Bret kicked a stone with his shoe. "I can't see how you could, but I appreciate the offer."

If he'd taken his safe, comfortable life for granted once, he certainly did not now. Tate raised his eyes to a pair of doves cooing in the oak above them. They mated for life, he'd heard somewhere. His heart gave a sad heave. He had expected life to unfold before him in an uncomplicated fashion, wed to the girl he loved. This was indeed a humbling experience.

IN THE ELEGANT ballroom, at the conclusion of a quadrille, couples left the dance floor chatting and calling to acquaintances. Ianthe, her hand resting on Ormond's arm, steered him toward Bret, who had just made an appearance. "The duke is our bereaved neighbor," she murmured to Ormond.

Reaching Bret, Ianthe sank into a curtsey. "Your Grace. Have you and Lord Ormond met?"

"I don't believe so," Bret said. "How do you do, sir?"

"Allow me to offer my condolences, Your Grace," Lord Ormond said in a flat, emotionless voice.

Bret nodded. "Good of you, sir."

"Please relay my thoughts to your mother and sisters and tell them I am thinking of them," Ianthe said. "I will visit them when I return to the country."

Bret nodded. "Mama will be pleased."

"Your Grace," Ianthe continued, sensing Ormond's impatience, "according to my father's groom, my mare, Freckles, is suffering a particularly worrying bout of colic. I wonder if we might discuss it. Your stable master has such a wonderful knowledge of horses, and may have imparted some of that to you. I am very worried. You know how special Freckles is to me."

"There was some method he mentioned which might help," Bret said with a slight frown.

"I should be very grateful." Ianthe turned to Ormond. "Would you please excuse us for a moment?"

"Certainly. Your Grace." Ormond bowed and left them.

"What is this? I know nothing about colic," Bret said when Ormond was no longer within earshot.

"I want news of Tate," she demanded.

Bret eyed her cautiously. "Tate is well enough. He does not want you involved. As you well know, my lady."

"Of course I know it." She huffed, frustrated. "Telling me his plans can't hurt, surely. I accept there is little I can do to help him. Is he in danger?"

"He is not in any danger." Bret raised his eyebrows. "And I don't renege on promises." With a stiff bow, he began to move away.

"I can help you with Lily," Ianthe said quickly.

"What makes you think...?" He turned back. "Is it that obvious?"

"Perhaps only to me."

"How could you help?"

"I shall befriend Lily and pass messages between you."

He blinked. "You would do that, my lady?"

"If you tell me the reason why Tate must dress that way."

Bret groaned. "I promised him I wouldn't."

"I shall tell him I coerced you. He won't hold it against you."

Bret turned and looked at Lily, where she sat with her mother. "He will. We have a gentleman's agreement." He glanced around them. "We can't talk here. Ormond waits with your mother. He has his eye on us."

"Meet me on the balcony just before the last dance is called. Ormond plans to leave before then."

"Very well."

Ianthe watched him disappear through an archway. Would he tell her the truth? Or still try to evade her questions? She hurried back to her mother, and Ormond, who still watched her.

"Tate has been like a son to us," her mother was explaining to him. "How is His Grace, Ianthe? He hasn't come to see me. I assume he still suffers, poor man."

"Yes, he is deeply upset, Mama," Ianthe said, pleased her mother refused to wear her spectacles. She turned to Ormond. "Thank you for waiting, sir. You promised to tell me more about your mother, who I believe resides in Bath. Such a delightful place in which to live." As she sank onto the seat, she gave him a brilliant smile, causing the suspicion to fade from his eyes.

"Indeed." He threw up his coattails and sat beside her.

"Mother prefers the Bath townhouse to living on the estate. She enjoys Bath society."

As he rattled on about the important personages among his mother's circle of friends, Ianthe nodded, but her thoughts were elsewhere. She would count the hours until she could speak to Bret again. It was impossible to guess what Tate was up to. Whatever it was, he wasn't about to tell her. She hoped to have more success getting the truth from Bret.

Chapter Seven

TATE SCOWLED. LUCK was not with him tonight. Vingt-et-un was not his game, but it might have helped had his mind been on it. He had intended to win enough to forestall a trip to the bank.

As the clock struck two, he nodded to the croupier and rose from the table. It had been crowded tonight, the air dense with cigar smoke and raucous chatter, the players' voices raised in exhilaration, alarm, or despair. All but two of the courtesans who visited tonight had gone upstairs with the men.

Donovan, who had been prowling the floor, approached him. "Another disappointing night, Mr. Bradley?"

"Unfortunately. I've had a bad few days, but my luck will turn. It always does."

Donovan folded his arms and scrutinized him. "I consider myself an excellent judge of men. But you perplex me, sir."

"Oh? I believe I'm a fairly uncomplicated character," Tate said warily.

Donovan's cold, calculating eyes met his, sending an uncomfortable chill down Tate's spine. "No, my instincts tell me this is not so. And I never go against my instincts, Mr. Bradley. They have served me well in the past."

Tate raised his hands and shrugged. "I am just as you see before you, Mr. Donovan. Someone making their way in a difficult world."

"Is there a special lady in your life?"

Tate was taken aback. "There hasn't been time for more than brief encounters." Uneasy, he adopted an affronted expression. "I wonder why you ask?"

Donovan chuckled. "I could offer you a lady for the rest of the evening."

"Thank you, no. I prefer to choose my own."

"Women would be drawn to you."

Wondering where the devil this was leading, Tate said wryly, "You are too kind."

"I have a proposition for you."

"Oh?"

"My club, Fortune House, in Soho, reopens in a few days. There will be a string quartet, fine food, and naturally, champagne and vintage wines. Ladies and gentlemen are welcome to play at the tables."

"I have been to such clubs on the Continent."

"I can offer you a handsome bank with which to bet, if you'll agree to squire a lady for the evening."

It would give him an intro to the club. Tate said, "I don't consider myself…"

"Do not feign humility, sir. I would find it difficult to believe you. A gentleman such as you will encourage a better class of women to spend time at my club. And keep them coming back."

"I will not take them upstairs," Tate said bluntly.

"No. These are not courtesans, sir. Wealthy widows and their friends, mostly. Whether you choose to bed them is your prerogative. While it will disappoint some ladies, you are merely required to accompany them for the evening and encourage them to play. Something I suspect will come easily to you. And one hundred pounds to sweeten the pot."

In Donovan's view, as Bradley, a hardened gambler down on his luck, he would welcome such a proposition. Tate nodded slowly, appearing to consider it while he'd already decided. He was excited at the prospect, in fact. This had fallen right into his lap. He hoped to make the most of the opportunity. "That seems fair."

"We agree?" Donovan said. "Excellent. Be at Fortune House on Friday at eight o'clock. I am confident this will prove to be a beneficial arrangement for both of us."

"I hope not to disappoint, Mr. Donovan."

Donovan chuckled and left him.

Tate went back to the inn, somewhat bemused. He was to be little more than a hired rake. It was an extraordinary request, but nothing Donovan did surprised him. Tate should be wary, though. Something may lie behind it. Donovan was, if nothing else, an astute businessman keen to climb another rung up the ladder and reach that pinnacle of wealth that would give him an intro into the upper echelons of society. And it gave Tate entry to the club, a legitimate reason to be there, and carte blanche to wander at will when Donovan was absent. But he didn't think for one moment the Irishman trusted him. Tate wasn't about to let down his guard.

On Saturday, he ventured out into the dreary morning. He greeted the hawker on the corner, which had become a daily ritual, and then walked to his usual inn to partake of his usual eggs and coffee. He raised his hat to Annie, a lady of the night, tiredly making her way home.

Annie curtsied and grinned broadly. "The offer is still there, ducks. I'd open me door for you anytime."

He grinned and raised his hat, then continued on raising a hand to a man driving his cart to the markets to sell his wares. Three weeks had passed since this deception had begun, and while Bret attended routs and balls, Tate marked time. This charade threatened to suck the lifeblood out of him. He found it hard to fill the hours while locked in his troubled thoughts. It had not been his intention for it to go on as long as this. He penned letters to his mother, his uncle, and sisters, telling them he was well, but felt cut off and powerless.

Tate turned up the collar of his great coat. It was a deuced cold day. He was glad he wore boots, for the ground was muddy. Raindrops from the overhead branches spattered onto his hat as he made his way across Hyde Park to the Serpentine. He found Bret sheltering beneath the leafy bows of the broad oak. The lake waters reflected the gray of the sky, the water fowl huddled along the bank. Tate's concerned intake of breath drew in smells of rain-sodden grass, mud, and reeds, as he acknowledged this could not go on much longer.

Bret straightened as Tate approached. He looked down at his feet. "I have to confess I've let you down."

Dreading the answer, Tate asked, "What happened?"

"I broke my promise to you, Tate. I told Ianthe you were visiting a gambling club."

"For the lord's sake, why?"

"She insisted on knowing what you were up to, and it was all I could think of. And I could hardly argue with her while Ormond observed us."

Tate tightened his jaw. "Watching Ianthe, was he?"

"Like a sparrow hawk and she a mouse."

"You told her everything?"

"Not everything. I don't know it all."

"How did she react?"

"Her eyes revealed some deep emotion, but I wasn't privy to her thoughts."

"She would never think me a hardened gambler." Any more than his father was. Ianthe would want to know more, and Tate doubted she'd give up easily. But really, there was nothing she could do.

"She scoffed," Bret said.

"That worries me."

"Ormond behaves as if they were engaged, although no announcement has been made as yet. Will we meet again next week?"

Tate pushed away the painful thought of Ianthe lost to him,

knowing the pain would come later when sleep eluded him in his room at the inn. "You've decided to remain in London?"

"Er, yes. I believe I will for a bit. If there's anything more I can do…"

"No, thanks. I hope to call a halt to this soon. The longer it goes on, the greater the likelihood our deception will be uncovered."

Bret agreed.

"I suspect Lily has something to do with your reluctance to leave London." Tate raised an eyebrow. "You are being careful with my good name, I trust?"

Bret grinned. "Have no fear."

Tate came away with the uneasy notion Bret kept something from him. This could not continue for much longer. He would search Fortune House the first chance he got, and if he failed to find the evidence he sought, he would need to come up with another means of outwitting Donovan. The man was a scoundrel who saw himself living in Cloudhill like a true gentleman. Tate was equally determined he would fail.

A few weeks before he died, his father had called Tate to his study and explained this quirk in his signature. Tate still had the example written on a piece of bond in his keeping. And then when his father returned from London, perhaps aware of his seriously ill health, he had hoped he could leave it to Tate to resolve. He was about to explain when he collapsed. It meant a good deal that he'd taken Tate into his confidence. Especially when his father had treated him as the younger son too inexperienced to be relied upon, even following Edward's death. It had made Tate determined to convince him he was well able to take over the management of the estate when the time came. Too late for his father to witness it, but it would be enough for Tate should he save Cloudhill and run the estate well. Perhaps his father would know of it.

But would he ever get the chance to prove himself? As he strode across the park, he felt disquieted. It was as if he was losing himself along with Cloudhill.

⟫⟫⟫⟨⟨⟨

IANTHE SAT IN the crowded ballroom with her mother. Lady Boyce had eclipsed last year's ball with a Grecian theme. Scantily-draped marble statues adorned every corner, some topped with laurel wreaths.

As Ianthe expected, Lord Ormond claimed the first dance, a cotillion. They moved through the formal steps, and when they briefly came together, he grasped the opportunity to praise her white Grecian-styled gown, trimmed with gold embroidery. As they left the floor, he leaned down to her. "I wonder if I should go down on bended knee here before the *ton*, would you refuse me, Lady Ianthe?"

She stiffened. "I should dislike such an outlandish display, Lord Ormond. But I am confident you would not do so."

"Does another gentleman have a claim on your heart?"

"I'm sure I don't know who you refer to."

"Your childhood playmate, perhaps?"

"You surprise me, sir. His Grace and I have danced once this Season. I've barely spoken to him."

"Your father has encouraged my suit, but I suspect he awaits word from you."

"Papa isn't here tonight," she said, attempting to put him off.

His eyebrows snapped together. "Perhaps tomorrow?"

Ianthe found him presumptuous. While aware her parents wished for the union, she had been careful not to make any promises. When she gazed up into his hazel eyes, she didn't find the warmth of an ardent suitor, but a man intent on having his way. She had not noticed this in him before. But maybe she hadn't been interested enough to study his character. If she married him, his charming manner might grow thin if she didn't obey him. It occurred to her he lacked a lightness of spirit. That he may not find amusement in the foolish things she and Tate laughed about. It was true Tate had spoiled her for any man, and perhaps she was not being fair to Ormond. But until Tate finished this risky business he was involved in, she would not commit herself to Ormond or any gentleman.

After he bowed stiffly and left her with her mother, Ianthe searched for Lily. She found her slumped in her seat beside her mother, who was chatting flirtatiously to the man at her side. Ianthe didn't like the look of him. He had a raw-boned face and a thin, cruel mouth. It appalled her how pulled-down Lily appeared. If Ianthe had harbored any reservations about helping Bret, they were dispelled.

"Mama, I must visit the ladies' withdrawing room."

Her mother tsked. "Really, is that necessary? You will miss the next dance."

Ianthe put a hand to her hair. "One of these gold flowers has come loose. I'll ask the attendant to secure it."

As she walked past Lily, Ianthe stopped and turned back. "Why, it's Miss Forth, isn't it?" She greeted Lily's mother, who stared at her with a good deal of interest. "Lady Ianthe Granville. How do you do?"

The man beside her rose quickly to his feet and introduced himself as Mr. Rowse, bowing low over her hand while her mother gushed an airy welcome.

Ianthe turned to Lily. "I wonder if I might have a word, Miss Forth? I believe I saw you engaged in conversation with Lady Anne Rosedale, at the Kendalls' ball?"

Lily's eyes widened, but she had the wherewithal to nod agreement.

"I'm afraid Lady Anne hasn't been well." Ianthe smiled at Mr. and Mrs. Rowse. She put her hand to her hair, causing a gold flower to shift beneath her fingers. "I am worried, as I don't see her here tonight. Might she have mentioned anything to you, Miss Forth? I need to tidy my hair before a mirror. It would create a scandal if it tumbled down!" She tittered. "Would you accompany me? We can put our heads together and compare notes."

"Go with Lady Ianthe, Lily," her mother urged, her speculative gaze taking in Ianthe's gown, her dainty pearl and gold pendant, bracelet, and earrings. "Although I'm sure I'd recall you meeting Lady Anne."

"I met her first on the dance floor, Mama," Lily said as she left her seat. "In a set for the quadrille. And the next time, I'm not sure where you were..." Her voice trailed off as she considered it.

Annoyed, her mother waved her away.

"Oh, well done. I can almost believe there is such a person," Ianthe said once they moved out of earshot. She laughed and took Lily's arm. "Bret wishes to talk to you. He waits for you in an alcove in the corridor."

Lily turned to her with shining eyes. "Thank you, Lady Ianthe. You are so very kind."

"I wish you well, Lily." Ianthe smiled. "But first, come to the withdrawing room with me. Mr. Rowse might watch us."

"He is hateful," Lily said, her chest rising with quick breaths.

"I'm sure he is," Ianthe replied. "But you must be careful. There is much riding on your discretion."

"I will! And thank you again!"

Whatever occurred between Bret and Lily Ianthe wasn't privy to, having left her in his care. Returning to the ballroom, she accepted another gentleman for a country dance, not wishing to dance with Ormond a second time. She drooped with tiredness as the carriage took her and her mother home. London, which promised such excitement, had lost its luster.

"Lord Ormond shows a great deal of interest in you," Mama said from her corner of the coach. "Why don't you encourage him?"

"I am not sure I approve of Lord Ormond," Ianthe said honestly.

"Oh? In what manner?"

"He is hot-headed. He kept that hidden until recently."

Her mother laughed. "He wants to marry you. Is that so hard

to understand?"

"I suspect there is something more."

"I fear we are speaking at cross purposes. More what?"

"I don't know. I shall have to see."

"Well, of course you must be absolutely sure he is the man with whom you wish to spend the rest of your life. Although Lord Ormond is quite a catch," she said regretfully.

"Papa wouldn't insist, would he?"

"Men don't always understand matters of the heart. They are rational beings. He would be disappointed, naturally."

Ianthe chewed her bottom lip and stared out the window as the coach drew to a stop on the sweep of white gravel outside their mansion.

She did not sleep soundly that night. It was late when she went down to breakfast. Her mother, seated at the table with her coffee, perused a letter. "I have bad news." She glanced up. "Bertie has contracted the mumps."

"Oh no, poor Bertie. First Frederick's broken arm and now this!"

"I shall have to go to him," Mama said.

"Do you want me to come home with you?" Ianthe tried to hide her dismay.

"There is no need. You can go to your grandmother in Sloane Square. She will be happy to chaperone you."

"Very well, Mama." She hoped her grandmother would be. While Ianthe had always loved her company, Grandmama was not one for attending balls.

"As Cecily and Gerald have taken a house in London for the Season, she and Gerald can be of support to you and your grandmother."

"They only have eyes for each other and speak of little but their wedding and their bridal trip to Paris," Ianthe said crossly and somewhat unreasonably. Weddings were not her favorite subject. Had she allowed herself to be swept along toward marriage with a man she didn't love? There seemed an awful inevitability about it. Why should a woman be defined by her marriage? It was not so for men.

"And one day soon that will be you," Mama said with amusement as they entered the foyer.

"I shall be so glad to see Cecily." Her sister was the only one in the family Ianthe could confide in. But she knew what her sister would say. It was because of Tate. And it was.

Chapter Eight

C OMPARED TO THE Lexicon, Fortune House was like another world. A string quartet played a Bach concerto in a corner of one of the two elegant salons. Italian crystal chandeliers hung from the painted ceilings, showering the room with dancing lights. A myriad of blazing candles were reflected in the gilt-framed mirrors and lit the baize tables and expensive artworks hanging on the gilt-paneled walls. Men's cologne and women's flowery perfume scented the smoky air. The ladies one might find at a *ton* dinner party. Their voices restrained, they sat at the tables or walked about, their silks, satins, and jewels on display. Most were accompanied by male escorts, but a few ladies were alone. Donovan brought one of the latter to Tate's side.

Mrs. Granger, an American lady in deep magenta and black lace, eyed Tate speculatively as Donovan introduced them. Emerging from mourning, she was in her late twenties with abundant chestnut hair and brown eyes. When Donovan left them, she appraised Tate with a confident smile.

"Shall we enjoy a glass of champagne while you tell me what game interests you?" Tate gestured to a pair of gilt-legged chairs upholstered with satin and signaled the waiter. A wealthy woman, if one could judge by her jewels and appearance, and Donovan's interest in her, Mrs. Granger was very attractive. She gave Tate her full attention as he explained the rules of Hazard prior to her joining a table, after which, she attempted to discover more about him.

Unwilling to concoct a fabricated story, Tate evaded her questions, drawing her out by asking more about herself and her life in America.

Her accent was appealing as she explained her husband had been a diplomat and they had lived in Washington. He had died unexpectedly while visiting London, and unwilling to go home, she had stayed. With a shrewd glance, she shrugged her slim shoulders in the lustrous silk gown. "I can see you prefer your privacy, sir. I shall refrain from urging you to divulge that which you wish to keep secret. But I confess I find you an enigma."

He raised his eyebrows. "May I ask why you think so?"

"Because I sense you do not belong here." She smiled sweetly and placed her hand on his arm. "And I feel a little out of place myself."

"Why then did you come?" Tate asked, making a further attempt to lead the conversation away from him.

She nodded toward a group at the faro table. "My friends invited me. And I am lonely." She sighed. "My husband was very dear to me. I miss the life he and I shared, especially the evenings." Her gaze held his and a rueful smile lifted her lips.

"I understand." Touched by her honesty, Tate did not remove her hand, although he disliked encouraging her.

"Are you married, sir?"

Tate shook his head.

"Might you be lonely?"

"No. I can't say I am." He pushed away the thought that he would always be lonely without Ianthe in his life.

"Perhaps you are and don't realize it? Or is there a lady?" She nodded wisely. "There is always a lady for gentlemen such as you."

Tate smiled and briefly placed a hand over hers. "You flatter me."

Turning when the door opened to admit more guests, it was

all Tate could do not to jump to his feet. Long thirsting for a sign of Ianthe, he thought he had conjured her up. She entered with her brother-in-law, Gerald, and sister Cicely. Ianthe saw Tate lift his hand from Mrs. Granger's. Her eyes widened, and her steps faltered, causing Gerald to lean over and speak to her.

Mrs. Granger gazed from Tate to the new arrivals and then back to search his eyes. "Which lady has such an effect on you, I wonder," she mused, removing her hand and sitting back. "My guess is the lady in pink."

Ianthe's gaze still rested on him. She wore a short-sleeved, pale pink gown, long white gloves on her slender arms and a silver shawl draped at her elbows; diamantes sparkled in her hair. She looked quite the loveliest he had ever seen her. The men in the room thought so too, most of them turning appreciative eyes upon her. It was a testament to her beauty, Tate thought, when she could turn a man's eyes away from his card play. He suffered a swift surge of jealousy and deep anguish.

Ianthe's eyes widened as she glanced from him to Mrs. Granger, seated so intimately close to him. She spoke to Cecily and Gerald. They looked his way then strolled over to watch a game of faro. He was relieved when it appeared they did not intend to claim an acquaintance. But his relief was short-lived. What would Ianthe think of finding him here with Mrs. Granger? And why had she come? Had Bret told her he was here? If so, Tate would take him apart limb by limb.

"Mr. Bradley?"

Mrs. Granger observed him.

"I beg your pardon, Mrs. Granger." Tate rose and offered her his arm. "Shall we begin?"

Tate led her over to the guests gathered around the Hazard table, watching the shooter toss the dice as Donovan emerged from his office.

Tate almost groaned. Ianthe was not about to become a person of interest for that scoundrel. Not now, when he'd given up so much to ensure that would never happen. It became increasingly urgent for him to give up this life with the vowel in his possession. Donovan must leave to oversee his other establishment soon, if not tonight.

He urged himself to be patient, but his shoulders were stiff, and he forced a smile for Mrs. Granger's benefit when she took a turn with the dice and tossed down a four and a six.

His subtle glance revealed Ianthe standing beside Cecily while they watched Gerald play. Raising her eyes to Tate, Ianthe shook her head. A slight action no one but he would detect. Had she given up on him? He could not blame her.

Donovan strolled across to Ianthe. Snapping his fingers, he called for champagne and a servant to bring two chairs for the ladies to be seated.

Ianthe offered the Irishman a gracious smile, which was so engaging it made Tate catch his breath. It appeared that Donovan thought so, too.

Mrs. Granger, having turned the dice over to the player next to her, asked him a question. He forced himself to give her his attention.

An hour had passed when Ianthe, without another look in his direction, left the club with her sister and brother-in-law. Even if he managed to keep Cloudhill for future generations, and even if Ianthe was still free, would she even want to marry him? Had he lost any hope of her love? While he prayed it was not so, he resolved to keep her safe.

He found it impossible to abandon all hope, however, and acted with haste when Donovan and two of his men left the club. As soon as the door closed behind them, Tate stood. He excused himself to Mrs. Granger, who was doing remarkably well, having taken the dice again.

After a quick glance around, he slipped into the office. A lamp burned on the wide, carved cedar desk, the glow behind the glass throwing an arc of dim light into the room. The replica of a gentleman's library, he noted wryly. Donovan would fancy himself one as he sat here. Bookshelves filled two walls, the floorboards covered in richly-patterned Eastern rugs. Tate went straight to the large cupboard and found it unlocked. Inside were ledgers, receipts, and correspondence in cardboard files. He searched through them then put them back.

A watercolor of a hare by Albrecht Dürer hung on the wall. Tate lifted a corner and peered behind it. His breath caught when he found a locked wooden box fitted into a space in the wall. His heart galloping, he tried the handle. No key. An eye on the door, he rummaged through the desk drawers. Did Donovan keep them on him? It was something he might do, Tate thought bitterly. But wait... He turned back to the ornate desk. The desk in the library at Cloudhill was like this one and had a secret drawer. Tate lost precious time prodding the protuberances before conceding that this one didn't. He looked under the blotter. Not there. With a creeping sense of failure, he lifted the erotic small bronze statue of Pan, which sat on a corner of the desk. Beneath it was a brass key.

Hurrying over, Tate removed the picture and placed it on the floor. He unlocked the box and opened it. He searched through a bundle of papers, which appeared to concern property transactions. Searching further, he found a folder tied with a purple ribbon. Lifting it out, he took it to the desk. Inside were a bunch of vowels. Many lives held in the balance by the greedy crook, Donovan. Sifting through them, Tate leaped upon his father's vowel, his pulse beating hard. With no time to scrutinize it in the poor light, he shoved the paper into his coat pocket and returned the folder to the box. After locking the door, he replaced the picture and returned the key to its spot beneath the statue. Then he checked to make sure everything was as he found it before leaving the room.

His heart still pounding, he returned to the widow.

She smiled up at him. "I am most pleased with myself, Mr. Bradley. I have won ten pounds!"

"Well done."

"Time to go while I'm ahead, don't you think?"

"That's wise." He pulled out her chair.

She rose. "I wonder if you might accompany me. My friends left an hour ago. But I wanted to keep playing."

"It will be my pleasure." Tate felt the vowel rustle in his pocket as he settled her cape over her arms.

When their carriage drew up outside Grillon's hotel, Tate escorted the lady into the foyer. She stopped him as he prepared to leave. "Would you care to come to my suite for a drink? I can offer you a splendid Cognac."

"I deeply regret having to refuse. The evening is not yet over for me. There is something I must do."

"The lady in pink?"

Tate shook his head. "Not a matter of romance." He lifted her hand to his lips and kissed her gloved fingers. "It has been a delight, Mrs. Granger."

She sighed. "For me also, Mr. Bradley." She walked to the stairs, her backward glance regretful.

When the hackney deposited him outside the inn, Tate raced up the stairs to his room. He lit a candle and closed the door. Dragging off his tight coat, he removed the vowel from the pocket and held it up to the light. His heart beat like a drum against his ribs. A simple dot above the I! The signature lacked the heart-shaped loop his father had been at pains to show him. Yet it bore the wax seal and was witnessed, although the signature was indecipherable.

Tate sank down on the bed and found he was shaking. "I'll set this to rights, Papa," he said in a husky voice, his throat tight. "If it's the last thing I do."

He tucked the vowel into his coin purse and looked for a hiding place. He found a loose floorboard near the corner of the room and jimmied it up, pushing the coin purse into the space beneath, then stamped it down and covered it with the rug mere seconds before the door burst open.

Two burly men shoved their way into the room. These were not Donovan's usual men, who were fearsome enough. These were thieves from some St. Giles gang with knives tucked into their belts. "Donovan wants to see ye," one said, his grin displaying several missing teeth.

"Tell him to come up. I'm happy to see him."

"Donovan takes no orders from anyone." The largest of the two grabbed Tate's arms and pinned them behind him while the other tied his wrists with twine. Tate struggled until punched hard in the solar plexus. He groaned and bent over painfully, breathing through his nose. "Not a word out of ye or ye'll get far worse."

They dragged him out into the corridor, down the steps, and outside.

Donovan stalked the alley beside the inn. He swung around as they shoved Tate toward him, making it hard to keep his balance.

"What the devil is this?" Tate demanded.

"Search him," Donovan ordered.

They subjected him to further rough handling while they examined his clothes.

Donovan watched, his arms folded, jaw rigid. "Take off his boots."

Pushed to the ground, Tate tried to kick out at them as they dragged them off. It earned him another painful jab to his stomach.

"Nothin' here."

Donovan scowled. "Where is the vowel, Mr. Bradley?"

"I don't know what you're talking about," Tate said, wincing. "Have you lost your mind, Donovan?" They would tear the room apart. Had he hidden it well enough?

"I've had my eye on you, Mr. Bradley. You're working for your relative, the Duke of Lindsey. That is why I kept you close. It doesn't matter if you found it. The old duke signed it, and his solicitors have seen it." He rocked on his toes, his mouth a mean harsh line. "But I should like it back to keep as a record. I advise you to hand it over."

"Go to hell."

Donovan turned to the two men, who stood with fists clenched. "Work him over."

The first few punches were excruciating before he sank into a welcome well of blackness, not sure he would ever see the light again.

>>><<<

"WHAT WAS TATE doing there with that woman?" Cecily asked in the carriage as they wended their way to their grandmother's townhouse.

"I don't know."

Cecily shook her arm. "And dressed so strangely? Has he become a fop?" She raised her eyebrows accusingly. You knew he'd be at Fortune House. That is why you asked us to go there."

Ianthe flushed. While Bret hadn't mentioned the name, she had hoped to find Tate there. Now she wished she hadn't. "I merely wished to visit a gambling house," she said, sounding unconvincing even to her.

"You should forget him, Ianthe. Don't you think so, Gerald?"

With a vague nod, it became clear Gerald considered it wise to remain silent.

Cecily frowned at him then turned back to her. "I've always been fond of Tate, but he appears to have taken a wrong turn since his father died."

"You always make hasty judgements, Cecily," Ianthe snapped.

"I don't believe I do," Cecily huffed.

Ianthe sighed. "I'm sorry. That was mean. I'm tired and I feel guilty for having dragged you both there."

"Nonsense, we enjoyed it, didn't we, Gerald? You won a little at cards, did you not, darling?"

"A few pounds, my sweet." Gerald smiled fondly at his new

wife.

As the newlyweds gazed at each other, Ianthe wrestled with her thoughts. She was angry and confused, but worse, he had broken her heart.

Once home, she undressed quickly and fell miserably into bed, turning restlessly. She couldn't banish the sight of Tate, seated close to the woman whose hand rested on his arm. On intimate terms, it would seem. And here she was, desperately concerned about him. Ianthe screwed her eyes shut. She would waste no more tears for the Duke of Lindsey! Minutes passed before his face entered her thoughts again, a warning in his green eyes. It seemed to her that he did not want to be recognized. For what reason? She moaned and thumped her pillow. She wouldn't think about it anymore. But she must see Bret. She might persuade him to tell her more.

Still exhausted, she slept late and went down to breakfast at ten o'clock. It astonished Ianthe to find her grandmother seated at the dining table when it was her habit to remain in bed until noon.

"I have been waiting for you, miss," Grandmama said. "Please sit down." She beckoned to the footman. "Henry, we shall have our tea and toast."

"What is it, Grandmama?" Ianthe asked as the footman hurried to obey.

"I have received a missive from Gerald, delivered at a most uncivilized time of the morning, expressing some concern about you. And well, he might! It was my belief you were to attend the theater, but apparently you persuaded him and Cecily to visit a gambling club afterwards."

"It is an elegant club, Grandmama. Many ladies and gentlemen were there."

"But you deliberately misled me when you knew I would refuse such a request."

"I am sorry. I was curious to see one when I'd heard so much about them. But we were quite safe with Gerald accompanying us. His footman stood outside the door."

"I have a good mind to send you back home to your mother."

Ianthe gasped. "Oh, please don't, Grandmama. I shan't do it again."

Her grandmother sipped her tea and eyed Ianthe over the rim. "I suspect it has something to do with Tate."

Ianthe widened her eyes. "Tate?"

"Yes. It was the family's expectation that he'd propose to you after Cecily married. He did not. But because he is in mourning, we must give him time to recover from the loss of his beloved father."

"Yes, of course," Ianthe murmured. Did grief send him into the arms of that woman? An attractive and charming American widow, as she discovered. Ianthe's shoulders drooped. When she'd spent most of her life in the countryside, how could she compete with such a person?

"Still, there is a lot you are not telling me. You can confide in me, child. I have withstood much in my long life and there is little you can say to shock me."

Ianthe swallowed. "You are the best of grandmamas," she said sincerely.

"No need for that. Remember, the offer remains, should you wish to talk." She addressed the footman. "Where is the toast, Henry? Will we have it before luncheon?"

"I have it ready, my lady." Henry carried over the rack of toast, butter, and strawberry preserve on a tray, obviously used to the whims of her grandmother.

Ianthe would love to confess all, but there was little her grandmother could do. Too little any of them could do. And she might act on the threat to send her home. Best to allow Tate to deal with this matter in his own way. Even though it led him away from her. She sighed, swallowed, and buttered her toast, aware of her grandmother's sharp gaze.

"Tell me more about your new suitor, Lord Ormond. I cannot say I warmed to him."

Ianthe put down her toast when crumbs stuck in her throat. "Papa approves of him, and Mama will always do Papa's bidding. But I know so little about him, Grandmama."

"Nevertheless," her grandmother said implacably. "Tell me what you do know."

"He is personable, and heir to a marquessate." She wondered if she should mention how forceful Ormond had been. Would her grandmother stand by her if her father urged her to marry him? Ianthe prayed she would.

"He sounds perfectly respectable. What is it you don't like about him?"

When Ianthe explained how Ormond had pressured her about an engagement even though she had yet to accept him, her grandmother raised her eyebrows and paused, spreading jam on her toast.

"Mama says it's because he is in love with me," Ianthe added hastily, not wishing to draw ire upon her parents.

"But you don't feel the same?"

"Not in the way I would wish."

"Then what do you feel about him?"

"I don't know what to think. I would like more time to get to know him. These things seem terribly rushed."

"Then you must take it, my dear. But don't use Tate as the touchstone for every gentleman you meet."

Ianthe drew in a sharp breath. "I don't," she blustered.

"Has Tate ever kissed you?"

She closed her eyes, remembering, the slumberous expression in his eyes, the hiss of his breath before he pulled away. "No. We almost kissed at a parlor game. Everyone was laughing and larking about. I wanted to kiss him. I suppose he's forgotten all about it."

Grandmama raised her brows, compassion in her eyes. "But you haven't, I gather."

Ianthe sagged in her chair and shook her head.

"And you don't feel that way about Ormond."

"Not yet."

"Then perhaps you never will, my dear. There are plenty of fish in the sea, as the saying goes. I hope your father understands that and gives you time to meet many more of them."

Ianthe smiled. "I am so glad I came to stay with you, Grandmama. Not that I wanted poor Bertie to get the mumps, of course."

"Of course not," Grandmama said with a faint smile.

Tate appeared charmed by the American. Ianthe chewed her lip. Did she no longer mean anything to him? She placed a hand against her heart to ease the anguish, and then hastily removed it before her grandmother saw and correctly interpreted the gesture.

Grandmama wished to help, but could she? Ianthe nourished the tiniest hope she would.

Chapter Nine

WAKING FELT LIKE rising from the dead. With a moan of protest at the fierce throb at his temples, Tate opened his eyes. Once his hazy vision cleared, a woman's freckled face appeared, leaning over him.

"Thought you might die on me."

He knew her. She always greeted him on the street with a friendly smile. "Sorry to worry you, Annie." He raised his head, causing more pain to wrack through it, and looked around her small room. It smelled of stale, cheap perfume and something he didn't like to put a name to. "What day is it?"

"Monday. You've been out of it since Friday. I washed you and got you to eat a few spoonfuls of soup yesterday."

He lifted the sheet. He was in his drawers and stockings, his chest bare. "I don't remember. Where did you find me?"

She poured him a glass of ale. "In the alley beside the inn, on me way back from a customer. It rained that night. You woulda died for sure if I'd left you."

"I am immensely grateful." He licked his bottom lip and discovered a sore split. Struggling up on his elbows, he drank some warm ale, grateful for it. His throat felt as dry as the Sahara. "How did you get me here?"

"Me pimp, Pete, hauled you up the steps."

"He'll be angry with you for looking after me. I'm bad for

business."

"Pete's all right. He thinks you'll be good for a bit of blunt."
She rubbed an eyebrow. "He helped himself to your watch. And
your waistcoat, fine silk, it is." She frowned. "I hid your boots and
wouldn't let him take your pantaloons or your shirt."

Tate eyed a raised red mark on her cheek. "Pete better not
have taken it out on you." He dragged himself up. Every part of
his body ached. He'd have some colorful bruises. "There should
be some money back at the inn. I'll bring it."

"No need to rush off. I'll get you some food."

"I'd appreciate something to eat. You're a grand girl, Annie."

"That's what they all say."

Annie hurried over to a cupboard and took out a loaf of bread
and a chunk of ham. She sliced them and served them to him on a
cracked plate. "No butter, sorry."

Tate took a bite. His stomach lurched, but he plowed on.
"This is the best meal I have had for years."

Annie grinned. "You wouldn't kid me, would you, lad?"

"Lad? Where are you from, Annie?" he asked as he ate the
bread and ham and washed it down with ale.

"Up Leeds way."

"Of course. You're a long way from home."

She shrugged her thin shoulders. "With nine children still
living at home and me father out of work, I couldn't stay. I hoped
to find a job as a maid in London, but had no luck."

"What happened?"

"Met a fella who promised to look out for me, but before I
knew it, I was on the street with all me savings gone."

"I am sorry, Annie."

She took the empty plate from him. "Life's not so bad."

Tate didn't believe her, but said nothing. He cautiously
swung his legs over the edge of the narrow bed and placed his
stockinged feet on the floor. "May I have my clothes? I could do
with some help with my boots."

She ran to get them. It was a painful struggle, but he was glad of them when he gingerly got to his feet. He felt woozy, but his head soon cleared. Why hadn't Donovan made a better fist of killing him? "I'd better go, but I'll come back tomorrow."

"You can stay awhile if you want."

He smiled and shook his head. "What would Pete say about that?"

"Oh, him." She shrugged. "I'd probably get a clip over me ear. Unless he thinks summat good will come of it."

"Tell him I'll be back with some money. But he won't get a penny of it if he hurts you."

Tate managed the narrow stairs to the street. The day was cool, and he shivered in his shirt sleeves, but passersby barely gave him a look.

The innkeeper was at his desk. He looked up at Tate and raised his eyebrows. "Mr. Bradley. I thought you'd gone for good."

"And leave my luggage? My key, please. I want to go to my room."

"You no longer have a room. You haven't paid."

Tate frowned. He put his hands on the desk. "Where is my luggage?"

The fellow leaned away from him. "In the storage room out back. Yer lucky. We don't keep things long here. No room."

"Lucky for you that you did. You could hardly have missed seeing me dragged outside into the alley beside this inn and beaten within an inch of my life."

He flushed. "A lot goes on around here. I don't get involved."

"You could have sent someone to Bow Street for help. It's just up the road." Tate shook his head. "I want to see the room."

"Why?"

"Never mind why. Anyone in it?"

"No."

Tate held out his hand. "The key?"

The innkeeper's gaze swept over him, noting the absence of a coat and his dirty and crumpled pantaloons.

"Any reason why I should, sir?"

"Will five pounds persuade you?"

The man's eyes widened. "Where is it?"

"It would be wise to believe me."

The man handed over the key to Tate. "I'll have that right back along with the five pounds, sir," he said, although his voice faltered at the fiery light in Tate's eyes. "You are welcome to stay should you pay for the night."

"My luggage?"

Some minutes later, carrying his portmanteau, Tate climbed the stairs and let himself into the room. He shut the door and locked it, then knelt down and pulled up the corner of the rug then levered up the floorboard. The coin purse was there with the vowel still inside, along with his money. With a surge of relief, he sank down on the bed, holding the piece of paper which could cause such hurt to so many in his hands. He would have to move fast before Donovan located him again. He hadn't seen any suspicious characters lurking outside, but they might come back to watch the inn. Was Donovan's intention to get the vowel back the reason he was still alive? But for how long?

Longing for a bath, he put on clean pantaloons and his dark blue coat, tying a cravat at his throat. Carrying his portmanteau, he left the inn by the rear entrance, climbed over the low back wall, and checking to see he wasn't followed, walked around the block before going up to Annie.

When he handed her twenty pounds, her eyes widened. "Lawks!"

With a rush of sympathy, Tate guessed she would never have seen such a sum in her life. For now, it was all he could do. He told her to give Pete half the money, and to hide the rest.

"Do you want me to help you find a position in a household, Annie?" Tate asked.

Hope filled her eyes only to be dashed again. "Pete would kill me."

"I can't do it now. But I won't forget you," Tate said.

Tate went downstairs. Annie probably didn't believe him. Her experience on the streets would make her distrustful of everyone.

Around the corner, a hackney waited at the stand. Tate directed the jarvey to Steven's Hotel on Bond Street. Known to be frequented by officers in the army, it would be difficult for Donovan to accost him there, supposing he could find him.

The jarvey pulled up outside the hotel, where two saddle horses and a tilbury waited. Tate entered the busy foyer and paid for a room, ordered a bath, a barber, and a good meal, after which he would make his way to the family solicitors.

He would now be recognized, and realized he'd have to get word to Bret to lie low. Feeling more like his old self, Tate emerged from his room some hours later and entered the hotel dining room. The hotel laundry had pressed his one good coat and polished his boots while he bathed, and a barber removed the dark stubble on his jaw and neatened his hair and sideburns.

Tate knew the fight for Cloudhill was far from over. After doing justice to well-cooked, flavorsome roast beef and vegetables, followed by several cups of coffee, he traveled to an office near Lincoln's Inn to consult Pendle & Pendle, the family solicitors. He would leave the vowel in their safekeeping. Should anything happen to him, his uncle could continue his fight to keep Cloudhill in the family. But Tate didn't fool himself. Donovan wasn't the sort to give in easily. No doubt the Irishman pictured himself riding over the Cloudhill estate. It would take a mighty effort and some swift action to thwart him. And the question yet to be solved was why his father didn't question it immediately.

BRET APPEARED AT Mrs. Tomlinson's card party. He looked uncomfortable. Ianthe knew he usually avoided small, intimate gatherings. When the opportunity arose, she strolled out into the small walled garden. He soon joined her, and they met behind a hedge out of sight of the house. How anxious he looked. Fear rippled through her. Was it Tate? She grew annoyed with herself when she remembered the last time she'd seen Tate. With the widow at Fortune House. "What has happened?" she asked Bret. "Is it Lily?"

He shook his head and drew her further into the shadows. "Tate didn't turn up at Hyde Park on Saturday."

"Are you sure you didn't mistake the day?"

"Quite certain. You haven't seen or heard from him?"

"Not since last Friday evening at Fortune House."

Bret scowled at her. "Why did you go there?"

"Why not? It's a perfectly respectable club. My sister and her husband accompanied me. I wanted to see what a gambling club was like. I didn't expect to find Tate there."

"But you hoped to." Bret groaned. "He'll think I told you about the club. I'm in for it." He rubbed his creased forehead, obviously concerned. "I wonder where he's got to."

"Tate was with an American lady. Perhaps he is with her now." Her breath caught in her throat, and it was a minute or two before she felt she could compose herself to speak. "Do you know where he is staying?"

"No. He never told me. Somewhere near Covent Garden."

"What hotels are around there?"

"I doubt he'd stay at one of the best hotels. He wouldn't want to be noticed."

"Why was he at Fortune House?" Ianthe asked anxiously.

"He's after proof to prevent a crime against his family." Bret held up his hands. "Don't ask me anything more. I'm in enough trouble already."

"At Mr. Donovan's club?" A chill ran down her spine. "If Tate contacts you, please send me a message straightaway."

"I will." He peered around the end of the hedge. "Your grandmother appears to be looking for you."

"Bother."

"We'll have to be patient," Bret said. "Wait for him to contact us."

Ianthe wasn't good at waiting. Her mother accused her of impatience all the time. She left Bret and hurried back to the house. Gerald had been reluctant to take them to Fortune House. He'd told her Mr. Donovan might look like a gentleman, but he was from the criminal class. She shivered and rubbed her arms. She wished Bret would tell her more. But Tate would always take risks if he felt the need for it. Suppressing a shiver, she entered through the door. The time might come when she wouldn't see Tate anymore, but just knowing he was alive would ease her torment. She couldn't bear it if he was no longer in the world.

Her grandmother raised her eyebrows. "Who did you talk to in the garden?"

"It was Tate, Grandmama."

"Tate? Why hasn't he come to greet me?"

"He had to leave and sought a quick word with me."

"About what?"

Ianthe crossed her fingers behind her back. "He intends to sell a horse to Papa, and asked my opinion."

"He meets you in the bushes to seek your opinion on horse flesh? You are making a May game of me, my girl. And you have to get up very early in the morning to succeed in that." She shook her head. "We shall talk further at home."

"Yes, Grandmama," Ianthe said meekly.

"You aren't planning on eloping with him, are you, Ianthe?" Her voice dropped. "I know your father isn't as warm to the idea of your marriage to Tate as he once was."

"No, Tate doesn't want to marry me, Grandmama."

"Now I consider that a bag of moonshine."

At first, startled by her grandmother's use of language, Ianthe gazed at her hopefully. "Do you really?"

"It was quite bad of him to lurk about in the garden in that fashion..." She frowned. "Listen, my dear. Don't commit yourself to this fellow, Ormond, until you are very sure."

"But Father..."

"I will handle your father. I could do it when he was in lead-ing strings. And I still can!" She sighed. "Here comes Mrs. Hollingdale to bore me to death. Find the waiter. I shall need champagne to endure it."

Ianthe hurried away. For all her Grandmama's fierceness, could a frail old lady still hold sway over her father?

Chapter Ten

THE CLERK SHOWED Tate into the office of Mr. Henry Pendle. He declined the offer of tea, produced the vowel, and got straight to the point.

"It's quite plain this is not my father's signature." He pointed to the dot over the *I* in Lindsey. "You must agree the extravagant loop, which looks like a broken heart, is missing."

Pendle smoothed his bald pate as he studied it. "We considered it authentic, but that was because the former duke failed to advise us it was a forgery."

"My father was ill and had his reasons. I believed he sought to slow proceedings, relying on me to deal with this fraudulent attack to despoil his character and claim Cloudhill."

"Extraordinary!" Pendle waved the vowel. "And it's to do with this man, Donovan?"

"Yes, the scoundrel who has grown wealthy by destroying men's lives. But beyond that I don't know. I intend to find out."

Henry sat cogitating while Tate grew more and more nervous. Then he sent for his son in the adjoining office.

William, a younger version of his father with a little more hair, took up a magnifying glass and studied the signature, then called for documents to be brought which were signed by Tate's father in past transactions to compare them.

"Yes, there is quite a marked difference." Henry looked at

Tate over the top of his spectacles. "However, it has the wax seal."

Tate nodded. "Could that not be forged?"

"Very difficult. Although most things can be from my experience," Pendle the elder said.

"However, should the executor of your father's estate, which is your Uncle Clive, Earl of Butte, refuse to sign the contract, which he will do in such a serious matter as this, I doubt Mr. Donovan will accept it without a fight," William warned.

"I foresee a court case." Henry's eyes lit up with the scent of battle.

Tate sat back, arms crossed. "What are my chances should it come to that?"

They frowned at each other. "We will produce these documents and more to show the consistency of your father's signature and refute Mr. Donovan's claim." Henry folded his hands on top of the desk. "But it would be helpful to learn the circumstances your father found himself in. Why did he not nip this in the bud? You say you believe he never gambled. Families sometimes aren't aware…" His voice faded at Tate's scowl.

Tate shook his head. "He did not."

"Some speculative investments which might have gone wrong, perhaps?"

William nodded. "There is that coal mine in the north. The coal seam ran out."

"Yes, but most of my father's investments are sound, as you know, and as his banker will attest," Tate said, growing annoyed. "You cannot possibly suggest he was on the brink of bankruptcy."

Henry nodded and twirled the quill in his fingers. "I shall advise the purchaser of the change of circumstances. Then we'll leave it to you to discover more while we await a response from Mr. Donovan."

Tate left their office. In the street, his elation at having at least delayed the sale of Cloudhill ebbed away when he considered how the matter was yet to be resolved. How difficult would it be to discover what lay behind all this?

He visited his bank, then returned to the hotel and penned a note to Bret to alert him to the potential danger and request a meeting at a tavern in the Seven Dials at six o'clock, where he trusted no one would recognize him.

Just before six, Bret walked into the taproom. Removing his hat, he sat and stared with concern at the bruise on Tate's cheek. "Donovan?"

Tate nodded to the pot boy, who placed two tankards of ale before them. "I found the vowel in the office at his gaming hell. Signed and sealed. I've left it with the solicitors. They have stopped the sale."

Bret's eyes widened. "I say, that's splendid news. That's the end of it?"

"Not really, even though it appears my father's signature has been forged."

"Donovan will dispute it?"

"I imagine the matter will go to court."

"And if he loses, he'll come after you again."

"I'm sure of it. Be careful. He believes me to be my cousin, acting on instructions when I stole the vowel."

"Then we are both in danger," Bret said, massaging the side of his neck.

"Knowing how the man thinks, Donovan will file the documents in court as a matter of urgency. Then he'll wait for the decision. But whether or not he wins, he'll want to finish this." Tate thought back to Donovan smiling while watching his men savagely beat him. "He's in league with criminals, but even worse, violence comes naturally to him."

"Here's to getting the better of him." Bret raised the tankard. "You want me to disappear?"

"It would be wise."

"Doesn't suit me to go off and leave you to deal with this alone. And nor will I leave Lily."

Bret had grown in confidence and stature. A different man to the one Tate met what seemed like a long time ago now. But might this newfound confidence lead him to disaster? "What are your intentions?"

"I must get her away, but I'll have to find the best way. Ianthe will help me."

"Yes. Ianthe." Tate frowned. "Did you tell her about Fortune House?"

Bret shook his head. "I didn't. Lady Ianthe is smart. It's a gaming house which welcomes women, and I suppose she hoped to see you there."

"She saw me."

"And she didn't like what she saw."

Tate shrugged. "I squired a lady for the evening. Donovan's orders."

"Lady Ianthe might not see it that way."

Tate hated her thinking so poorly of him. He tightened his jaw. "She's going to marry Ormond, though, isn't she?"

"He's always there, conversing with her parents, or dancing with her. There can be no doubt he's preparing the ground."

"Bloody hell."

"Just what does she mean to you? If I can be so presumptuous as to ask."

Tate scowled. "It's never held you back before." He whipped off his hat and raked through his hair. "I love Ianthe, and it's killing me! I hoped for us to marry, before…" He looked away from Bret to calm himself.

Bret put a reassuring hand on Tate's shoulder. "Then why not tell her? You should fight for her if you love her."

Tate shook his head. "Her father has made it clear he no longer favors me. He wants Ianthe to marry Ormond, who can offer her so much more than I can." Calmer now, but not resigned to it. He never could be. "A duke without an estate and limited funds isn't good enough for his daughter. And even if Lord Granville could be persuaded to change his mind, I wouldn't agree to it. Live off her dowry in a small estate miles from anywhere? Accept financial assistance from her father? No, I won't do it to Ianthe. The only way marriage is possible is if, and when, I can go hat in hand to her father with the confidence of knowing I'm the best man for her."

"You should let Ianthe decide. It's obvious she loves you. Why not elope as we plan to do?"

"It's not that simple, my friend." Tate's fingers grasped tight around his tankard. "Ianthe is not in any danger. She is a cherished daughter with a bright future. Which seems not to be the case for Lily."

"That's true. Lily has told me how they shut her in her room for hours without food. That rotten devil who controls her mother will force her into this marriage. And there are rumors about Baron Bolton. They say he has a contagious disease." Bret groaned. "True or not, I would rather they throw me into Newgate than see her married to him." He traced a bit of spilled ale on the table with his finger, and then looked up as if to judge Tate's reaction. "I still think you should tell Ianthe how you feel. Where will this strict sense of honor get you?"

"It's the way I was raised. That is what my family expects of me."

"I'm glad I wasn't born into the aristocracy, although I wish I could offer Lily a more comfortable life. When we marry, tutoring will not be possible. I'll need to find a suitable position quickly." He hesitated. "I rather hoped you might help."

"Anything I can do. Depend upon it. When is it to be?"

"I was confident you would help us, and we very much appreciate it," Bret said with a relieved smile. "But we must wait until the family leaves London during mid-summer."

"But that's weeks away. Lily could be engaged or even married to Baron Bolton by then."

"Engaged, perhaps, but not married. Lily says Bolton is set on an autumn wedding. He wants his relatives who are traveling in Italy to attend."

"Do you realize society won't sanction this? You will be ostracized."

"It won't bother us once we leave London. We shan't tie our lives to the dictates of the *ton*. Lily wishes to live quietly, and so do I."

Falling silent, Tate uneasily contemplated his future while Bret stared into his ale. Both their plans depended on so much going right, which at this moment, seemed very unlikely.

Tate stirred. "While the solicitors deal with this, I need to get out of London. I'm traveling to the country to visit my mother. On my return, I'll move into Lindsey Court. It will give you time to make other arrangements."

"I have to admit to being glad it's over. While I'm not sorry I agreed to it, especially meeting Lily, it's been unnerving at times. Especially now when a missive has arrived from the Prince of Wales. He plans a party after his return from Brighton with music selected from Handel's compositions, listed on the invitation. I'll gladly leave it for you to answer. And your valet wrote. He returns to London next week."

"Good." Tate eyed Bret's crisp cravat. "The laundry maids are serving you well."

Bret flushed. "Can't say I enjoy having to dress so carefully. At least I was spared a valet putting his hands on me."

Tate laughed.

"I'll attend the last spring ball of the Season and try to have a quick word with Lily. By the time you return to London, I shall have slipped back into obscurity."

"So, you won't miss this life even a little?" Tate asked.

"It's exciting, but no, I'm not cut out for it. All I need in life is Lily beside me."

Tate nodded, understanding. If he had Ianthe, he could bear anything that came his way. Ianthe had loved him. But he couldn't be sure now. Stripped of his standing in society, he didn't feel the same man. But if, like Lily, Ianthe still loved him, and was deeply unhappy with what her father proposed for her, he would fight for her in a heartbeat. Although, right now, it seemed a nearly impossible mountain to climb.

They finished their ale and left the table. "Write to me at Lindsey Court and tell me how you go on and where I might find you. I'd like to help with your elopement if I can."

"I would appreciate it. And I won't be far away," Bret said. He grinned. "I have a feeling you might need me."

Tate put a hand on his shoulder. "Thank you. Donovan is a vicious devil. Watch your back."

Putting on his hat, he stepped out into the lane. Something good had come of this, his friendship with Bret. He hoped one day to trace the family connection.

He walked down the street, his thoughts on Ianthe. If only he could do as Bret suggested and tell her of his feelings. If only it was that simple. But if she gave him some sign she loved him, he may not be able to resist.

⇒⇒⇒≪≪≪

WHEN IANTHE LEFT the room at a card party to seek some air, Ormond appeared in the corridor. "Shall we take a turn around the terrace?" He took her arm and ushered her through the doors a footman had opened for them.

Out in the cool air, her heart in her throat, she drew away from him but could think of no polite way to refuse. She went to the balcony rail to gaze into the small walled garden, barely aware of the picturesque floral display.

He stood beside her, his hands near hers on the rail. "We have spent a fair amount of time together these last few weeks, have we not?"

"Yes." But not at her request, she wanted to add.

"I hoped you might come to know me. I am confident I know enough about you, Lady Ianthe, to want you for my wife."

She turned to look up at him. "But you don't know me, Lord Ormond. You know nothing of my hopes and dreams."

He laughed and looked down his long nose. "I know they are the dreams of a young woman, highly romantic and not always practical."

Incensed, she clamped her lips on a rebuke which would get back to her father. There was something relentless about Ormond. He was not used to being thwarted, she suspected, and he did not like it. "What are your hopes for the future, sir?"

He raised his eyebrows. "Mine? To marry, naturally. As my father's heir, I am expected to have sons, but this you would know."

"And what if we marry and I cannot give you an heir?"

His assessing gaze roamed over her body. "You are a healthy young woman. It seems unlikely."

"You have no daughters by your first marriage?"

His eyes were like hard brown agates. "My wife could not bear a living child." He forced a smile. "That is highly unlikely to happen again."

"I might have only daughters. Will you be content to love them?"

"Of course not. Daughters are of no importance. I need a son and heir. But I find this conversation distasteful. A young woman of your breeding should not speak of such things."

She raised her chin. "We are talking about my future, my lord."

"Which will be in excellent hands." He leaned forward, his breath hot on her neck as he kissed her cheek. "Now, shall we stop this? And talk instead of wedding plans?"

"No!" His lips on her skin had repulsed her. She could not keep up the pretense a moment longer. "I consider it fair to tell you now that I won't marry you, Lord Ormond."

He drew back as if she'd slapped him.

His eyebrows snapped together. "You've kept me hanging on, believing..."

"I have done no such thing."

"Your father will wish to hear of this. A slip of a girl has no say over her future."

Suddenly afraid, Ianthe side-stepped him and rushed to the door, fearing he might compromise her. Would her grandmother be able to deal with her father's anger? Papa was sure she would marry Ormond. He merely gave her time to warm to him. Her mind in a whirl, she hurried back to the card party.

Her grandmother looked up and saw the obvious distress on her face. She noticed Ormond coming in behind her. She laid her cards down and left the table. Taking Ianthe's arm, she drew her into a quiet corner. "You're trembling. What is it, Ianthe?"

"I won't marry that man," Ianthe murmured. "He wants a wife for only one reason, to give him an heir. He doesn't care a whit for me. And he takes no heed of what I say. There's something about him I don't trust."

"Calm yourself, my dear. I shall not allow him to browbeat you further tonight. I'll request your father come to see me tomorrow."

Ianthe released her breath. "Thank you, Grandmama."

"Now, I see Tate has arrived, and looks your way." She gave Ianthe a gentle push. "Speak to him. He will put a smile back on your pretty face."

Vaguely aware her grandmother was still hopeful of a match with Tate, she made her way over to Bret.

"I hope you are well, Your Grace." She curtsied.

He took her gloved hands as she rose to her feet. "I am, thank you, Lady Ianthe. I can see you are in excellent health, as you have a fetching color in your cheeks."

It was due to anger and distress, but she smiled up at him as they strolled over the floor.

"I plan to leave London shortly. To visit my mother," Bret explained. "Might I write to you?" he asked in an undertone.

"Yes. Please do." She glanced over her shoulder to where Lily's mother and her new husband were at the faro table. "Come to the morning room in ten minutes. I will go directly to make sure no guests are there, and then I'll bring Lily to you."

He nodded, then strolled away to watch a game of whist.

After seeing the two lovers together, Ianthe left the room and found her grandmother. She was grateful not to have seen Ormond again, and shortly afterward, they took their leave.

"Tell me what happened between you and Ormond to upset you," Grandmama said in the carriage.

Ianthe, her voice strained, related the conversation she had with Ormond. She prayed her grandmother would not view it the way her mother had, as a man madly in love and keen to marry her. She knew it was not so.

"I shall send a letter to your father at his club," Grandmama said. "A friend of mine knew Ormond's wife. I will ask her about him."

She sagged back against the squabs in relief. "Oh, how splendid, Grandmama."

"It might be useful to have something extra to include in our argument," Grandmama said thoughtfully. "But for now, you must not upset yourself, child. Leave it to me."

"Yes, Grandmama," Ianthe said meekly. She wished she could be more confident of the outcome. Did sons obey their mothers when they were men?

She barely slept for the rest of the night, and was up not long past dawn, pacing her room. At twelve o'clock, her father arrived, summoned by her grandmother. They were closeted in the library for half an hour while Ianthe waited, heart beating hard and feeling sick.

Then she was called inside.

Papa looked angrier than Ianthe had ever seen him. "A letter arrived this morning from Lord Ormond, informing me you have refused him. And now your grandmother tells me she agrees with you, that the man is obnoxious. But as he is nothing but politeness itself in our company, I find it impossible to imagine he's any less so with you! It has occurred to me that your wish to marry Tate is behind your reluctance to marry Ormond, and we both know that is impossible."

"Papa..."

He held up his hand. "You need time to reflect on your behavior, Ianthe. You shall go home to your mother for a week. You are to write him a note of apology and explain you are leaving London for a brief stay."

"Surely, Granville, you don't wish to consider..." Grandmama said.

"Please, Mother. I have not forced Ianthe to wed Phillip Ormond. I shall give her time to realize what an advantageous marriage this would be. Which most fathers would not do, I might add. Let us end the matter." He drew out his watch from his waistcoat pocket. "I have a luncheon engagement." He rose and kissed their cheeks. "A few days in the fresh air of the country will do wonders. You must miss your mother." He patted Ianthe under the chin. And with that, he was gone.

"I suppose a week's grace is the best we can hope for," Grandmama said. "Never fear, child, I have yet to consult my friend. If there is anything untoward to learn about this man, and I suspect there must be by the way he has treated you, your father will learn of it."

"Oh, Grandmama!" Ianthe came to hug her.

She turned away, close to tears, fearing there was little Grandmama could do. Would she be forced to marry Ormond? *Tate!* She cried silently. But he seemed far away from her now.

Chapter Eleven

ON HIS WAY home to Cloudhill, Tate rode into the stable yard of The Black Horse Inn in the hamlet of Thurnham, scattering chickens in all directions as he pulled up his horse. He dismounted, a stable hand turning from forking hay to look at him. An ostler left a roan he'd been grooming and hurried to take Tate's horse. Tate smelled roasting meat on the breeze and his stomach growled. He'd left London before breakfast.

Once he gave his instructions for the care of the animal, he headed for the inn door. Removing his riding gloves, he lamented the absence of his favorite horse, Bayard, languishing at home. Riding him over the estate acres again would bring both pleasure and pain.

There'd be many important matters awaiting him his uncle would want to discuss. Tate must also see the land steward and the gamekeeper. And possibly the bailiff. There'd be a pile of correspondence and no secretary to assist him.

The year before, after Edward died so unexpectedly, Tate, shocked to find himself the heir, worked hard to learn all that was necessary to run Cloudhill, the family's five-thousand-acre principal seat. For his own edification, but also to reassure his father, who grieved for Edward. Normally, he would enjoy visiting tenant farmers and the home farm, but he expected to be besieged with questions as to the future of the estate. People were nervous, and he had little to say to reassure them as of yet. He prayed for good news from the solicitors when he returned to London. Whatever the outcome, Donovan must be dealt with. What that might entail remained to be seen, but he suspected, having gained a fair idea of Donovan's nature, he would turn on him with violence. Was he capable of killing a man? When Tate thought of his father's distress, which brought on the apoplexy and claimed his life, his hands formed into fists and a hot and bitter rage consumed him. Yes, he could deal with Donovan. But as angry as he was, his conscience would rule him. He would never strike a man down in cold blood.

The first thing he intended to do after seeing his mother and Emily would be to search his father's papers in the library for some clue as to what led them to this sorry pass. The shock of losing his father had cast him so low he'd avoided it, believing it more important to discover what he could in London. Now, he geared himself to look carefully through them, although it was doubtful he'd find anything.

With one foot on the inn step, Tate turned as a fine carriage pulled into the forecourt. Such equipages would rarely be seen this far from the main road. Only those who traveled in the same direction as Tate.

An ostler ran to the horses' heads, and the footman jumped down to open the carriage door.

Two women he knew very well descended. The elderly lady swathed in shawls wore mulberry wool while Ianthe was striking in a lilac pelisse, her bonnet adorned with silk flowers and soft feathers. The unexpected sight of her here, and so utterly desirable, made his heart race.

Before he considered whether it might be ill advised to show himself to Ianthe's grandmother in the bright light of day after she'd seen only Bret for some weeks, he swept off his hat and walked over to greet them.

"Lady Caldwell, Lady Ianthe." He winced at the pain from a bruised rib as he bowed. "I trust your journey was pleasant?"

"No carriage journey is pleasant at my age," Ianthe's grandmother grimaced. "I abhor being jostled about and long for a glass of Madeira and my bed. But I shall have to endure many more miles before that."

Tate smiled. "I was about to partake of some luncheon. Will you join me? I can certainly promise you a glass of madeira."

"We shall be delighted." Lady Caldwell gazed shortsighted at him from beneath the wide brim of her hat draped in net. "We saw little of you in London. I was saddened to hear of your father's death. It was sudden, I believe. I have written to your mother and will call on her."

"Thank you. Yes, it was sudden and a great shock."

Ianthe searched his face, frowning as she noted the fading bruise. "Did you suffer an accident?"

"A mishap while riding in the park," Tate replied.

She narrowed her eyes. "A riding accident? In Rotten Row? *Lud*. What a Banbury story."

"Ianthe," her grandmother admonished.

With an amused glance at Ianthe, he escorted them into the inn, where Lady Caldwell ascended the stairs to tidy herself.

Shown to a table in the busy dining room, redolent with tasty aromas from the kitchen, Tate assisted Ianthe into a chair.

"Why didn't you keep your appointment with Bret?"

"Another matter took precedence on that day."

She glared at him. "You won't tell me the truth, will you?" she said in a fierce whisper.

"While I appreciate you leaping to my defense, I fear you are making mountains of a molehill." Tate smiled. Even though she was cross with him, he enjoyed being with her. Having her to himself. He took far too much pleasure in her company, he thought as his gaze drank her in: her blonde curls, disordered as she took off her bonnet, her pretty mouth, her lips set in lines of disapproval. "That color suits you. You should wear it more often."

Her gaze pinned him. "I do, but you would not be aware of it when we so rarely see you. Will you continue to avoid me, I wonder?"

Tate fiddled with his napkin. He hated to keep the truth of his situation from her. "I won't have you involved, Ianthe."

"Was that...really an accident?" she asked, gesturing to his bruise, her eyes anxious. "Are you in the most dreadful danger?"

"No such thing." He signaled to the hovering servant, who hurried over to take the order for wine. "Right now, I'm hungry."

"We can't discuss it here. Grandmama will be back in a moment. Will you call on us? I am home for a week."

"What has brought you back to the country in the middle of the Season?"

"To see Mama." Her gaze slipped away, and she chewed her bottom lip. "Bertie has the mumps, but the doctor says he's no longer infectious."

What was this? Was there more to this visit than she wanted to tell him? "I'm sorry to hear about Bertie. I'll ride over tomorrow after luncheon and see the poor fellow. But can we meet somewhere first?" He steeled himself to be plagued with more questions he couldn't answer, but fool that he was, he wanted desperately to see her alone.

"I'll wait in that spot where the willows grow along the stream." It reminded him of their last meeting. The painful time when his father's death was raw. He'd just learned Cloudhill had been lost and was forced to accept he must give up his cherished plans for the future: marrying Ianthe and raising their children in the home he loved. "You can tell me the truth about what caused that bruise," she said, confirming his fears of an interrogation. "You winced. Are you badly hurt?"

"No." He smiled. "I am still on my feet, as you see."

She narrowed her eyes. "You are remarkably good at dissembling."

"You should not have gone to Fortune House," Tate countered. "Gambling clubs are dangerous places. I beg you not to return there."

She shrugged indifferently. "The place holds no interest for me." She scowled at him. "Unlike you, it seems. What were you doing there? Bret refuses to tell me. Enjoying the company of the

American lady, perhaps?"

Her grandmother had entered the dining room and paused beside Ianthe. "My goodness, Ianthe, you should not speak to Tate in that fashion. Have you learned no manners in London?"

Tate rose to draw back her chair. "It is my fault, my lady, and I fear I deserve it."

"Do you?" Lady Caldwell looked at him with interest. "Now why would that be, I wonder."

Fortunately, the waiter, who had been anxious to take their order, stepped forward and coughed. "Would you be wanting the cauliflower soup and the lamb stew? Or we have roast pork. And there's a tasty, fresh baked peach pie."

Once their orders were placed and the servant hurried away, Tate met Ianthe's eyes, which asked silent questions of him. Lord, how he loved her. Could he trust himself when they were alone tomorrow? She might have decided on a new life with Ormond. He must not forget that. The prospect served to chill him like a dash of ice water.

"I heard that Lord Ormond has been squiring you about town," he said, hoping to discover what he thirsted to know.

She looked down at her hands. "He has, yes."

The engagement had not yet been announced. Tate's relief was palpable, but brief as other worries crowded in. How long before they became engaged and ended his hopes for their future together?

A polite repast followed where they spoke of mere pleasantries. And certainly not what he wished to say.

Several hours later, Tate rode along a lane bordered with flowering hedgerows and red dog rose, as it meandered through meadows where sheep grazed to the tall elaborate gates of Cloudhill. He passed through with a nod to the gatekeeper, Bickle, who had emerged from the gatehouse to greet him.

Tate's pulse quickened as he rode from the avenue of elms and took in the majestic house above him on a rise, crowned by a bank of white clouds advancing slowly across the blue sky. Parts of the building were Elizabethan, others added through the years, but it remained an elegant structure of golden stone overlooking sweeping lawns and gardens where rhododendrons and dogwood trees flowered, the air perfumed with lilacs. Spring always put on a good show, but he loved every season. This was his home. He was born here. The sight of it wrenched at his heart while its beauty still took his breath away.

Returning from the stables, a footman stood at the open door.

"Welcome home, Your Grace."

"Thank you, James." In the marble-columned great hall, Tate removed his hat and gloves and laid them on the console table. "Where is my mother?"

"Her Grace is in the morning room, Your Grace."

When Tate entered the comfortable, sunny morning room, he viewed the small group huddled on the sofas and chairs around the fire that were now his responsibility. Clara, the elder of his two sisters, had returned from convalescing with their Aunt Mary in Kennington. She sat beside his mother while Emily's despondent green gaze viewed him from a chintz-covered chair.

"Tate." His mother held her arms out to him.

"Well, what a bevy of beauty to greet a fellow," he said more heartily than he felt. He kissed his mother. In unrelenting black, she seemed to have aged. Beside her sat his father's favorite daughter, his sister, nineteen-year-old Clara, the beauty of the family. Her dark hair had lost its shine, and her face was pale and thin. Her big, doe-like dark eyes looked red-rimmed and strained. The difference in her shocked him. So unlike the girl who had gone so eagerly to London for her come-out last year. A gentle, loving soul, Clara had captured everyone's hearts. But how ill was she?

He sat beside her. "How good to see you back home. Have you recovered from your malaise?"

Her eyes sought his, soft and hurt, reminding him of a wounded deer. It sent a cold shaft through him. "Indeed, I am much better." He thought her voice lacked conviction.

Tate searched his mother's troubled green eyes. She made no

comment, nor did she try to reassure him. Another chill passed down his spine. Was something being kept from him? Or was it the distress of their father's sudden death?

"Should you have undertaken such a journey?" he asked Clara gently.

She glanced at their mother before speaking. "I couldn't stay with Aunt Mary forever. I had to come home." She dropped her gaze to her fingers curled together in her lap. "Papa said that once I had recovered, I must return to London next Season. That I cannot let life pass me by."

"Certainly, if you wish to. But for now, here you shall stay until you are completely well." He gave her hand a firm squeeze before releasing it.

"Tate, what is London like? Is it very thrilling?" Emily asked. Her nervous fingers fiddled with a loose fair curl. "I shall still be able to make my come-out next year, shan't I?" She turned to Clara. "We can go to London together. When you are perfectly well again, we will set London ablaze!"

Clara smiled and nodded with little enthusiasm.

"Let's see when the time comes," Tate said, hating that he could not set Emily's mind at rest. "Is my uncle here?"

"We expect Clive this afternoon. I must consult the house-keeper and speak to Cook about dinner." His mother rose and slowly walked from the room.

Tate's throat tightened as he gazed after her. He'd been so pleased to come home, but now, the weight of his family's troubles seemed to bow him down.

His thoughts turned to Ianthe and their meeting tomorrow. Had he been foolish to suggest it? As much as he yearned to see her, he feared he might lose the tight hold he had on his emotions.

WHEN AT THE inn, Ianthe had watched Tate ride away; she was

ready to scream with frustration. There was so much she wanted to know. *Have patience*, she urged herself. Tomorrow, he would not evade her questions so adroitly.

She must act while she was free, and before her father condemned her to a life of misery with Ormond. She felt as if she was tied up in knots and struggling helplessly to free herself. Would Mama join with Grandmama to help her? Ianthe wished she could be sure of it.

When they arrived at the Granville mansion, Bertie rushed out to meet them with their dog, Felix, close to his heels.

Grandmama took him by the shoulders to keep him still as she studied him. "You appear to have recovered, Bertie. It is to be hoped you will no longer cause your mama anxiety." She turned to Ianthe. "Tell her I shall come down when body and soul are restored." With that pronouncement, she entered the hall, requesting their butler to have tea and a bedwarmer brought up to her chamber, and to send her maid to her.

Ianthe hugged Bertie and bent down to pat the exuberant dog. "How well you look. I suspect you have been malingering to avoid your studies."

Bertie grinned. "There are much better ways. And I am never ill for long."

"I'm glad. Come inside, I want to see Mama."

Her mother was writing a letter at her desk in her sitting room. She rose as Ianthe entered. "You're here at last, dearest." She stood and held out her arms.

"Mama." Ianthe stepped into them and was overwhelmed by her mother's familiar scent, afraid she might cry.

Her mother drew away and gazed at her, concerned. She put a hand to Ianthe's forehead. "You look a trifle peaky. I hope you're not coming down with an ague."

"No, Mama. I'm not ill."

"You will benefit from a few days in the country." She smiled. "We'll have tea, and you can tell me your news. Where is your grandmother?"

"She has gone up to her bedchamber. The journey fatigued her."

"Carriage travel is grueling for one of advanced years. I shall see her directly. I wish to hear all the goings-on in London. Shall we go down?"

Ianthe almost groaned aloud. Her mother would not like to hear that she'd refused Ormond and been sent home in disgrace.

"I saw Tate when we stopped for luncheon at Thurnham," she said as they descended the stairs to the morning room.

"He's home? He will have much to occupy him."

"He plans to visit us tomorrow."

"I should like to see him."

During their tea, Ianthe resisted confessing all, preferring to wait until Grandmama came down. Even though she knew her mother wanted what was best for her, it would be good to have an ally who could explain the situation without the emotion Ianthe would bring to it.

But Grandmama did not come down. Tired out by the coach trip, she remained in her bedchamber. Her mother went up to see her, but Ianthe didn't know what was discussed between them. Later, at dinner, Mama referred briefly to Ormond, and said she would wait to hear from Papa before they discussed it further.

The next afternoon, Ianthe rode her mare, Freckles, to their arranged meeting place where the willow trees bent graceful fronds over the stream. It was a few miles from the house, a pleasant ride through the woods and meadows. Clouds sailed across the azure sky, the sun warm. Ianthe remembered how she and Cecily used to lie on the grass and study the clouds to pick out animals and objects in the interesting shapes and tell stories about them. It all seemed so long ago when life was less complicated. For a moment, Ianthe yearned to be back there as she perched on a fallen log beneath a willow and listened to the gurgling stream. She took off her bonnet and raised her face to the sun, even though it would bring out her freckles and horrify her mother.

Riding Bayard, Tate cantered toward her over the meadow. As he dismounted, Freckles, who had been roaming the meadow unfettered, galloped to meet Tate's gelding, and the horses nuzzled each other.

With a smile, Tate walked over to Ianthe with his familiar loping stride. How imposing he was. His leather riding breeches fit him like a glove. Watching him, she no longer wished for the past, but yearned for a future where they could be together. The man was frustrating and headstrong, but she knew him to be honorable and gentle. She'd watched him with his dogs and tending his horses with those long-fingered, capable hands. He would never deliberately hurt her. Neither would he lie to her.

"There's more than a hint of summer in the air." His easy smile failed to hide the recent upheaval in his life, although the bruise, at least, had almost gone.

"Are you staying long?"

"A few days only." Tate's outward sign of calm didn't fool her as he joined her on the grass. Their gazes collided, his intense with emotion. So maddening! She veered from wanting to pound her fists on his chest to throwing herself in his arms to pull his head down to hers, to kiss him like a wanton trollop. She couldn't, of course. Not when she feared it would embarrass him. She felt bruised after the brutish way Ormond had spoken to her. No man had ever made her feel worth so little. As if she was necessary to his life only to give him a son. Through the years she had known Tate, he had sought her advice and valued her friendship. He would never treat her in that manner. But that he didn't want her lay heavily on her heart. She couldn't forget the American lady at the gambling house, her hand on his arm in a proprietary gesture.

Ianthe realized she still foolishly clung to the hope they might one day be together. Mortified, she glanced away to watch swallows busily building their nest in a nearby oak. If Tate changed his mind, he would have to propose, formally, on bended knee. She still had at least a remnant of pride left.

Chapter Twelve

BIRDS FLUTTERED IN the trees above them. While Ianthe's gaze rested on the birds, Tate watched the emotions flitting over her lovely face. He fought the urge to declare his love for her, to discover if she felt the same. He couldn't resist dropping his gaze to the enticing curve of her breasts and her long legs beneath the habit. Had fate robbed him of the one woman in the entire world he wanted? The dappled sunlight through the delicate willow fronds created a curly golden halo of her hair. He longed to reach out and touch the silky strands. Frustrated, he tensed. What would happen if he reached for her? Madness, but heaven knew how many more times they could be together like this.

Her blue eyes met his. "You must be keen to return to…your life in London."

"Not right now," he said. "Are you?"

She shrugged.

"You appeared deep in thought as I rode over the hill."

"It's the warm sun. It makes one daydream." When she dropped her gaze, concern brought him alert. What troubled her? For something surely did. Should he ask her? "Your grandmother seems in remarkably good spirits," he said instead.

Ianthe picked a piece of grass and shredded it in her fingers. "Grandmama is wonderful."

"Why have you come home?"

"I thought I told you."

"I don't believe you did."

"To see Mama, of course."

"Yes, you might have mentioned that," he said ironically, knowing that was not the reason.

She finally looked at him. "You've cut your hair."

"Better?"

"Yes, much. I found the other style disconcerting. You didn't look like yourself."

The clothes he'd detested to wear in his guise of gambler would be given to the poor. He stretched his legs out, feeling much more himself in his favored riding breeches and boots.

"Has Bret left London?" she asked.

"No, but he is relieved to no longer be impersonating a duke."

She nodded. "It did not sit well with him."

"It didn't. But he made a valiant effort. I am sincerely indebted to him."

"So, this scheme, which you refuse to tell me about...is it at an end now?"

"That part of it, yes."

"When I found you at the gambling club with the American lady, I wondered if you'd decided to embark on a new life."

"No, Ianthe. The life I want is here. The American widow was a means to an end. It allowed me to gain access to the club."

The stiffness in her shoulders eased a little. Above them the soft breeze stirred the branches and a leaf settled on her shoulder. Tate leaned over and plucked it from her velvet habit, close enough to breathe in her feminine, sweet fragrance. At the rush of desire to kiss her, he sat back and drew up one leg, resting an arm on his knee. "I can tell you about it now. It was unfair not to, but I considered it necessary."

"You trust me now?" she asked dryly.

"I always did. It's just...it wasn't safe."

He knew her reply would be scathing, but he had to say it.

"You really should not ride about the estate without your groom."

"And why not? I have been riding alone since I was twelve years old. Have you forgotten?"

"Times have changed, Ianthe."

"Have they?"

How could she understand the lengths to which a villain like Donovan would go? The Irishman would stop at nothing, even murder, to get what he wanted. "It's become a more dangerous world."

She leaned closer and her finger, feather-light, stroked his bruised cheek. "Were you being truthful when you said you weren't in danger?"

He didn't reply, but smiled, shook his head then caught her hand, small and soft, holding it for a moment.

"You wouldn't tell me if you were, would you? But I should like to hear it all now, please."

Tate didn't miss the beseeching note in her voice. Surely, for now at least, Ianthe would be safe from Donovan's notice. The Irishman would have his eye on the prize, Cloudhill. And she was right. She deserved to hear what lay behind his extraordinary behavior. If the *ton* learned of the masquerade, their censure would be harsh and swift. It would hurt his mother and his sisters. But nothing would stop him from pursuing Donovan to the bitter end.

He eased his back against the tree, and began with what he had learned after his father's death while she listened, interrupting now and then with a question or a distressed moan, which sent a shaft of painful longing through him. His arms ached to hold her.

When he was done, he felt profoundly relieved. He'd hated the coolness that had formed between them. Even if nothing came of the court case and he was forced to leave England for a time, he would go knowing Ianthe knew the truth and wouldn't judge him too harshly. But he omitted telling her about Donovan's vicious attack. "The solicitors aren't very confident the signature on the vowel can be proved a forgery. As it is legal tender, Donovan will most likely contest the matter in court. If he does, ownership of Cloudhill hinges on the result."

She twisted the stings of her bonnet held on her lap, her voice low with distress. "Oh, Tate. Not Cloudhill!" When she looked up, her eyes were filled with tears. "You've been through so much. I wish I'd known. And I'm sorry I doubted you with the American woman."

"Your father would be rightfully outraged had I drawn you into this." He shook his head with a brief grin. "Although, you made it devilishly hard for me not to."

He caught a little of the girl he recognized in her eyes, lit with fiery determination. All those times she'd tagged along and raced him and Stephen, riding hell for leather over the fields, determined to beat them, and she might have on a better mount. The way she'd scolded Tate when she thought him wrong about something he'd said or done. As he inevitably was. When had the warmth of friendship changed into a passionate yearning? The moment he'd almost kissed her at that house party? Almost, because he'd feared his feelings would be writ large for all in the room to see. "I can tell you now because things have moved on. I've left it in the hands of the lawyers. But...we are not there yet, Ianthe. There's a very strong chance I can never call Cloudhill mine again."

Her bottom lip quivered. "I cannot bear to think of it."

Tate swallowed, his heart heavy, and gently wiped a tear from her velvet soft cheek with his finger, longing to banish them with kisses.

For a moment, neither spoke.

"If the court case doesn't go in our favor, I'm afraid we must," he said finally, his husky voice betraying him.

She sighed. "Oh, Tate how dreadful. So you...just wait?"

"We all remain on tenterhooks: my mother, my sisters, and my uncle. These matters move slowly. It may be a long wait. But at least my intervention has held up the sale of Cloudhill."

"And if Cloudhill is never returned to you, what will you do?" she whispered.

He shrugged, adopting a casual pose to hide his distress. "Leave England."

"Tate—"

"See a bit of the world now that the war has ended," he added hastily, fearing what he would do if she begged him to stay.

Her lashes lowered, hiding her expression. "Oh."

As the minutes lengthened, Tate felt that intimacy they'd always enjoyed stirring between them. It would take very little to reach for her, but where would it lead? Her father could be planning for her to marry Ormond. He could hardly ask her to wait for him. Her father wouldn't allow it in any event. And he'd be a selfish brute not to wish her happiness should she choose to marry the fellow.

But Tate clung to the dream of them being together at Cloudhill. He needed to hang on to that dream now, even if it proved in the end to be only a fantasy.

Before his emotions got the better of him, he rose to his feet and held out his hand to her. "Let's ride to the house. I wish to see your mother and Bertie. And for a moment, we can pretend that everything is as it used to be."

She pulled on her gloves then settled her hand in his and climbed to her feet, arranging the skirts of her riding habit. "If only it was." With a troubled glance, she put on her riding hat and briskly tied the strings. Then they strolled together to the horses, over the daisy-strewn grass.

"Bret is determined to rescue Miss Lily Forth. I fear for them, but I have promised to help them," she said, darting a peek at him as if defying him to warn her not to.

"I worry for them too. It's a desperate plan."

"I admire Bret for his passionate commitment to Lily, though."

Tate wondered if that was meant to be a criticism of him. Bret had advised he declare himself. Whisk Ianthe away to

Scotland. But he was not Bret. As much as he wished to flaunt society and escape over the border with Ianthe, he had a family to protect. "Leave it to me to assist Bret. These things have a way of turning nasty, Ianthe. If it all goes wrong, it could rebound on you. Imagine if your father got to hear of it."

She frowned. "I'll be careful. I am not a fool."

He assisted her onto Freckles. "There have been times of late when I wished you weren't quite so smart."

Bayard pulled on the reins when, with a flap of its wings, a swift swooped down over his head. A hand on the horse's glossy neck, Tate asked, "Are you enjoying London?"

She sighed. "London hasn't been as exciting as I expected."

He'd noted the traces of tiredness beneath her eyes. He mounted up and rode alongside her. "Why not?"

"I fear I am most dreadfully ungrateful. Grandmama has been wonderful, and I can see Cecily. But the Season is a frightful rush. One doesn't have time to catch one's breath. And I missed Mama when she came home to care for Bertie."

She did not mention Ormond. "Life in London is a good deal faster than the country, and the smoky air can be injurious," he said. "Clara certainly found it so. But she has returned home."

"She's home? Poor Clara. We were all so worried about her. I must go to see her. Is she well again?"

"She says so, but is still fragile, I fear. She needs to rest quietly at home, and it's my hope this business won't disrupt her convalescence."

They cantered over the meadows and entered the wood along a bridle path. Leaving the horses at the stables, they walked over the gravel drive to the house.

At the front door, Tate greeted Walter, the Granville butler whom he'd known since he was a young lad. They crossed the hall as Bertie rushed in with his boisterous terrier, Felix.

"Will you play a game of drafts with me, Tate? Stephen has gone back to Oxford, and it's frightfully dull here. I can't wait to go away to school next year."

"I'm afraid I won't be able to this visit, Bertie," Tate said. "The next time I come, I will. I promise." But could he hold to that promise?

He steeled himself to return to Cloudhill and face the up-heaval. He'd made a start on the estate files the secretary, Cedric Lynch, appeared to have kept in good order. It made Tate wonder what reason his father had to dismiss Lynch. He'd never explained. Neither did Uncle Clive know.

→》》《《←

AFTER TEA, IANTHE saw Tate off at the stables.

A hand on the horse's bridle, he turned to her. "I shall see you in London. Will Lord Ormond object if we have that waltz?"

Before she could reply, the family coach rattled down the driveway toward the stables from the house.

Ianthe rubbed her arms. "Papa has come home."

Tate swung up into the saddle. "Your father will not wish to find me here with you."

She chewed her lip to stop it trembling. "I shall save you that waltz."

He nodded; his green eyes shadowed by his hat seemed dark and serious.

She raised her hand in farewell as he rode away, disappearing through the trees. Should she have told him she loved him? And how horrid Ormond had been to her? To have Tate hold her and promise to protect her? With aching sadness, she faced the bald fact that Tate clearly didn't want a future with her. She couldn't depend on him to protect her.

She walked back to the house to face her father. As soon as she entered the house, a footman came to summon her.

Ianthe entered his study. "Did you have a good journey, Papa?"

He looked up from the letters on his desk. "I did, thank you.

Sit down, Ianthe."

As she slid into a chair opposite, he tapped his quill on the desk and then put it down. "I'm told Tate was here."

"He is home for a few days to see to things, and came to visit us."

"Did he?" He sighed and looked at her for several minutes while she fidgeted. "You have not gotten that young man out of your system, I see."

"He doesn't wish to marry me, Papa."

"No, he's a decent fellow, Tate. Always liked him. Very sensible. He knows he is not right for you. It is for you, Ianthe, to realize it."

"I do... I..."

Her father held up his hand. "Lord Ormond has been to see me. He is outraged by your extraordinary declaration that you will never marry him. And points out that if you refuse him after he has courted you, he will appear a poor thing in the eyes of the *ton* and suffer extreme embarrassment."

Her throat tight, she said, "But I never said I would marry him, Papa."

"Nevertheless, the understanding was there."

"And he was quite mean to me," she said, fearing she sounded desperate when she wished to remain calm.

"Hard to believe. His manners are impeccable."

"Lord Ormond doesn't love me. He made it plain he only wants to marry me to give him an heir."

"He's put it badly. Perhaps he acted out of hurt at your cool rejection of him. But foolish girl, it's clear he feels very passionate about marrying you." He folded his arms, leaning back, making his chair give a protesting creak.

Ianthe clamped her lips on the urge to argue. Angering her father was not wise and would never work in her favor.

"You have much to offer him, Ianthe, apart from your womanly charms. You are intelligent and good company, although you've shown him little of that it seems."

"Something about him repels me, Papa. I don't know why. It's a sense I have."

"Not this womanly sense your mother has accused me of lacking on occasion?" He smiled. "You don't know him well enough to make such an assumption. You need to think rationally about your future. He's not an ogre. Phillip Ormand is an attractive, affable man, who will one day be a wealthy marquess. He can offer you a wonderful life."

"If I should give him an heir."

"Most men wish for an heir to carry on their heritage. It is not unusual."

Ianthe could see her position was hopeless and to continue in this vein would get her nowhere. "I need time to think, Papa."

"There is no rush. Although, I should like your betrothal to take place within the next few months. It has been an expensive couple of years: the cost of Cecily's dowry and wedding, the boys at university and Eton, and other unexpected expenditures." He frowned. "And Ianthe, you will be twenty this year, older than most debutantes. Ormand might have looked for someone younger. But he has chosen you. I might remind you I had agreed to you making your debut at the same time as your sister, although the cost of bringing two daughters out together made me shudder, but you strenuously refused. I was quite aware you did so because Tate was home mourning his brother. And I agreed at the time because I expected you to marry Tate. Naturally, that is not the case now." He shook his head. "Cloudhill lost to the Lindseys. Unthinkable. Matters have changed. I hope you understand that."

It was foolish of her to continue to hope that one day they would be together. But no matter what her father said, she still did.

Her father thought he was doing the right thing. It was wise not to annoy him, she decided, for when anyone did so, he could become quite determined. "You are the best of fathers, Papa," she said, coming around the desk to kiss his cheek.

He smiled. "Be off with you, girl. I have letters to write."

As she left the room, her one hope was her grandmother would learn something about Ormond to change her father's mind.

Her mother waited for her in the corridor. "You must change out of your habit." She slipped her arm around Ianthe's waist, and they walked together to the stairs. "Dearest, your papa believes marriage to Lord Ormond is the best course for you."

"Grandmama doesn't think so."

"And she is entitled to her opinion, of course. But what your grandmother thinks will make little difference to your father. He will merely resent her interference."

Although Ianthe didn't know how she might manage it, she had no intention of entering meekly into a marriage with Ormond. She left her mother and climbed slowly up the stairs, seeking the comfort and reassurance of her grandmother, her legs leaden.

Chapter Thirteen

A S TATE RODE back to Cloudhill, he considered what passed between him and Ianthe. She had exhibited no pleasure at the mention of Ormond, her eyes dark and troubled. But it gave him little pleasure to think she didn't love the fellow. An urgent surge rushed through his veins, frustrating him. This appalling business he was desperate to put an end to moved far too slowly.

In the secretary's room, Tate searched through the accounts for the last six months, listed in Lynch's ledger. An item caught his eye. It mentioned a Dr. Robert Manners in Kennington, where his Aunt Mary lived. It must surely be something to do with Clara.

Wishing to understand the seriousness of his sister's illness, he removed the bills filed away in drawers and flicked through them until he found the one he sought.

A note accompanied Dr. Manners' account. *I can assure Your Grace of my discretion,* Robert Manners had written. *Your daughter's health improves, and I grow more confident of her full recovery, although she remains troubled. I'm told the church will ensure the babe finds a suitable home.*

Shocked and sickened, Tate sat back and stared at the piece of paper held in his shaky fingers. His dear, gentle sister had given birth to a baby? Anger swiftly followed. It must have happened in London. Some man had attacked her? Who was this mongrel?

And why hadn't Tate been told? He caught his breath as concern and compassion for Clara made him want to go immediately to find her. For several minutes, he attempted to calm himself while he wondered how he might best help her. Then he rose and left the room, encountering a footman in the corridor. "Ask my mother and Lady Clara to come to the library, John."

Tate entered the large chamber lined with bookshelves and went to the drinks tray to pour himself a brandy. No fire had been lit, the lofty room cool, but none of the other rooms would offer them the privacy required for this conversation. He took a sip of the mellow liquid, and holding his glass, roamed across the blue-and-gold patterned swirl of dense carpet. While deeply concerned about Clara, other questions arose. How did this happen to a gently reared girl like his sister? And might this be the reason behind his father's inexplicable behavior?

Moments later, his mother hurried in with his sister. "What has happened, Tate? Do you have news?"

"Nothing concerning Cloudhill, Mama. I've ordered tea, but perhaps you would prefer a glass of ratafia?" Tate said as they seated themselves on the sofa before the marble fireplace.

His mother glanced worriedly at him as she sat. "Tea, thank you, Tate."

Tate crouched down beside Clara's chair. He looked into her sad, pale face and took her slender, cool hand in his. "Clara, I've only now discovered the truth. I am deeply sorry for what you have endured. I wish I'd known. That I might have helped."

Clara flushed scarlet and burst into tears. After he gave a reassuring squeeze of her hand, he rose to his feet and sat on a chair opposite the sofa.

His mother's nervous fingers plucked at the fringe on her shawl. "Your father forbade me to tell you and Emily. He wished to handle this himself." Her voice trembled with distress. "He believed he could make it all go away, but then that awful man, Donovan, threatened us. He said he was going to spread the news of Clara's disgrace throughout the *ton*."

"What did Papa propose to do, Mama?"

"Your father told me very little. He said not to worry. But then, of course, he couldn't..." Her distressed voice died away.

Clara put a hand to her chest as a sob rose. "It is all my fault."

"I don't believe that for a moment. But could you tell me what happened?" he asked, his voice gentle.

"I won't have Clara blaming herself. I am to blame," his mother interrupted. "It was my duty to protect her and keep her safe from fortune hunters and rogues." Her breath caught. "And I failed."

"No, Mama." Clara turned to her tearfully. "I was foolish to agree to stroll in the gardens with him when you left the ballroom with Mrs. Abercrombie to visit the ladies' withdrawing room."

Tate clamped down on his teeth. "Which ball was it?"

"It was the Forsters'." Clara fumbled for her handkerchief. "The gentleman said the moon shining on the pond was a remarkable sight, and everyone was going out to see it. He assured me we would only be gone a few moments...but he took me deep into the gardens, we were alone, and then he...he...grabbed me..."

She burst into tears, comforted by their mother's arms.

"Who is the rake?" Tate repeated grittily.

Clara sniffed. "Lord Farnley."

"Edmund Farnley?"

"Yes."

Tate had encountered the lord at boxing matches and disliked his arrogance. He would deal with him, but now was not the time to think of vengeance. Clara's needs mattered more. But he would not escape Tate's wrath for long. His family would not be safe until the Irishman had been dealt with. What was of vital importance was how Donovan came to hear of this and threaten his father with the signed and sealed vowel. Although, he believed he knew. He understood the course his father took, although fury, deep emotion, and concern for Clara, whom he must have feared would not survive such a distressing ordeal, made him decide on a course of action which had proved to be devastating to them all.

He looked at his mother. "Did Papa contact Farnley?"

"He was furious. He went up to London to have it out with him."

"And did he?"

She shook her head. "He was told that Farnley had been killed. Shot in Hyde Park a few days earlier in a duel. Farnley had ravished Bebbington's daughter, Anne, and she had not lived..." She faltered.

The footman opened the door for the maid who carried in the tea tray. She placed it on the occasional table before them, bobbed, and left the room.

"You cannot blame yourself for any of this, Mama," Tate said as his mother presided over the teapot. "An evil man crossed our path. The world is better off without him." And another would soon be dealt with, Tate thought grimly.

His mother nodded. She fussed over Clara, placing a slice of pound cake on a plate before her.

Clara sat silent, acknowledging it with a slight nod, but did not eat a morsel. Her tea cooled on the table in front of her.

Tate was painfully aware his father had considered him too inexperienced to be involved in such a sensitive affair. Well, he was involved now, and in this, he would act according to his own dictates. He put down his glass and leaned forward in the armchair. "What do you want to do, Clara? It's entirely your decision."

Her doe-like brown eyes flew to his. "My decision?"

"Yes."

She put her hands to her face. "I'll die if I can't have my baby daughter with me. It's been almost a month since I've held her. Her name is Rosamunde," she murmured, her voice muffled.

Clara was so fragile he feared she would pine away. Tate made up his mind. "Then that is settled. We must bring

Rosamunde home." *And think of some way to protect them both.*

"You'll find her and bring her home?" Clara cried, removing her hands to stare at him.

"I promise."

"Tate, perhaps Clive…" His mother began.

"I will deal with this," Tate said firmly while wondering what difficulties awaited him in Oxfordshire.

"My son, I know you will do your very best, and we all depend on you, but the scandal…"

"We will put it about that Clara married secretly and has since been widowed," he said.

"But I don't know where the baby is," Clara interrupted. "After Papa died, the vicar came and took Rosamunde away, Tate…" Her words rushed out with her breath as if held in for too long. "They told Aunt Mary they'd found a couple who would love and care for her, and Mary thought it best, as that was what Papa had discussed with her before he died."

Hiding his dismay, Tate said smartly, "Then I shall make haste to Oxfordshire. How is Nanny Pettigrew?" he asked his mother. "Is she in good health?"

"Yes, I believe so."

"Good. We'll take her along. And Mama, you must come too."

His mother nodded, looking pleased, and Clara smiled through her tears.

Dear lord, Tate prayed, *do not let me fail in this.* This was not what his father had intended. It played into Donovan's hands and placed Cloudhill further at risk.

After his mother and sister left, he stared through the long windows at dusk approaching in the gray sky above the woodland trees. He wouldn't fail his family, whatever it took.

IANTHE COULD THINK of nothing during the night and the next morning but Tate's grim news about Cloudhill. It was the reason her father no longer considered him as a prospective son-in-law. Could it be the reason Tate wouldn't ask her to marry him? She wished she had been more honest with him about Ormond. But she doubted it would change his mind, even if he loved her, and he did, of that she was sure. But women must wait to be asked. Who made up that silly rule?

In the afternoon, Ianthe rode over to Cloudhill to visit Clara. Of a similar age, they had been good friends through the years. Ianthe missed seeing her since she'd been convalescing with her aunt. She'd been eager to hear all about Clara's London Season, but it was sadly interrupted through her illness. Ianthe wondered how she would find her. Tate appeared to be concerned about her.

The butler smiled a welcome and admitted her to the morning room where Clara sat, her embroidery ignored on her lap. She looked up as Ianthe came in. "How good it is to see you, Ianthe. I'll ring for tea."

"I'm so pleased you're better," she said, although Clara was not herself, her face too pale and her eyes red-rimmed. Ianthe took the two books from her basket, and sitting beside Clara, placed them on the table beside her. "I thought you might enjoy these while you are convalescing."

Clara turned them in her hands, opening one to glance inside. "*Pride and Prejudice.* Thank you, Ianthe. I enjoyed a book by this author."

"You might like *Mansfield Park* too. If you wish, I shall send that one to you."

"You are very good to me."

Ianthe worriedly studied her friend. "How are you, Clara?"

A flush climbed up Clara's neck. "I'm much better today. Especially now Tate has gone to Oxford with Mama."

"Oxford? Why there?"

"To visit our Aunt Mary." Clara hesitated. "I shall tell you my secret, because I trust you, Ianthe."

Startled, Ianthe smiled warmly. "Well, of course you can trust me."

Clara put the books on the table. "While I was in London, something horrible happened to me."

Ianthe nodded. "It must have been very disappointing to fall ill during your debut."

"No, Ianthe. I wasn't ill. A man attacked me at a ball. In the gardens."

A chill passed down Ianthe's spine. Horrified, she stared at her. Poor Clara! "Oh, my dear! How utterly terrifying."

"You need to be very careful, Ianthe. Men aren't to be trusted. Well, some of them are. My wonderful brother, and my uncle, and indeed the doctor who cared for me in Kennington."

Her throat tight, Ianthe put a hand on Clara's. "Oh, Clara! I can't believe such an appalling thing happened to you. Did he...hurt you?"

"It was dreadful," she whispered. "He forced himself on me."

Tears sprang to Ianthe's eyes. "Oh, dear lord!" She swallowed, trying not to cry when Clara was dry-eyed and strangely subdued. "I am so sorry."

"But something wonderful has come of it."

"Really?" Ianthe said doubtfully.

"I have a beautiful daughter. Her name is Rosamunde. Tate and Mama have gone to fetch her and bring her home."

Ianthe forced a smile, astonished at the news. A baby out of wedlock would surely cause a dreadful scandal and ruin Clara's life. "A daughter? How wonderful."

Clara's expression grew uneasy. "But I'm terribly afraid they won't find her. The vicar took her. We were told a good family would be found for her." She put her hands to her face, her voice muffled. "I didn't want to give the baby up, but my father ordered it."

Ianthe felt sick. Her friend had gone through an appalling ordeal. To have to give birth without a husband to care for her.

And then to have it taken from her. It was unimaginable. And her reputation would be ruined. "Tate will find her," she said bracingly, although she struggled to believe there would be a happy ending to this.

"Yes, Tate has promised, and he never breaks his promises." It seemed as if Clara tried to convince herself.

"No, he never does," Ianthe said firmly.

A maid brought in the tea tray, and Ianthe had time to dwell on what Clara had told her. It was shocking, and might hurt her friend's chance of a happy marriage. Had the old duke ordered a home to be found for the baby to protect the family from scandal? But Tate had taken a different course. He would honor his sister's wishes. How good he was, and how she loved him.

"I look forward to meeting Rosamunde." She accepted a cup of tea from Clara. "I'm sure she's a lovely baby."

Clara nodded. "She has big brown eyes and dark hair."

"She'll be as beautiful as her mother." Ianthe was relieved the baby didn't appear to favor the father, whoever the brute was. Would Tate confront the rake? She felt sure he wouldn't shirk from what he considered his duty. Her admiration and love for him made her sigh. Hating the thought of him confronting a ruthless rake, she gently drew the conversation back to books.

Later, after she left her friend, she thought about how cruel life could be. How unfair it was that ruthless, unprincipled men could force themselves on a woman, and leave them to bear the consequences and the disgrace.

Ianthe paused on the path and stared sightlessly at the bees buzzing around a flowering bush. She knew of husbands who were cruel to their wives, having overheard talk among the women at an assembly dance. And once they had power over a woman, who was to stop them? How could anyone, even her father, help her if Ormond was such a man? She gasped and rubbed her arms. Suddenly, the breeze felt cold.

Chapter Fourteen

SINCE DAYBREAK, THE coach had traveled through villages, woodlands, fields of crops, and green meadows. It now neared Kennington town in Oxfordshire. Tate rubbed his stiff neck. Could he bring the baby home as he'd promised Clara? Was the outcome he sought even wise? Had his father been right to find a home for the baby? His mother was quiet during the journey, and he knew it troubled her as much as it did him. In the corner, Nanny, now in her sixtieth year, snored softly after embracing the journey with enthusiasm, eager to see the blessed babe.

"Do you approve of my decision, Mama? I could not deny Clara, but is it the right one?"

"I wish I knew, Tate." She looked anxious. "Your father thought Clara would stand a better chance of a good life without a child born out of wedlock, hard as that may seem." She sighed. "But I care little for society's dictates in a matter such as this. Rosamunde is my grandchild, and I cannot help wanting her with us. To know she is well cared for and loved. But what if this Mr. Donovan learns Rosamunde is at Cloudhill? He would spread his shameful gossip, and society would turn their backs on Clara. A respectable life would not be possible, as she'd be forced to live as a recluse. And as for the child…" She shook her head.

Tate was sure Donovan had his spies watching them. "We

shall have to come up with a plan for Clara, and I might have an idea." He sighed. "But right now, I must deal with this villain who threatens us."

"Do you mean through the courts?"

"Yes, Mama. I think we have an excellent case." He was not about to voice his violent thoughts about putting an end to Donovan permanently.

Her troubled eyes searched his. "Tell me about your idea for Clara."

"She must marry, and soon."

"Yes. I agree. But he must be someone she likes and trusts. And she trusts so few men now. I won't have her distressed."

"I will ensure she is not."

"That's assuming we can find Rosamunde."

"Aunt Mary might know where she is."

"I hope she insisted on being told. She's a dear person, but not having married and had children, she may not see things as we do."

When the coach pulled up beside Mary's manor house set in acres of pleasant gardens, she hurried out to welcome them.

The footman jumped to the ground and put down the steps. After he assisted Tate's mother and Nanny from the coach, Mary rushed into her tearful sister's arms.

Tate was instructing the coachman to drive to the stables at the rear when Aunt Mary came over to hug him. "Tate, how good of you to bring your mother to see me. And Nanny Pettigrew, it's been years, how are you?" After Nanny's assurance she was well, his aunt turned to him. "What is the reason for this visit?"

"We'll discuss it inside. I wished to tell you how grateful we are that you took such good care of Clara." He took her arm, and they started out for the house.

"Poor Clara. I became very fond of her and the sweet baby. There was a time when we feared Clara would not live. How is she?"

"She will be much improved when she has her baby in her arms."

Mary turned to him as they walked into the hall. "But Tate, how can she? It will cause a dreadful scandal."

"Leave it to me, Aunt Mary, to find a solution."

In the drawing room, his maiden aunt's taste in furnishings was a surprise: a riotous floral paper on the walls and crimson swags decorating the windows.

His mother asked anxiously, "Mary, where has the baby gone? Do you know?"

Aunt Mary shook her head. "The vicar wouldn't say. Richard's instructions were for him to keep it secret. I supposed he thought Clara might try to find her."

His mother put a hand to her forehead and sagged at the knees. Tate put his arm around her waist and helped her to a chair, where Nanny fussed over her.

Aunt Mary ordered the maid to bring tea.

"The vicar must be persuaded to reveal her whereabouts," Tate said. "We won't leave without Rosamunde. She is to come home with us."

Mary looked astonished. "To Cloudhill? But Tate, everyone will know the baby is Clara's. What about the scandal? Your father wanted Clara to marry. He said she will have more children and eventually forget. Especially after such a dreadful experience."

"Clara won't forget," his mother said with a solemn shake of her head. "A woman never forgets her child."

"Aye," Nanny said forcefully. "There is nothing like a mother's love."

Aunt Mary nodded. "Dr. Manners said the same. I had the impression he wasn't entirely in agreement with Richard's decision, although the doctor never uttered a word of criticism. He was very protective of Clara, however, and tried to help her all he could."

"He sounds like a good man. Give me his address, Aunt

Mary. I'll see him." Tate bent down to his mother, who looked exhausted. "You must rest, Mama; you too, Nanny. I'll go alone."

Mary hurried to pull the bell. "Your coach horses will need to rest. I'll order Jim to bring the landau."

"Do you have a suitable mount for me? I prefer to ride," Tate said.

"There's my mare, Daisy," she said doubtfully. "She's a sturdy animal. I've had her for some years, but I rarely ride these days. She is rather a slow top. I hope she doesn't take exception to a man riding her."

When the footman brought the luggage in, Tate went upstairs to change into his riding clothes.

At the stables, he viewed his aunt's horse with misgivings. She'd been correct in her description of Daisy. Used to a sidesaddle, the mare first tried to unseat him, then refused to rise above a trot. After wrestling with her with a firm hand, she reluctantly came to accept him as the one in control and broke into a halfhearted canter.

Fortunately, the doctor's house was only a few miles distant, and in less than half an hour, Tate tied Daisy's reins to the fence outside a neat two-story brick cottage with ivy growing over one wall and cream-painted shutters. Tate walked through the well-tended garden. He could hear chickens somewhere nearby. At the left of the house to the rear were the stables, and Tate could see a large vegetable plot and a cow in a field.

A maid in a crisp apron answered his knock.

"Duke of Lindsey to see the doctor," he said as she admitted him. After a startled curtsey, she led him wordlessly into a parlor where he waited for the doctor to appear, impatiently tapping his calf with his crop.

He did not have to wait for long. A tall man, younger than Tate expected, perhaps in his early thirties, with fair hair and a serious but kindly face, hurried in.

He shook Tate's proffered hand. "How is Lady Clara, Your Grace?"

"My sister is still very fatigued, but resting comfortably."

"Be seated, please. I am happy to answer any questions you may have. But first, may I offer you a libation?" He shrugged with a smile. "I'm afraid I can only offer you sherry, and you may not find it an excellent vintage."

"No, thank you, Manners. I wish to get on. The vicar has a home in mind for Rosamunde, I believe. I intend to take the baby back to her mother. If you'll first tell me about the baby's health, I'll go to see him. Is Rosamunde well enough to undergo a long journey?"

"The babe is in perfect health, Your Grace." Manners frowned. "But she is not at the vicarage."

Tate cursed under his breath. "Where is she? Do you know?"

"I did ask, but I'm afraid the vicar, Mr. Wellbright, wouldn't tell me. He said the duke instructed him to remain silent on the matter."

Tate tightened his jaw. "He will tell me."

"I imagine so, but in case he is reluctant, I shall accompany you," Manners said forthrightly. "I'll just give my housekeeper my direction."

"I'm afraid I rode here on an unfortunate beast of my aunt's, doctor."

"My curricle is at your disposal," Manners said as he took his coat and hat from the peg in the entry. "It won't take me a moment to hitch up the horse."

They traveled along the road while Tate prayed the baby was still in Kennington, so he and his mother could take Rosamunde home to Clara tomorrow.

In the church, the choir was rehearsing, their voices rising in excellent harmony.

As Tate and Manners walked down the aisle, the vicar, who was conducting, turned around. Their voices died away.

The vicar came forward. "Good day to you, Doctor Manners." He glanced at Tate inquiringly. "May I be of service?" He was gray-haired, of middling height, and above sixty years of age.

His face bore the compassionate lines of his years in service.

Tate introduced himself. "I have come on an urgent matter, Vicar."

The vicar shook his hand. "Mr. Wellbright, Your Grace. I was indeed sorry to hear of your father's death. A fine, highly-principled man." Mr. Wellbright dismissed the choir and led them to the presbytery. "My housekeeper will bring us tea." Once seated in the small, modestly furnished room, Mr. Wellbright turned to Tate. "How may I assist you, Your Grace?"

As Tate explained, the vicar's eyes grew alarmed. "But, Your Grace, your father insisted the babe be sent away. I was instructed to find a good home for her. That is what I did. She is no longer here in Kennington. Not in Oxfordshire, in fact." He faltered at the thunderous look on Tate's face. "Rest assured, I was discreet. The child's new parents do not know who her mother is. I understood the secret was necessary to protect your sister from scandal and was most assiduous in the matter. If anyone was to ask, I was to say it was a widow's child."

"But what about the mother's wishes, Vicar?" Manners said. "Was she not to be considered?"

The vicar looked confused. "This was for her sake. That was the duke's wish."

"Where is Rosamunde, sir?" Tate demanded in a manner his father would approve of, if not his motive for asking it.

"Cricklade in Wiltshire. The family's name is Nott," Wellbright said reluctantly. "The family was merely visiting here. Their relatives are my parishioners. I can assure you they are decent folk." He rose and went to his desk. "This morning, I received a letter from them. They've called the baby Anna and assured me she's settling in well."

Tate emerged from the church with the doctor soon afterward, having gained the address from the vicar, who was clearly unhappy about revealing it, and the turn of events which went against Tate's father's wishes. He did not try to argue, but it was clear he felt it best to leave matters as they stood.

The setting sun cast shadows over the grass as they climbed into the curricle.

"I'm afraid I must visit a patient, Your Grace," Manners said, taking up the reins.

"I am grateful for your help. I'll return my Aunt Mary's irascible horse to her." He spoke distractedly, wondering what he should do. Nothing in life had prepared him for this.

"Please give my best wishes to Lady Clara." Manners' fair skin flushed slightly. "An exceptionally brave young woman, if I may be allowed to say so."

"Clara told you what happened to her in London?"

"Lady Clara needed to speak to someone, and I was there," he said with a slight nod.

"I'm glad you were," Tate said, and meant it.

As Manners drew up outside his house where Daisy waited, he said, "You can rely on my discretion."

Tate nodded. "I know we can, Manners."

Could a horse actually look bad-tempered? Tate thought as he mounted her and turned her head toward his aunt's house. He hated to have to relay the bad news, which would disappoint his mother. But he wasn't about to return to Cloudhill and face his sad sister without her baby.

"But if Rosamunde has found a loving home," his mother said when he'd explained, her trembling voice betraying her distress, "perhaps it is better to leave things as they are?"

Tate heard the appeal in her voice, his mind busy with what lay ahead. "Are you able to embrace another journey, Mama?" he asked. "You don't have your maid, and I imagine very few clothes."

"I am not made of gossamer, Tate," she said crossly. "And my accompanying you will not be an impediment. It's just that I have some concern for the family who has taken the baby into their care. Removing her could break their hearts."

"I dislike that as much as you, Mama. But a mother's love surely must take precedence."

"Remember your Bible," Aunt Mary said in a solemn voice. "When Solomon announced he would cut a child into two so that each mother should have half, the birth mother, unable to bear her son being killed, offered it to the other woman to save the child's life. If Rosamunde is safe and happy with her new family, should Clara decide what is best?"

Tate studied his mother's troubled face. He knew she feared burdening her desperate daughter with such a decision. And any delay would make matters worse. "No," he said finally. "The decision must rest with me. We go to Cricklade in the morning." He turned to the elderly woman who had been a large part of his childhood and now lived in a cottage in the village on the estate his father had gifted her on her retirement. "Nanny? Will you come?"

Her cross expression reminded him of when he was a young boy and was caught out for some misdemeanor. "Of course I shall come. The duchess and the babe will need me."

Smiling, his mother stood. "I must organize my clothes."

"I shall arrange supper." Mary went to the door.

"Aunt Mary?" Tate followed her. "Is Dr. Manners married?"

"He is a widower. Lost his wife very young. It was very sad."

"He seems a good fellow."

"Robert Manners is a dedicated doctor. He hails from the gentry. His family has lived in this area for generations," Mary said. "It's my belief he should marry again. He needs a wife to take care of him. But he works such long hours; I doubt he has the time to find one."

She slipped out of the room, leaving Tate with his thoughts.

An hour after supper, bone weary, Tate followed his mother, Nanny, and Mary up the stairs to bed. It was much earlier than he usually retired. He yawned, sure his busy mind wouldn't allow him to rest. But surprisingly, he did.

IANTHE DROVE THE curricle to Cloudhill to visit Clara again the following day. A footman accompanied her with a basket of treats to cheer Clara, including the book she promised, although Ianthe doubted anything would be of much interest except news of her baby, and that might not happen for a week or more.

"It is so good to see you," Clara said as a footman showed Ianthe into the morning room. "I've been most dreadfully lonely. Emily is spending a fortnight in Bath with the Suttons. I am pleased for her. At almost eighteen, she should enjoy Bath society, and I fear it has become dreadfully dreary here since I came home."

"We have all been concerned about you, Clara. I pray you will hear good news soon. Will you write to me when you do?"

"I will, Ianthe. You must see Rosamunde before you return to London."

"I should like that very much."

Clara's conversation was all about Rosamunde: how adorable she was, so sweet-natured.

Ianthe listened with compassion and a growing sense of unease. What if Tate came home without Rosamunde? Clara seemed so delicate, Ianthe feared for her.

She drove away a half-hour later with the footman, hoping to see Tate and the baby before she returned to London. She wanted to tell him how much she admired him for doing this for his sister. Many men would not have agreed to it, including his father.

Her mother met her in the hall at home with unwelcome news. "Now that Bertie has recovered, your father wishes us to return to London. We will go in the morning," she said. "There's no longer any need to stay with your grandmother. Don't forget to thank her."

"So soon, Mama?" Ianthe cried. "Weren't we to stay until the end of the week?" She would miss her chance to see Tate, and Clara's baby. "Can we not stay a few days more?"

"I'm surprised you prefer the country to the delights of the city," her mother said, raising her eyebrows. "It is your father's wish. Have your maid pack, Ianthe."

"Very well, Mama."

Ianthe trailed up the staircase to her bedchamber. Back to London. How she hated to go. Ormond would be waiting, sure of her parents' approval. Would his manner toward her have changed? Might he become the appealing suitor once more? Or was he now set against her? Yet still determined to marry her? The horrible thought made her put a hand to her stomach. It wouldn't matter what manner of speech he employed, she would see through it to the man beneath. She paused on the stairs and clutched the banister, bowing her head. All her hopes rested on learning something about Ormond's treatment of his first wife, which her father could strongly disapprove of.

She entered her bedchamber and threw herself onto the bed, gazing up at the flowery swathe above her. She hated to miss seeing Tate and the baby. How long before he came up to London? Would he appear in society? Might he come to see her?

In her whole life, Ianthe had never kept a secret from her mother. But even though it felt wrong, she kept Clara's baby to herself because her father would learn of it. She wasn't sure what Papa would make of it, but she wanted nothing to confirm his opinion that a Lindsey wasn't right for her.

It was to her grandmother Ianthe turned, finding her at her knitting by the morning room fire. The news shocked and saddened her. "A woman's lot in life isn't always easy, Ianthe. And being wellborn doesn't prevent heartache." She'd smiled and touched Ianthe's cheek. "I want you to be happy, dear child. And I will do all I can to bring it about. I am sure a reply to my letter will soon arrive in the post."

It rained in London, the gutters streaming with dirty water, the air smelling of damp, soot, and horse dung. Pedestrians scuttled about to find shelter. She averted her face from the coach window. She should be grateful to be dry and safe, but she couldn't conjure up a shred of gratitude right now.

Once settled in their Mayfair house, her mother called her to her sitting room. A pile of invitations sat opened on the desk.

"We have a busy few weeks ahead, my dear." Mama gazed at Ianthe anxiously. "I pray you will enjoy the Season after this unfortunate disruption."

"Yes, Mama." Ianthe looked away so her mother couldn't see the misery in her eyes.

"And there's a note from Lord Ormond. He wishes to call on Sunday after church to see you. Now, doesn't that sound as if he still wants to marry you?"

If he attempts to charm me with his lies as he does my father, I'll stamp on his foot, Ianthe thought darkly.

Chapter Fifteen

Cricklade in Wiltshire

A S THE DUCAL coach traveled down High Street, people turned to stare. Tate engaged three chambers at the White Hart Hotel, and arranged accommodation for his servants for the night, then left his mother to rest. The innkeeper directed him to Nott's house, and he left with Nanny.

The Notts' terrace house lay at the far end of High Street. Tate stepped up to the narrow porch and rapped on the knocker.

A ginger-haired man of about thirty answered the door. He stared wide-eyed at Tate and Nanny. "May I help you?"

"Duke of Lindsey, and this is Miss Pettigrew. May we come in?"

Nott's eyes widened. He opened the door. "Yes, of course, Your Grace."

After they were seated in the comfortable parlor, Tate came straight to the point. "I'm sure this will be very difficult for you, Mr. Nott, but the baby's mother has changed her mind about the adoption," he explained.

Understandably, Nott looked confused. "She has? But why..."

"The baby was removed from the mother without her permission."

"But the vicar assured me..."

"I have spoken to the vicar. He acted in good faith. He was not aware of the full facts of the matter."

"May I ask if you are the father, Your Grace?"

"No. The father is deceased."

"She is a beautiful baby. We thought perhaps she is a royal by blow, if you'll forgive me, madam." He quickly averted his gaze in response to Nanny's fierce expression.

"No not royalty." Tate glanced around. There was no sign of Rosamunde or Nott's wife. "Where is the baby?"

His expression pained, Nott's Adam's apple jerked. "We have called her Anna. But she is not here."

"Is she with your wife?"

He shook his head and glanced at Nanny again, who looked ready to bite him. "My wife became...unwell and could not care for Anna. We had to leave the baby with a woman in the village who takes in children. Just until my wife is well enough to care for her, you understand."

Nanny murmured something Tate was glad he couldn't hear. "I'll have the woman's address, if you please, Mr. Nott."

"Yes, certainly. It's best for you to take her," he said with a sigh of relief. "I understand. It might take some time for my wife... If you'll step outside, I will direct you."

The coach stopped at a small cottage on a narrow plot of land a mile beyond the township. Weeds had taken over the garden and the thatched roof needed repair. A shutter hung by one hinge from a window.

Tate strode up and knocked briskly.

A woman with untidy brown hair and a stained skirt opened it. Her eyes widened. And filled with fear. "What do yer want, sir?"

"I have come for the baby you know as Anna Nott."

"Ye can't take her, sir," she said with an alarmed shake of her head. "They entrusted her into me care."

"Yes. I can." He moved her aside none too gently and strode into the small parlor.

There were eight children in the room, which smelled of rancid fat. Some slept, others wandered about strangely subdued. A baby lay in a drawer.

"Is this Anna?"

"Yes sir."

He strode over and looked down at her, seeing that she slept. Her small fingers curled into a fist against her smooth cheek, her mouth a perfect rosebud. He would know Rosamunde anywhere. She was the image of her mother.

Nanny hurried over and picked her up. "The mite smells of liquor," she cried, outraged.

"Dear God, woman. Did you give the baby spirits?" Tate demanded.

She took a step back. "Just a drop. Needs her sleep, poor babe."

"I've a good mind to call the constable and have you thrown into prison."

Her scared eyes darted around the room. "Better the children be with me than at home on their own. I look after 'em well, I do."

Disgusted, fearing he might take her by the shoulders and shake her, Tate strode to the door and held it open for Nanny. She sailed through it with Rosamunde held snug against her breast.

His mother waited at the inn door. She had sent for milk and a cradle. In Nanny's room, Rosamunde was quickly tended to, and showed remarkably few effects of her experience, waking with a happy smile.

On the journey home, Nanny proved a Godsend. She cared for the baby tirelessly, only resting when Tate's mother insisted.

A week after departing from Wiltshire, stopping to spend the nights at inns and rest the horses, the coach pulled up outside Cloudhill, and the weary occupants alighted.

The front door opened. Clara rushed over to Nanny as she carried Rosamunde onto the porch. "Give her to me, Nanny."

Clara eased back the blanket to peer anxiously at Rosamunde's face. "Oh! She looks a little too pink. Is she well, Nanny?"

"Hush, my lady," Nanny said. Outrage at Rosamunde's treatment made her Scottish brogue more pronounced. "The bairn is in good health. She needs her sleep. The journey has tuckered her oot."

Tate insisted Clara was not to be told about Rosamunde's adventure in Wiltshire and he saw he was right.

"Give her back to Nanny for a moment, Clara."

Hesitating, Clara carefully placed the baby back in Nanny's arms.

Tears spilling down her cheeks, she went to hug her mother and then threw her arms around Tate. "Thank you," she whispered against his coat.

"She is beautiful, Clara." Tate rubbed her back, noting worriedly how thin she'd become. "Nanny, take Rosamunde to the nursery," he said. "This is her home now." He took her arm as Clara jerked away from him. "You can go up in a minute. Come into the library. I want to have a quick word with you."

Clara watched Nanny mount the stairs, and looked as if she would argue with him, then allowed him to lead her inside. "What is it, Tate?" she demanded. "I must go to Rosamunde."

She stood before him on the library carpet, fidgeting like a fawn about to flee.

"What is your opinion of Dr. Manners?"

Her pale cheeks flushed, and her eyes softened. "He was wonderful. He spent so much time caring for Rosamunde and me. I doubt I would have survived without his skill as a doctor."

"Yes, but what do you think of him as a man?"

Her lashes fluttered. "He is very kind. I like him very much."

"I thought I might invite him to visit Cloudhill. Would you like that?"

The shy smile which warmed her brown eyes told him what he wished to know. "It would be nice to see him."

Tate nodded. "That is all I wished to say, Clara. Go to your baby."

He watched Clara hurry from the room with a smile.

At the desk, he dipped a quill in the inkwell and began to write. While he intended to tell Manners and the vicar in what condition he had found Rosamunde, it could wait for a later time. It served no one to cause a fuss now, least of all Clara.

Dear Dr. Manners, he wrote, *the baby is now home with us at Cloudhill. I found Mr. Nott in Wiltshire in a worried state. Mrs. Nott had fallen ill and could not take care of the baby. I must thank you for your valuable help in this matter. I am also writing to invite you to visit us at Cloudhill. Assuming you are able to take time out from your busy practice. I know Clara would like to see you.*

Manners may be surprised and suspect matchmaking on his part. But this was no time for subtlety. Tate signed it, heated the wax, and applied the ducal seal to the folded missive, extolling the advantages of a secretary which he must find.

He put the letter aside and took out another piece of bond to write to Bret. His address was now in Smithfield and Tate planned to visit him there when he returned to London at the end of the week.

Other letters awaited his perusal. One from his solicitors. Tate breathed deeply as he slit it open with a paperknife and read the contents. As he'd expected. Donovan had contested ownership of Cloudhill, intending to prove the validity of Tate's father's signature. They had set a date for the court hearing in six weeks. Two weeks had passed, four remained, then Tate would know.

A day later, a letter arrived by return mail from Dr. Manners expressing relief that Rosamunde was well. He would be delighted to visit as soon as a locum for his practice could be arranged.

Tate rode over the estate on Bayard, enjoying the familiar scents. Reaching a grassy rise, he reined in and looked toward his neighbor's property. Clara had told him Ianthe had called to see her before she returned to London. She had confessed all to Ianthe and found her most compassionate and understanding.

Ianthe would be, even if she might question the wisdom of his actions, he thought with a sigh. When could he see her? Would the engagement have been announced? Tensing his jaw, Tate rode on, returning only when his horse tired. For the next hour, still with his love in his thoughts, he curried Bayard, gave him his feed bag, and with a fond pat, returned to the house.

His mother was in the morning room, the baby in her arms, while Clara looked fondly at them. He found the baby's smell quite pleasant as he bent to kiss the tiny, dark head. One day, he would have babies of his own. He would like a girl and a boy. He pushed the thought away. There was only one mother he wanted for his children in the entire world.

On Saturday, Tate bade farewell to the family. Nanny had moved back to the nursery wing for a time to assist with the baby, and a wet nurse from the village had been engaged. If Rosamunde's lusty cries were any sign, she thrived. Clara fussed over her and questioned him daily about Manners. When might he come? Tate didn't know, but if the doctor was the man he thought he was, he would arrive soon.

There was little time to waste. Once the court decided, his family would again be in Donovan's sights. He didn't fool himself that whichever way it went, the man would attempt to take revenge. Tate placed guards about the house and grounds to be on the safe side, and instructed the gatekeeper not to admit any strangers.

Arriving in London, Tate found it strange to take on the duke's mantle in his father's house. His wily butler, Knox, greeted him as if he hadn't seen him for some time, which, of course, he had not. His valet, Wallace, took charge of Tate's clothes while expressing sympathy for His Grace having to dress himself.

As the days passed, he realized his world had changed forever. Invitations were delivered daily, most of which he put aside. He could not ignore the one from the Prince of Wales, however. Tate had barely had time to come to grips with his beloved parent's passing, yet it was apparent society considered his mourning period to be over. He must take his place in society and be the duke his father expected him to be. Tate spared a thought for his brother, too. Illness had cut Edward's life short, and all this was taken from him. Tate would do his best to honor them both. He grinned ruefully, admitting he hadn't done very well thus far. And there was still the matter of Bret's elopement. Another escapade the *ton* would frown on should they learn of it. He wished he could persuade Ianthe not to get involved, but she was determined.

London celebrated Wellington's great victory. The church bells pealed, and visitors crowded the streets and parks, the taverns and inns doing a roaring trade. Lightness of spirit filled the capital after the long years of war took such a dreadful toll on the country.

As he drove his curricle around London, Tate noticed the same hackney following him about. The sorry nag had a white star on its forehead, like Bayard. The next day, the hackney was there again. Tate drove into a narrow, empty laneway and jumped down as a few minutes later; the hackney carriage rattled in after him.

The thin fellow stopped and attempted to back the horse, but Tate was upon him before he could. He grabbed the jarvey by his coat and pulled him to the ground.

"Eer, wot you about?" The man straightened up and spat, wiping his mouth.

Tate loomed over him. "Why are you following me?"

He banged his dusty hat and jammed it over his sparse hair. "A fellow's allowed to drive down this 'ere lane. Unless you own it?"

"I am waiting for an answer. If you don't furnish it quickly, we'll take a trip to Bow Street."

He looked alarmed. "No need for that. I was paid to watch you. Meant you no 'arm, mind."

"Who paid you?"

"The man didn't give 'is name."

"What did he look like?"

"Tall, an Irishman."

"When you see Mr. Donovan again, please give him a message from me. There is no need to waste his money. I remain in plain sight and intend to see him again presently."

"I'll tell 'im. Don't worry." He scurried back to his hackney.

As he climbed into his curricle and drove on, Tate doubted the jarvey would rush to tell Donovan he had failed. So Donovan was keeping an eye on him, Tate mused. Perhaps he hoped to find Tate's cousin, the gambler who had robbed him of the vowel. He doubted this jarvey would follow him again, but there would be someone in his place soon enough.

He would have to act fast. Now he'd discovered his father's secretary's address among his father's papers, he intended to pay him an unannounced visit. If what he suspected was right and Donovan got wind of his interest, Lynch could be in danger of ending up in the river, like poor Walmer, who had damaged Fortune House in a rage after his son killed himself.

Tate drove on to Greenhill, a small hamlet of farms at the foot of Harrow Hill. Lynch's parents lived on St. Ann's Street. Tate soon found it, a small farmhouse on a few acres.

He tied off the reins and went through the gate.

An upright gentleman, his face heavily lined from years of hard work out in all weathers, stood at the open door.

"How do you do? Duke of Lindsey," Tate said. "I would like to speak to your son, Cedric."

Lynch eyed him curiously. "Please come into the parlor, Your Grace."

His wife appeared at the kitchen doorway, wiping floury hands on an apron.

Tate was invited to sit in the scrupulously clean parlor, a room apparently little used. He remained standing, wondering if Cedric would make an appearance. Beyond the door, after a few whispers, a hushed silence fell over the house.

When he glanced out the window, he saw Cedric striding

down the drive toward the front gate.

Tate ran out of the house. He caught him up on the road, grabbing his arm. "Avoiding me?"

Lynch swung around. In his late twenties, Cedric had brown hair but did not resemble his father. He had a weak face and an undershot jaw. He pulled away, his hands going to his dislodged hat, his face crimson as he struggled for breath. "No, Your Grace." He swallowed. "I wasn't aware…"

"Let us return to the house," Tate said, cutting him off. "I want a word with you."

Lynch's gaze darted about, seeking a means of escape. Finding none, he said, "Yes, of course, Your Grace."

Once again in the parlor with the door closed on Cedric's inquisitive parents, Tate placed a wooden straight-backed chair before him and ordered him to sit. He viewed the nervous man before him. "Why did my father give you notice?"

"He wished to employ someone recommended by a friend."

Tate shook his head. "Try again."

Lynch's shoulders jerked. "I don't know what you want from me, Your Grace."

"I think you do. I believe you forged my father's signature and applied the wax seal to a vowel for a gambling debt at the Lexicon, the gambling club owned by Bernard Donovan. One which my father never visited."

"I didn't!" he blustered.

"I would tell the truth if I were you," Tate advised. "Do you realize how precarious life has become for you?"

Lynch's eyes widened. "Why…how?"

"Do you really think Donovan will allow you to live with the knowledge of his fraudulent attempt to gain ownership of Cloudhill?"

Lynch wrung his hands. Sweat dripped down his forehead into his eyes. He blinked it away. "Can you protect me?" he asked, his voice hoarse.

Tate would prefer to beat the man to a pulp, but he asked,

"What did Donovan hold over you?"

Lynch looked down at his nervous fingers. "A gambling debt I couldn't pay. He approached me some months ago. Told me he'd waive it if I could find something to blackmail the duke with. I didn't want to do it, Your Grace," he said, rushing on. "I liked your father, but if I didn't, his thugs would kill me. When I discovered your unmarried sister was in the family way, I...gave him the information. I wasn't proud of it. I'm deeply ashamed."

Tate scoffed at that. The man just wanted to save his hide. "And my father guessed it was you."

"He let me go without a reference. Told me if I spoke of it to anyone, anywhere, he'd come after me with the law. But then he died, and I thought I was safe."

Tate looked into the man's soft, self-indulgent face. His father must have worked his fingers to the bone to give his son a good education. Tate fought to suppress his anger. He wanted to wring the man's neck, but fortunately for Lynch, he needed him. "You'd better watch your back, Lynch. Donovan is probably plotting your death as we speak."

"No!" he cried. "You said you'd help me."

"Court sits in less than a month. If you testify and admit to your culpability, I will ensure you stay out of jail. I'll help you leave the country, should you wish it, which I strongly advise you to do."

"I'll do it," Lynch uttered in a broken voice.

"Pack a bag. I'll send you where Donovan can't find you until the day of the hearing."

Lynch stumbled to the door. Outside in the corridor, he faced a barrage of questions from his parents.

After he'd said goodbye to his father and sobbing mother, Tate drove him back to Lindsey Court. Sending for the coachman and a footman, he ordered them to take Lynch to the hunting box in the Epping Forest. "Stay with him, John, at all times. Arm yourselves. I don't expect trouble, but keep looking over your shoulder. I want him back in London in three weeks."

John nodded. "Yes, Your Grace."

"If he tries to escape, shoot him."

Lynch uttered a strangled sound and his face paled.

An hour later, Tate watched them until the coach was out of sight. He checked up and down the street for a sign of anything unusual, but saw nothing to concern him. Would he manage to get this coward to admit to his crimes?

He returned inside. The Ashwins' ball was this coming Friday, and Ianthe was likely to be there. Despite everything, they would have their waltz, because he refused to let that villain Donovan rob him of everything he treasured.

>>><<<

AFTER CHURCH ON Sunday, Ianthe waited with a beating heart for Ormond to visit. She had been ill with nerves since she'd woken up and couldn't eat a bite of breakfast, causing her mother to remark on it.

When the footman admitted Ormond into the drawing room where she and her mother sat, his face was wreathed in smiles. He crossed the floor and took her mother's hand. "You look like sisters in those yellow gowns, my lady."

Her mother laughed and smoothed her cream skirts. "What nonsense, Lord Ormond. Only a young woman would wear that shade of yellow."

He turned to Ianthe, and his eyes swept over her. She noted the possessiveness in his gaze. "Indeed, Lady Ianthe reminds one of a yellow rose. A delight to the eyes."

"Thank you, sir," she said with a stiff nod of her head, wondering how her mother could fall for so trite a line.

"A lovely day. The walk to church was most pleasant." He seated himself in the chair directly opposite her, where he could watch her without turning his head.

Her mother gave a pleased nod and rose from the sofa. "We

are short of staff on Sundays as some of the maids attend church or visit their family. I'll see to the tea tray."

Left alone with him, Ormond's manner changed to testiness as he observed her. "I see absence has not made your heart fonder, Lady Ianthe."

Ianthe didn't know what to say to that. If she agreed, he would have something to complain to her father about. "I'm sorry I was so abrupt the last time we met. It was unkind of me."

He sat forward in his chair, a flicker of triumph in his eyes. "It was indeed. Does this mean you have changed your mind about us?"

She sighed. "I don't love you, Lord Ormond. Surely you would want to marry someone who did."

He rose abruptly and joined her on the sofa.

She stiffened as he reached for her hand and held it in a tight clasp, as if to prevent her from moving away.

"Perhaps I like a challenge."

She went cold and gazed up at him in horror.

He chuckled. "How serious you are, Ianthe. And so very young. And spirited. You have much to learn. It shall be a delight to teach you."

The door opened and her mother came in smiling when she saw them together. A footman with the tea tray followed.

The rest of the half hour was a blur while Ianthe's mind grappled with what he'd said. He liked a challenge. When more callers arrived, Ormond took his leave, and Ianthe breathed more easily. He was still determined to marry her. She feared there was nothing she could say or do to deter him.

Her mother took up her knitting. "Has your view of Ormond changed?"

"No, Mama."

"I am sorry, dearest, when I saw you holding hands I thought..."

"I dislike that man with every breath in my body," she said fiercely.

"Oh Ianthe," Mama put down her knitting and gazed at her sorrowfully. "It's Tate, isn't it? Seeing him again. Did he make any promises he cannot keep?"

Ianthe gasped. "Tate would never do such a thing. He is an honorable man. Unlike Ormond."

"Why do you say that about Lord Ormond?"

Ianthe couldn't put into words how she believed Ormond preferred a spirited woman because he enjoyed breaking her. Had he been like that with his wife? "He...he..." Robbed of breath, she fought for words. "He said he looked forward to teaching me..."

Her mother looked perplexed. "I don't see what is wrong with that, my dear. Many husbands would wish to instruct an innocent young bride in the ways of the world." She took up her knitting again. "As my words appear to fall on deaf ears, it's best we say no more about it now."

Mama's busy knitting needles clicked in the silent room.

Ianthe stared at a painting on the wall of a rider galloping over a field and thought about Tate. What was happening at Cloudhill? Had he brought the baby home? Clara would be so happy! Ianthe wanted so much to be there with them it hurt.

Chapter Sixteen

T HE BUTLER ANNOUNCED Tate at the door to the ballroom. He beheld the dazzling scene before him, the colored streamers swinging in the draft in patriotic splendor celebrating Wellington's victory, the women's sumptuous gowns and sparkling jewelry, the candelabra casting lights over the crowd. Joyous laughter and chatter everywhere.

More confident of success in keeping ownership of Cloudhill with the secretary's evidence, Tate welcomed the thought that this life would be his. His and Ianthe's? Hope flooded through him like a burst of adrenaline as the guests turned to watch him move through the room in search of a familiar face. He found Hart, who had sent a note to advise Tate of his return from the country.

Hart pushed his way toward him. He looked closely at Tate standing directly beneath a magnificent Italian crystal chandelier. "Ah," he said, "it is you."

"Good to see you," Tate said with a wry grin. "How is your father?"

"As grumpy as ever. I am to write and advise him of the success, or failure, in my search for a suitable bride."

"Well, you can begin tonight." Tate glanced around the long room. "There are some lovely young women here."

"I would prefer to hear what's been happening with you since

I left London."

"Shall we meet at the Crown at nine o'clock for breakfast? The day after tomorrow," Tate said. "There's little point in attempting to raise you from your bed tomorrow morning."

Hart cocked an eyebrow, and he grinned. "Not if there's a lady in it. I'll be there." He moved away through the throng.

Tate strolled along the rim of the dance floor where the Roger De Cloverly was in progress. He looked for Ianthe, wishing to ensure she kept the waltz free for him, and found her among the dancers. Her partner was a fair-haired man he thought might be Ormond.

Tate retraced his steps to Hart, who stood in conversation with a few friends and promptly introduced him. Tate nodded his head toward the dancers. "Ianthe's dance partner. Is it Ormond?"

Spotting her, Hart nodded. "That's him."

So that was Ormond. He danced well, smiling at Ianthe. Should he forget his promise of the waltz and walk away? He fought to conquer his jealousy, and failing, joined in a discussion about how much lighter the mood in London was now that Napoleon had been vanquished. Most approved of the splendid parades, the busy hotels, restaurants and eateries, the magnificent theater entertainments, and dances. But Tate knew the long war had cost England a great deal, which would leave people struggling for many years. And he was keen to support any bill in the House of Lords which would benefit his tenant farmers.

He saw Ianthe and Ormond leave the dance floor at the conclusion of the dance. Instead of returning her to her mother, Ormond steered her out through the French doors onto the terrace. Ianthe had no wrap. The spring weather was unpredictable and the evening quite cool.

Tate excused himself from Hart's circle. He strolled over to observe them through the glass doors. Ormond and Ianthe were the only people on the terrace, the braziers flickering and smoking in the damp air. They appeared to be arguing. Ormond took hold of Ianthe's wrist. She tried to pull away, her face alarmed.

When Ormond kept hold of her, Tate pulled open the door and strode out. "The lady wishes you to release her."

Ormond swung around, surprised, but kept hold of Ianthe despite her struggling to wrest her hand away. Ormond glared. "This is not your concern, Your Grace. It is a private matter between my fiancée and me."

Tate halted. Had he blundered into a lover's quarrel?

"Lord Ormond is not my fiancé." Ianthe tugged at her wrist, a fiery light in her eyes.

"Unofficially," Ormond said smoothly, making no move to release her. "Lord Granville has as much as agreed to our marriage."

Tate's initial relief at Ianthe's denial of their engagement turned to anger at the man's brutish insistence to hold her against her will. "Take your hand off the lady."

Ormond obliged, but with a show of bravado. "You reveal far too great an interest in Lady Ianthe, Your Grace," he said. "Some secret history between you, perhaps?" He turned to Ianthe. "Something your father would wish to know about, my dear?"

Fury made Tate see red. Fists clenched, he took a step forward and punched Ormond hard, determined to wipe the sneer off his face. Ormond fell back against the banister rail, his eyes wide.

"You have shown your true colors, Lindsey." He rubbed his jaw. "I might lower myself to your level and fight you, but I have no need to." He straightened up, shrugged, and shot his cuffs. "You have done me a favor. If Lord Granville ever considered you as the man for his daughter, now he certainly won't."

Ormond strode to the door, flung it open, and fought his way through the crowd which had gathered to watch them.

Ianthe gazed up at him, dismay in her eyes. "Oh Tate, I wish you hadn't done that."

He frowned. "Should I have stood by and let him assault you?"

She shook her head. "We can't talk here. Meet me in the park tomorrow. The oak tree by the lake where we met before. I'll come early, before breakfast."

"No, Ianthe, you shouldn't..."

"But I will," she said fiercely, and turned away.

Tate opened the door for her. She hurried inside, head lowered. He followed while the guests watched, some shocked, some intrigued. There were a few titters as he passed. He gritted his teeth. He should regret such an impulsive action, but only felt sorry he hadn't hit the brute again.

As he made his way across the floor, he passed Ianthe, now seated with her mother. Lady Granville frowned at him.

Tate gloomily left the ballroom, ruing his first appearance at a ball since his father died. His parent would turn in his grave. He flexed his fingers, his hand sore. He needed a drink. No, not one, several.

In the early morning, he made his way to the lake, the air damp with mist threading through the trees. His head ached from imbibing too much brandy, and lack of sleep. Would Ianthe be able to get away? He should have refused to let her come. He'd made life difficult enough for her as it was.

She was there, sheltering beneath a leafy bough. He expected her to be angry with him for causing a scandal. Instead, she ran and flung her arms around him.

She laid her head against his shoulder. "My gallant knight," she murmured as he put an arm around her. "Ormond is a horrible man. I can't make my parents understand. He's sly. Did you see how he had his back turned to the ballroom so my mother could not see how badly he behaved? He says nothing in their presence to alert them to his true nature." She sobbed into Tate's coat. "He only wants me to give him an heir." She caught her breath on a gasp. "He said I have a lot to learn to be an obedient wife, and he would delight in teaching me."

Bloody hell. He wished he'd hit him harder.

While he desperately wanted to protect her, he had no right

to interfere in her life. Jealousy had been a factor when he'd punched Ormond. Tate's arm tightened around her. Her bonnet fell back on its ribbons and her soft hair tickled his chin. "I'll speak to your father," he said gruffly as his unruly body responded to their closeness. "Tell him my side of it."

"No, Tate, you mustn't. Papa is furious with you. Ormond wasted no time last night in telling him. His version of events, of course."

"But surely after this, your father will support you?"

Resting her head against him, she clutched his lapel. "I don't think he will," she murmured, her voice muffled. "He likes Ormond and thinks he's doing the best for me."

"You will not marry Ormond," Tate stated flatly.

She drew away to look up at him. Tears clung to her lashes. He hated to see her so upset. He could have roared with frustration.

"Can you help me, Tate? Really?"

He bent his head and pressed a kiss to her damp cheek, then pulled away before he kissed her mouth. "Believe it. I will be your big brother in Stephen's absence."

"You are not my brother." She shook her head. "It is you I love, Tate. Ormond knows it's you I want."

The breath whooshed from his chest. He groaned. "Oh, Ianthe, with all my heart, I wish it could be so."

She rested her head against his chest. "I can't look at you. I've thrown myself at you."

"Sweetheart," he said gruffly, raising her chin with his hand to gaze into her eyes. "It cannot be."

She lifted her head and pressed her lips to his but briefly. When she would have pulled away, he hooked his hand around her nape and kissed her passionately. As if he wasn't hamstrung but as carefree as the waterfowl preening their feathers on the bank. Then he pulled away, breathing hard. He looked away, surprised at the lack of shame he felt to have kissed her when she wasn't his to claim. When his gaze came back to her, her blue eyes searched his. "You *do* love me."

"It's makes little difference, does it?" he said bitterly. "When I can't marry you. If I have nothing to offer you, I'll go away. You must forget me."

"Forget you? When I've loved you since I was in the school-room?"

His fingers traced the beguiling dimple in her cheek "Have you?"

"You must know I have." She sighed. "Now, when I'm in your arms, I don't care what happens."

"Your father won't agree to us marrying, Ianthe," Tate said huskily. Not as things stand now.

"We could elope, like Bret and Lily?"

He sadly shook his head. "And alienate you from your family? When I can't offer you the life your father wants for you?"

"In time, Papa will come to accept it," she said fiercely.

"He would hate me, and rightly so. I cannot do that, sweet-heart."

She frowned and turned her head away. "Then perhaps you don't love me enough."

"Oh, Ianthe." He wanted desperately to kiss her, to convince her of his love, but two men strolled along the bank toward them.

He turned her head to screen her face from their view. "Once the court decides the outcome for Cloudhill, I'll know where I stand. Should the verdict be in my favor, I will go to your father with the knowledge I can support you in the way he wishes, and should he agree…"

She gazed up at him, tears in her eyes. "If it is not too late."

Tate wanted to sound confident, but the way wasn't clear. Ianthe's father would be outraged if he heard of them helping Bret and Lily elope, and would oppose their marriage for that reason alone.

The men had moved on, but shouts came over the water from a rowboat out on the lake. The park filled up with people. "We must go."

She sighed. "Not yet."

"The sunlight catches your hair and turns it to gold." Tate brushed away a lock from her neck. "And that look in your eyes... You are in my blood, Ianthe. I would fight for you with my last breath. But I can't fight your father when he sees me as a poor choice." Nor could he draw her into his life while Donovan was a threat. But soon, would it end soon?

"And if you don't get Cloudhill back? That is the end for us, isn't it?" she said despondently. "You will leave England, and Papa will make me marry Ormond."

Tate flexed his hands into fists. "I'll stop Ormond."

He hated to see her look at him so doubtfully. "I should return home. Mama has become more vigilant, and it wouldn't do for Papa to learn of this meeting."

"And if he hears we've helped Bret and Lily to elope, that will be the end for us. You do realize that?"

She frowned. "Then he mustn't hear of it."

They walked back along the path to the park gates. Ianthe gazed up at the patch of blue forming above them. "It's so pleasant to see blue sky," she said in a sad little voice. "It is always so gray in London. The arch of blue seems to stretch forever when you view the sky from Ide Hill in Kent."

It saddened him to hear the longing in her voice, wishing they could be there together.

They drew closer to the gates, where her maid waited. She turned to him. "I'll try to prevent father accepting Ormond's suit for as long as I can, Tate. You'd best leave me here. Someone might see us and tell Mama. There's no sense in making matters worse."

She pulled her pelisse closer and hurried away.

Tate scrubbed his face with his hand. She sounded resigned. He bitterly hated that he'd disappointed her, that he couldn't do what she wished. The one thing he would do was stop Ormond from marrying her, whatever it took. He followed them, keeping Ianthe in sight. The thought of eloping, and the vision of them escaping to marry in Scotland, was so tempting he could taste it.

WHEN TATE'S LIPS met hers and he enfolded her in his arms, Ianthe felt warm and safe, as if the world had righted itself. He loved her. Her heart beat madly before reality struck. Was she foolish to believe that love could conquer all? She could think of little else but Tate, his lips, his smell, the feel of his body against hers as she hurried up the street with the blessedly silent Aggy. The maid was always sensitive to her feelings. She sighed. She had to believe that she and Tate would be together soon. But when she reached her family's London home, her mood sank desperately low. Her father was close to deciding, which meant Tate could not keep his promise to her.

When the footman opened the door, she held a finger to her lips.

Ronald grinned as she and Aggy slipped past him.

Her father emerged from his study into the corridor and stood in her way. "Ianthe! Send your maid upstairs and come inside." He shut the door behind her. He pointed to a chair. "Sit down."

Ianthe bowed her head and obeyed him. She wriggled uncomfortably, glancing up at him.

Behind his desk, Papa looked dreadfully stern. He no longer trusted her, which hurt her dreadfully. But she wouldn't lie to him.

"Please explain where you have been with your maid at this time of the morning."

"I met Tate in Hyde Park."

He frowned. "It did not bother you that such behavior would upset your mother and me?"

"Yes, of course I did, Papa, but I had to see him, to…thank him. Tate came to my rescue when Lord Ormond upset me."

He raised his eyebrows. "Ormond upset you? How?"

"Ormond held my wrist. He wouldn't let me go."

Obviously skeptical, Papa leaned toward her, his hands flat on the desk. "Tate interfered in something that didn't concern him. What was this disagreement between you and Ormond?"

"I disliked his officious manner, and I told him so."

"I expect that upset him. Hardly an assault. Did Ormond threaten you?"

"No...but..."

"So, you would thank Tate for causing a scene in front of society, and making you the subject of scandal? Because he was jealous," he added heavily.

"Tate wasn't jealous," Ianthe cried. "I was distressed, and he came to my aid."

"That is not Ormond's version of events. He said you were having a lover's squabble concerning some gentleman he thought you were flirting with on the dance floor. Then Tate strode onto the terrace and threatened him. When Ormond told him politely to leave, Tate struck him down." Her father leaned back in his chair to observe her. "I would never have expected such behavior from Tate. Always a gentleman, like his father. To behave like a thug at a victory ball! Losing Cloudhill must have upset the balance of his mind."

Ianthe clutched her hands together, her heart beating so hard against her ribs it hurt. She drew in a ragged breath. "I am never a flirt! You would believe Ormond instead of me, Papa?"

"Whom I choose to believe is none of your affair, Ianthe. I have been too lenient with you. You have behaved like a hoyden all your life. Following Tate and Stephen around like a puppy. It might have been appealing when you were young, but now you are a young lady. Running around the streets with your maid when the sun is barely up? Such behavior is deplorable. No man would wish such qualities in a wife. You are stubborn and wish to go your own way, and that will end in heartache." He folded his arms. There was no sign of the affection she'd always enjoyed in his eyes. "I don't intend to see that happen. You must take advice from those who know better."

Tears gathered behind Ianthe's eyes, and a lone tear ran down her cheek. She brushed it away, annoyed with herself. "I shall be all that you wish, Papa, if you will refuse Ormond's suit."

Her father pushed away from the desk and stood. "I am not about to bargain with you, my girl. Go to your bedchamber and remain there until you are told otherwise."

Ianthe trudged up the stairs. Her parents were very disappointed in her. Cut adrift from all she had known, if she could only speak to Grandmama, the one person who truly understood.

Grandmama! Ianthe sat down at the small desk in her bedchamber and took a sheet of paper from the drawer. She scribbled madly. Had Grandmama any news? Frustration and misery drove her to blot the page and make several attempts before she finished her letter.

When a maid came to tell her she was to come to luncheon, Ianthe was sure she couldn't eat a bite, despite missing breakfast. She tucked the letter into the sleeve of her morning gown, planning to ask Ronald, her favorite footman, to deliver it to Grandmama's house, which was only a few streets away.

As she passed the door to her mother's bedchamber, she heard raised voices. She had never heard her parents argue. Her mother always remained stoically in agreement with Papa about everything. Knowing it would concern her, Ianthe hovered near the door. She heard her mother say something about his misjudged handling of her. "She is your beloved daughter. You know she never lies or deliberately does anything to spite us. Please listen to her, Arthur."

Ianthe gasped. Her mother was sobbing.

"My love, you must see…"

"I see two people in love," Mama said, sounding unusually determined. "Who cannot be together."

"And never can be, Caroline," Papa said, apparently unmoved. "Surely you're not so foolish as to wish it so when the

Lindseys' fortunes are in danger of collapse? I am in business. And business supersedes love in a successful marriage. I know more about these things than you do."

Ianthe put a hand to her mouth. What Tate faced made her tremble with horror.

There was a moment's silence. Ianthe was about to go to the stairs when her father spoke again, his tone softer, as if her parents had been consoling each other. "You must calm yourself, my love, and consider Ianthe's future. One day, you will see I am right."

Ianthe fled downstairs. Mama stood up for her! Ianthe was terribly grateful, and felt less alone, even though her mother had failed to change her father's mind. Could Grandmama help? She went in search of the footman.

Chapter Seventeen

"**W**HY DID YOU punch Ormond, Tate?" Hart asked Tate during breakfast at the inn. "Wouldn't it have been wiser to wait until after the ball? Everyone talks of it."

Remorseful at the gossip spreading for Ianthe's sake rather than his, Tate shrugged. "If I had waited to get him alone, I would have beaten him within an inch of his life. Especially after what Ianthe confided to me about him."

Hart raised his eyebrows. "Still, it's unlike you to act so rashly, my friend. Although, I gather he deserved it."

Tate sawed into his bacon, conscious of the noise from the tables around them. "He does, and more."

Hart eyed Tate carefully. "Ianthe has always been in your blood. Are you sure you're thinking clearly?"

"My mind has never been clearer," Tate said, gritting his teeth. "Ormond's a mongrel." A man such as he, who liked to control women, must have a history of offense with the fairer sex. Now sure he was right to stop the engagement, Tate had given a lot of thought to how he might put an end to Ormond's aspirations. He'd look into his background.

When he returned to Lindsey Court, Knox presented the post to him on a silver salver. Tate went into the library to read it. At his desk, he picked up a letter opener and sliced through the missive from his mother. Dr. Manners had come for a brief visit, she wrote. He'd examined Rosamunde and declared the baby in perfect health. Blissfully happy, Clara rode out with him to show him the estate. His mother wasn't privy to what occurred between them during their outing, but they were both subdued when they returned, and she caught a look passing between them, which gave her pause to think. *Manners left the next day. Clara saw him off at the stables and returned with tears in her eyes. I believe she has formed a tender regard for the doctor, who is an impressive gentleman, well-educated, genteel, and very sensible. Clara was calmer in his presence than I've ever seen her, even before—Am I foolish to hope—?*

Tate put down the letter. "No, Mama, you are not foolish," he said to the empty room. He rose from his chair to roam the carpet, her letter dangling from his fingers. He had hoped for this. The perfect answer for Clara, which would give her the chance for a contented, meaningful life. But would she, as a duke's daughter accustomed to the trappings of wealth and position, want to give up so much to live a simple life in a modest house with few servants? Her life would be starkly different. Knowing Clara, Tate decided she would. She was always a shy, gentle soul. Not suited to be the wife of a man of consequence. The only snag was Manners. Would he agree to a marriage where there was a stark imbalance between their birth and fortune? Tate believed he was a proud man, who would probably refuse her dowry, if Tate could pay it.

Well, Manners had come all the way to Cloudhill to see her and Rosamunde, had he not? And while the ownership of this estate remained unsure, perhaps their present circumstances evened things up a little.

He frowned. If their courtship was to be, it must be hurried along. For until she was safely married to Manners and living in Kennington, she would not be free from Donovan's malicious intent. Yes, their marriage was the perfect answer. Scandal was unlikely to touch them in a small remote village many miles from London. To prevent talk among the parishioners, he planned to ask Aunt Mary to make a few comments in the right ears about how tragic it was for Clara to be widowed so young. Hopefully, that would lay any gossip to rest. They esteemed Manners in the village. Talk would eventually die down. In time, Clara would gain their respect as the devoted and caring doctor's wife he knew his sister could be.

No courtship flourished when the couple was miles apart.

Returning to his desk, Tate took up his pen and furnished his mother with a request. If Clara and the baby were in good health, could Clara make the trip to Kennington and stay with Aunt Mary?

He sent it off, confident his mother would agree.

On Saturday evening, he attended a sumptuous dinner at Carlton House and met many interesting guests, politicians, visiting dignitaries, and some minor royalty. As he and the other guests left the table to partake of cognac and listen to the fine orchestra, Prinny sent for him.

In the sumptuous Blue Velvet Room, so named because of the blue velvet décor, priceless artworks hung on the paneled walls. The furniture was exotically Egyptian in style. The overweight regent, resplendent in extravagant evening dress, beckoned him forward. His thoughtful gaze rested on Tate as he rose from a low bow.

"You do not physically favor your father, Lindsey."

"So I am told, Your Highness."

"And from what I hear, neither do your manners."

Having nothing to say in his defense, Tate remained silent.

"A lover's quarrel, perhaps?" Prinny prodded. Amusement and curiosity brightened his sovereign's blue eyes.

"A matter of bad timing, Your Highness."

Prinny guffawed. "Do you say so? I disagree, you have provided the *ton* with a delicious scandal which should last for at least a week or more."

Relieved not to be banished to the far New Hebrides, Tate smiled.

"Took a dislike to Ormond myself," the regent professed. "However, I wouldn't want to take a poke at him." He eyed Tate. "But you would strip well."

"I enjoy the odd boxing bout," Tate confessed. "Preferably in the right arena."

"Didn't like the cut of his jib, eh? Ormond would be wise to watch himself."

"I am not by nature a violent man, Your Highness," Tate said, feeling the need to explain, but Prinny merely waved the comment away. Tate suspected he'd disappointed him.

Prinny drew him on to other matters, inviting Tate's opinion. With a chuckle, he spoke of Napoleon's criticism of the Duke of Wellington. In Bonaparte's opinion, the duke made a bad tactical move to fight him at Waterloo, and he was confident history would agree with him.

For all the criticism leveled at the prince, and much of it justified, Tate had enjoyed his company, although he wasn't fool enough not to realize the regent's attitude toward him could change in a moment.

He rode out to visit Bret at High Holborn the next day, but after a few blocks, he saw again that he was being tailed. With a casual glance over his shoulder, he took measure of the tough thuggish man astride a bay. He did not try to gain on Tate, but kept well back, although always in sight.

Tate cursed. He wouldn't lead Donovan to Bret, which was obviously his intention. He could outride the fellow, who was too heavy for his mount, but Donovan could have prepared for such a contingency. Another of his scoundrels could lurk somewhere nearby. The risk to Bret was too great. Tate pulled the reins and rode down a side street, returning to Lindsey Court. He considered his options. There'd been no tail this morning when he met Ianthe in the park. He made certain of it, taking a roundabout route. Meeting up with Bret at dawn seemed a better option.

Having penned a note requesting Bret to meet him beside the Serpentine at first light tomorrow, Tate handed it to a footman.

He ordered him to wait until Tate had ridden away before leaving to deliver it.

Tate rode to Hyde Park. Before long, his shadow fell in behind him, keeping half a block away.

The man remained out of sight while Tate cantered down Rotten Row and spoke to a friend, then appeared again when Tate left the park. It was all he could do not to turn his horse's head and ride back to confront him, but he cautioned himself not to go off half-cocked. He admitted ruefully that taking matters head-on had proved unwise in the past.

Restless and feeling caged at Lindsey Court, Tate found the ride had done little to rid him of his nervous energy. He longed to be back at Cloudhill, riding over the estate lands once again. He dwelled on Ianthe's passionate declaration with heartfelt longing. To be with her on that hill she spoke of beneath blue skies and inhale the sweet country air was so bittersweet he moaned.

Shortly after dawn, Tate rode to meet Bret beside the lake. The weather remained fine, the birds' chorus filling the air as they rose from their roosting places on the wing, the lake rendered mirror-like by the soft morning light.

Bret stepped out of the trees to greet him as Tate dismounted.

"I hired a horse. Rode out to Staines-Upon-Thames, where Bolton has an estate," Bret said after they'd caught up on their news. "I spent a few hours in the village tavern. It's common knowledge that Bolton suffers from syphilis."

"Good God!" Tate said.

Bret nodded, his eyes dark and worried. "Rumor has it the same complaint killed the baroness."

"The man's a monster! I'm impressed, though, Bret. You would do well at Bow Street."

Bret laughed.

"What next?" Tate asked.

"Lily wrote. Her parents plan to leave London for Aldbury, their country home in Herts, within a few weeks. There's little chance of her evading them there. They watch her too closely. We will make our escape at the Bellman's summer ball in Richmond. It's my hope that Ianthe can help Lily slip away. I'll be waiting outside. Can I call upon you to drive us to the Bull and Mouth in Smithfield? The next morning, we'll go by stage to Scotland."

"Yes, my coach will collect you at the Bull and Mouth. You'll await Lily at the garden gate to the rear of the property in the lane which runs alongside the river."

Bret smiled with obvious relief. "I knew I could count on you, Tate. Lily hopes to see Ianthe before then, but in case she doesn't, could you tell her what we have decided?"

"Not so easy," Tate said. "I'm in her father's bad books at present."

"Why?"

As Tate explained, Bret's eyes widened. "If you need help with Ormond, I'm happy to oblige. Waiting at the inn is interminably dull."

"Feel like traveling to Aldbury? Ormond has a country estate there. I'd appreciate it if you could find out something about him which might be of use to me."

A keen light brightened Bret's green eyes. "I'd be pleased to."

"Donovan is having me followed. He's trying to get to you," Tate said. "You must be doubly careful."

Bret nodded. "I will. Have no fear."

"Are you short of funds?"

Bret shook his head. "I'll leave in the morning."

Tate clamped a hand on his shoulder. "Send me a message on your return. We'll meet here again." He glanced around. "I'd best leave first."

Hopeful that Bret might learn something, Tate rode home with no one following him. One thing he knew about Donovan's men, they stood out like a sore thumb.

⇛⇛⋗⋖⇚⇚

IANTHE ATTENDED THE Carringtons' ball. A collective gasp rose from the guests as the Prince of Wales appeared accompanied by his brother, the Duke of York, and his mistress.

Moments later, the prince's aide came to request Ianthe's appearance. Surprised, she turned to look at her mother.

Why would the regent wish to see her? A lump in her throat, Ianthe nervously smoothed her white satin and net gown while her speechless mother fussed with her hair.

Ianthe followed the aide and curtseyed low before the regent as he casually sprawled in a chair. His gaze roamed from the white feathers and diamantes in her hair to her white satin slippers. He beckoned to her. "It is you who has the Duke of Lindsey dancing attendance, Lady Ianthe?"

Ianthe stared at him, her throat dry. "No, Your Highness. He isn't… I mean…"

"I believe the lady protests too much, Your Highness." The Prime Minister, the Earl of Liverpool, one of the regent's party, chuckled.

Ianthe feared she might faint. She couldn't think of a thing to say in Tate's defense.

"I wish him well in his…passionate pursuit," the regent said. "My compliments to Lord and Lady Granville." He turned away.

Dismissed, Ianthe hurried away, annoyed with herself. Should she have at least said something? But what? The prince must have thought her stupid.

Her father stood with her mother. They smiled as she joined them. At last she had done something right, although what it might be exactly eluded her. Their gentle praise would have pleased her if Ormand had not joined them with his usual proprietary expression. She longed to tell him what the regent said. He would not act as if he owned her then.

"What did the regent say, Ianthe?" Papa asked.

"He merely wished me well."

"Was that all?" Her mother looked disappointed. Then she brightened. "I think I know what it is about. They have chosen you to be crowned belle of the ball."

"As she should be," Ormand said silkily.

Ianthe longed to poke her tongue out at him. When he claimed her for the next dance, she had to satisfy herself with treading on his foot.

As they danced, her thoughts inevitably returned to Tate. She thought the regent's comment about him was decidedly odd. But he must have gained the regent's approval. She smiled to herself.

"What makes you smile?" Ormond sounded piqued.

"Something the regent said."

"What was it?"

"Nothing of importance," she threw back at him as the dance sequence separated them. She caught his scowl before she turned and enjoyed a warm burst of satisfaction. Was it possible he'd give up his pursuit of her? She wasn't foolish enough to believe it. Ormond was ambitious, determined to marry an earl's daughter. It occurred to her, not for the first time, that he found her father's money more attractive than he did her.

Chapter Eighteen

B RET'S MESSAGE ARRIVED three days later. He had spent two nights at the local tavern making inquiries about Lord Ormond. *What I have gleaned is probably not what you hoped for,* he wrote. *Ormond is not well liked by the villagers, but that's hardly unusual. One fellow who worked on the estate for a time offered the opinion that Ormond was short of funds, as he failed to pay his bills. Some claimed that he doesn't get on with his father, the marquess. But that's the extent of what I could learn about him. I'm sorry I haven't more to offer you.*

With a muttered curse, Tate addressed the rest of his mail. Among them was a letter from his mother. Clara and the baby were in Kennington with Aunt Mary, and Dr. Manners called in every day to see them. *Mary said Clara was calmer and more content in this quiet place on the edge of the Common,* his mother wrote, *but she made no mention of a proposal.*

"Early days," Tate said to the empty room, rubbing the back of his neck. He refused to give up on what he considered to be an excellent outcome. One where Clara would be safe from Donovan and the *ton's* censure.

Two days later, a letter arrived from Manners. *Your Grace, I am but a humble man, not wealthy, but comfortably situated. My parents bequeathed me some money, which I have invested. They were good folk who enabled me to study medicine. My sister nurses a habitual invalid, a member of a wealthy family. I'm painfully aware of how presumptuous it is of me to request the hand of your sister, Lady Clara. She is a brave and beautiful lady who should rightly marry a wealthy, titled gentleman. But matters have changed. I can offer her understanding and tender care. I have come to love her deeply and will raise Rosamunde as my own. Should you agree to our union, we will marry quietly in the church here in Kennington after the banns are read. I await your reply with some anticipation. Yours sincerely, Robert Manners.*

While it had been what he hoped for, Tate studied it a long time. Could it be the answer? Did his sister want it? There was no question of her marrying a titled gentleman now.

Clara's letter came in the same post, begging Tate to agree to Manners' proposal. Tate immediately replied, giving them his blessing, and wishing them well. Unfortunately, the way things stood here, he doubted he'd even be able to attend their wedding.

The following day, a message arrived from Tate's footman who stayed with Lynch at the hunting lodge. Cedric Lynch grew restive and proved to be troublesome. Tate groaned and scrubbed his hand over his jaw. He hoped his father's former secretary hadn't changed his mind. He must go to Epping Forest and reassure him. It would be disastrous if everything he had arranged fell apart at the last minute.

His uncle's letter stated in bald terms the urgent need for a secretary at Cloudhill. *You must come home, Tate. There is much that needs your attention here.*

He could not leave everything to his uncle. He would depart for Cloudhill in the morning and stop at the hunting lodge on the way to make sure the secretary wasn't about to renege on his promise.

Early the next morning, Tate ate a hasty breakfast, pleased to be going home. Was the time drawing near when Cloudhill would no longer be his home? Unthinkable. The court case was next week. Lynch would give his evidence if Tate had to tie him up and drag him into court.

He set off in his curricle at the crack of dawn. No one appeared to follow. Once he'd left the city and was out in the country, Tate breathed the fresh air with relief, suddenly aware of how tense he'd become.

A breeze whispered through the trees, carrying familiar loamy smells, the great forest quiet and undisturbed out of hunting season. Tate pulled up his horses outside the brick dwelling. His footman emerged from the house. "When are we to return to London, Your Grace?" he asked as Charlie, Tate's groom, ran to take the reins.

"Not long now, John. Where is he?"

"In the parlor," John said.

He entered, finding Lynch chewing at a fingernail. He jumped up as Tate came in.

"Your Grace! I don't know why I agreed. I cannot appear in court. They throw forgers into Newgate! You must help me leave the country before Donovan finds me. He'll kill me."

"I don't doubt he would get his thugs to deal with you," Tate said coolly. "The only way to prevent him is to do as we agreed. That court will not deal with your crime, Lynch, so don't fear they will arrest you. After you give evidence, you board a ship, set to leave for France on the evening tide. And, although you deserve nothing from me, you'll take a tidy sum with you to begin your life on the Continent."

Lynch's chin wobbled. "The same day?"

"That very night. I will book your passage myself."

He released a heavy sigh. "Very well, Your Grace. I will do it."

"I might add that if you fail to keep your side of this bargain, you will also have me to deal with." Tate obviously looked as menacing as he felt, as Lynch paled. "And I can be every bit as deadly as Donovan, should it prove necessary."

Lynch took a step back and held up his hands. "No, Your Grace. Have no fear. It will be done."

Tate instructed his footman, a big, burly fellow, to bring Lynch to the court the following Monday. "And don't let him out of your sight."

When Tate finally arrived at Cloudhill and wearily entered the house, his mother rushed into the hall clutching a letter. "It's from Clara," she gasped. "Manners has proposed."

"That's remarkably good news, Mama." Such a marriage would not have been considered before the tragedy which befell her. But Manners was a kindly man. Tate felt confident that he would make Clara a good husband. And that could not always be said of titled gentlemen. He frowned, thinking of Ormond. Did Ianthe still have to endure the obnoxious man? If only Tate had found something damning to use against him. He longed to see her, to hold her in his arms and tell her she was safe, because he would always make her so. But her father forbade them to meet, and should the court case fail, she was lost to him forever. He must win, for surely, God was on their side.

IANTHE DIDN'T COME down to breakfast until eleven o'clock. She had woken early, but felt so despondent her appetite had deserted her. She'd tried to read, but the words faded as her thoughts turned inward. Nothing cheered her, but she was glad of the hot chocolate her maid brought her.

She expected that after such a late evening, her mother and father wouldn't rise until midday, so she sat alone at the table. As she buttered a slice of toast, the noise of the front door opening broke into her thoughts. She heard Grandmama addressing the footman. Ianthe leaped up and hurried to meet her. Grandmama had just removed her bonnet and pelisse, handing them to a maid. Swathed in her usual shawls and smelling of lavender, she submitted to Ianthe's enthusiastic hug.

"How are you, Grandmama? Did you get my letter?"

"I am well, thank you, dear. Yes, a number of them," Grandmama said with a hint of a smile. "I shall sit down; my bones dislike the early morning. Please order some tea."

Ianthe gave the order, then they sat in the morning room where sunshine came through the high windows. Grandmama fussed with the cushions on the sofa while Ianthe impatiently waited to hear what brought her here at this early hour. In the end, she could bear it no more. "Have you heard from your friend, Grandmama?"

Her grandparent nodded. "I have, yes. Mrs. Fairweather has been traveling the Continent, but has since returned. She promptly answered my letter."

"What did she say?" Ianthe felt breathless. "Something about Ormond?"

"Yes, indeed. Ah, here is the tea," she said as the maid carried in the tray. She removed the letter from her pelisse. "Pour me a cup, please, Ianthe, and I'll read this to you."

Ianthe added tea leaves from the caddy and hot water to the teapot. Allowing it to steep, she watched her grandmother unfold the missive. Ianthe's hands shook as she poured the brew into floral china cups, adding a lump of sugar and a slice of lemon to Grandmama's. Just the way she liked it.

Grandmama paused to stir her tea. She held up her lorgnette as Ianthe wriggled impatiently. "Mrs. Fairweather came to know Clarissa Ormond quite well. They were part of the same social circle. When she found Clarissa with a bruise on her face, crying in the withdrawing room at a sewing party, she tried to comfort her. Clarissa confessed Ormond was cruel to her. Concerned, Mrs. Fairweather prodded her until the truth emerged." She took another sip of her tea. "Well! Apparently, he *is* a brute, as you always suspected, clever girl. He forced her to have relations with him and berated her constantly because she could not give him an heir. He also criticized her appearance, and toyed with her, sometimes refusing to allow her to leave the house or attend the functions she most enjoyed. She confessed to Mrs. Fairweather that Ormond made her so unutterably miserable she wanted to die." Grandmama, lorgnette in hand, hovered over the page.

"Mrs. Fairweather writes, *I felt so sorry for her. She had endured several miscarriages, which infuriated him. I was so pleased for her when, after five months, it appeared she would give birth to a healthy babe. She hoped for a son because it might make him be kinder to her. Poor dear, it was not to be. Both were lost.*" Anger flashed in Grandmama's blue eyes. "Is your father at home? I wish to show this letter to him."

Ianthe's hands shook, and she had to put her cup down before tea sloshed over her lap. He and Mama had not yet come down. Her parents were very disappointed with her. Ianthe spoke quickly, nerves fluttering in her stomach. "We were very late to bed. Mama was upset when Millicent Tyndale was crowned belle of the ball and not me. And Papa made it plain in the carriage on the way home that my manners needed a good deal of improvement." She struggled to believe that Grandmama held the evidence of Ormond's cruelty in her hands. Would it be enough to convince Papa?

They were on their second cup of tea when her parents entered the room.

Her mother hurried over to Grandmama to greet her.

Her father bent and kissed his mother's cheek. "You are an early bird, Mama."

"I am. And I find it most inconvenient. But I bear important news, Arthur. You need to read this." She thrust the letter at him. "It is from a friend who knew the Ormonds well."

With an exasperated glance at his mother, he took out his glasses and, donning them, rattled the paper impatiently before reading it.

While he did so, silence fell over the room.

Mama raised her eyebrows at Ianthe in inquiry.

Papa tore off his glasses and thrust the letter down onto the table as if it burned him. "Can this be true?"

"There is no doubt, Arthur," Grandmama said staunchly.

Mama reached for the letter and read it.

Papa leaned back in the chair, a hand over his eyes. When he gazed at Mama, he said, "I have been a frightful fool, Caroline."

"No, Arthur." Mama dabbed at her tears with a handkerchief. "You wanted the best for Ianthe."

He looked humbled. Something Ianthe had never seen before. "Yes, I confess I did. And I still do."

"I consider myself very fortunate, Papa." Ianthe swallowed a sob. She hated to see him distressed. But the sick sensation in her stomach eased. Dare she hope he would now put an end to Ormond's pursuit of her?

"I deeply regret not listening to you, Ianthe," he said. "Dear God, it would have been disastrous for you had you wed him. I tremble to think of it. What happened to the Lindseys unnerved me. We cannot rely on anything in this world, it seems. It made me want to see you safely married." He took the cup and saucer her mother held out to him. After a moment, he recovered himself enough to say, "But that doesn't mean I will change my mind about Tate. There have been few of Ormond's stature in search of a bride this year. But the Season is not yet over."

Ianthe rose and hurried from the room. As she closed the door, she heard her grandmamma say, "You always were a stubborn child, Arthur."

Her father believed her. But he did not budge an inch in his refusal for them to wed. She wanted to go home to the country. There she could ride and try to deal with the abject misery threatening to consume her.

In the evening, she attended a card party with her parents. Ormond appeared and made his usual attempt to join their party as if he was one of the family. Her father, looking thunderous, took him aside. What was said between them, Ianthe didn't know. Neither did she care, for after a long look of smoldering dislike at her, Ormond took his leave.

Chapter Nineteen

ON WEDNESDAY OF the following week, apprehensive, Tate took the seat behind his barrister. The door at the rear of the bench opened. Tate glanced across the room at Donovan glaring at Lynch, who had earlier given evidence against him. Lynch now sat, head bowed, his hands tightly clenched.

"All rise," ordered the court usher as Judge Lionel Frobisher entered the courtroom and took his seat. The judge announced his verdict. "After hearing the evidence in this case," Judge Frobisher commenced, "I have no doubt that the signature on the vowel in question is not that of the late Duke of Lindsey's. It is a forgery by Cedric Lynch, the duke's former secretary, at the instigation of Bernard Donovan. Therefore, I find the transfer of the property, known as Cloudhill, did not legally pass to the said Bernard Donovan. It remains part of the late duke's estate. I further order that the relevant authorities investigate Bernard Donovan and Cedric Lynch for the crime of fraud." He struck his gavel. "The court is adjourned."

Greatly relieved, Tate thanked his barrister. As they filed out of the courtroom, Donovan looked long and hard at him. Lynch hurried up to Tate at the door. "I am ready to leave, Your Grace."

Tate's town carriage waited in the street with a footman at the horses' heads. "To the docks, John," Tate said as they climbed inside.

A half hour later, Tate watched Lynch, carrying his portmanteau, scurry up the gangway like one of the dockside rats. Then he gave John the order to return to Lindsey Court. He sat back, his body sagging with relief. A chuckle burst from him and then he laughed so loudly that his footman called anxiously, "Are you all right, Your Grace?"

"I am very well indeed," Tate said. Cloudhill was safe! Tomorrow, he would visit Ianthe's father, hat in hand, with a most humble apology for his reprehensible behavior, and express his love for his daughter. But tonight, he would celebrate with Bret, who for safety reasons, did not come to court and risk being seen by Donovan. They were to meet at the Old Star tavern by the docks at eight after Tate made sure the secretary sailed away from England on the tide, although Tate would have preferred to see him punished for a crime which had brought about his father's death.

Returning in the evening, the Thames beneath the moonlight was crammed with schooners and sailing ships forming a sea of masts among smaller craft. The brackish smells of the river, refuse, and mud fouled the air. He and Bret watched the schooner sail down the Thames with Lynch at the rail. Tate stared at him, relieved to see the back of the fellow he heartily disliked. He hated saving him from the law, and from Donovan's thugs. But that was their agreement.

"A celebratory drink." Tate nodded toward the Sea Shanty, where candlelight and noise spilled onto the street. Entering the busy taproom, they ordered ales. Nothing could spoil Tate's ebullient mood, not even the smoke hovering beneath the low-beamed ceiling and the rank smells of sweaty, unwashed bodies of sailors and dock workers.

Bret raised his tankard, yelling to be heard above the cacophony of fierce arguments and riotous laughter. "To success!"

Tate raised his tankard. "My deepest thanks, Bret. Without your invaluable help, the outcome would have been very different."

"It was an adventure not to be missed. I've enjoyed seeing how the *ton* live," Bret quipped. He grew serious. "And I met Lily, for which I must sincerely thank you, Tate."

"The adventure is not over yet." Expecting trouble, Tate had a pistol tucked into the back of his pantaloons beneath his coat. He glanced around the room. "I won't breathe easily until you are safely away with Lily. Donovan will want to take revenge. I only hope he wishes to confront me, and not stab me in the back." He shrugged. "I rather think he would favor the former. Killing me easily would not be his style."

"Do you think they have followed us here?"

"I wouldn't discount it. I shall have to deal with him eventually, and I prefer to be ready for the encounter instead of being taken by surprise. Although I'd rather you were not involved."

Bret looked offended. "What? You think I can't handle myself in a fight? That I'd get in the way?"

"I'm sure you can. But it won't be a clean fight with Donovan's men." Tate studied his friend. Bret was tall and broad-shouldered, but a scholar, not a fighter. Despite Bret's protests, Tate would prefer to handle whatever Donovan threw at him on his own without concern for his friend's safety.

"I am in this until the bitter end," Bret protested.

Tate grinned wryly. "I hope it's not bitter."

When a group of noisy men burst through the door, and it became impossible to carry on a conversation, he and Bret walked out into the damp night air. The moon sailed regally above them in a clear sky, providing enough light for them to find their way back to where Tate had left his armed footman guarding the carriage.

They retraced their steps along the narrow laneway to the road along the waterfront. Turning a corner, three men stood abreast, blocking their way. They brandished vicious-looking knives.

"We have no money," Bret called.

"Donovan ain't after yer money," the biggest of them said

with a snigger. "He'd like a word with ye. Best ye come obliging like, before we rough you'se up some."

"I'm afraid I have to decline your invitation." Tate pulled the pistol from beneath his coat and raised it. "It would be wise to let us pass."

The men looked at each other, but made no move to leave. Did they doubt a gentleman would shoot them? Or did Donovan want him alive?

"I can't shoot all three of you before reloading. So, who shall I choose?" Tate asked.

The rogues had shuffled closer, but now stopped and muttered to each other.

Then they moved as one, rushing them. Bret stepped in and put out his leg to trip the heavyset man who cursed and tumbled. Tate struck him down with the butt of his pistol and he crumpled at Tate's feet. Then Tate blocked the second man's knife arm and delivered a savage blow to the side of his neck. His head hit the cobbles with a thud and he lay still.

Bret stood over the third man, fists clenched, ready to hit him again. The fellow climbed to his feet and stared in stunned silence at his fallen mates.

"Do you wish to join your friends?" Tate asked, his gun pointing at the man's midriff.

He turned and ran, the echo of his feet slapping the cobbles until the dark swallowed him up.

"Donovan should employ better thugs," Tate observed. He tucked his pistol away into the back of his pantaloons and he and Bret ran to the carriage waiting with his footman in the main thoroughfare.

Before they'd left the alley, Donovan emerged from the shadows, a gun in his hand. The man beside him fingered a knife with his thumb and grinned, his face an ugly mask.

"Don't move a muscle or I'll shoot," Donovan warned. "You two do look alike. The men I most wished to see apart from Lynch. I have nothing to lose now, do I, Lindsey? You have taken from me what I most cherished. So you can watch your friend die first."

As Donovan took aim at Bret, Tate pulled out his pistol. He shouldered Bret away and pulled the trigger.

Two explosions echoed around the alley, followed by a cry, a groan, and a thud.

"For God's sake, Tate!" Bret yelled, falling to his knees.

⟫⟪

THE DAY FOLLOWING the court case, Ianthe was called into her father's study before luncheon. When she sat, he placed *The Times* newspaper on the desk before her. Her heart banging against her ribs, she picked it up and read the headline blazoned on the front page. The article read: *The Duke of Lindsey was successful in a case involving a property dispute yesterday against Mr. Bernard Donovan, the gaming club owner. Lindsey left the court immediately. Mr. Donovan was unavailable for comment.*

The following day, Mr. Donovan and another man were found shot dead in an alleyway near the docks. When this reporter called at Lindsey Court for a comment, the butler informed him the duke was away from home. The staff in His Grace's stables was questioned. The duke had been away for two days, along with the footman who accompanied him. Has he left London?

Alarmed, Ianthe clasped her hands in her lap. "Tate isn't involved in the murders. He wouldn't go to the docks. Why should he?"

Her father shrugged. "There's another article here about the details of the case. I knew of the financial problems, of course. But it shocked me to learn the extent of it. Tate came within a whisker of losing Cloudhill to that fraudster." He shook his head. "Unthinkable."

"Have you changed your mind about Tate, Papa?"

He frowned. "I'll make no judgement until we know more."

"Tate is innocent."

"I suspect you are right, my dear. We shall have to wait until he returns from wherever he has gone."

Ianthe stared at him. "Oh Papa, you don't think they have hurt him...or worse!" She bit her lip, fighting not to cry.

Her father rose and came to put his arm around her. "Ianthe, I admit to being impatient to learn what is behind all this myself. But Tate is a strong, healthy young man and nobody's fool."

She rushed to her bedchamber, shut the door, and collapsed on the bed. Donovan was the sort of man to seek revenge. She was glad he was dead. *Where are you, Tate? Please, please come soon.*

Ianthe did not leave her room for the rest of the day, her mind filled with agonizing doubts. She refused the dinner tray brought up to her, and lay awake for most of the night. In the morning, she hurried downstairs for the newspapers and took three from the footman before her father asked for them.

She scrutinized each page. There wasn't a word about Tate. Nothing!

Her mother entered the breakfast room, where Ianthe read the last of the newspapers. "You must calm yourself and eat something. You did not eat your dinner last evening."

She put a hand on her stomach. "No, Mama. I cannot."

"At least drink some hot chocolate and have a little toast. I am sure there will be news soon."

"But what if there isn't? What if we never hear from Tate again?"

"You are being too dramatic, dearest."

"People are assaulted and killed in London all the time."

"Not a duke. He would travel with armed footmen."

It suddenly occurred to Ianthe that Bret might know. But how to find him? Lily! "Mama, aren't we to go to a party this evening?"

Mama stared at her. "I assumed you wouldn't wish to—"

"But I do," Ianthe said impatiently. "Someone there might have heard from Tate."

Her mother's eyes softened. "Then we shall attend it. But you must eat, Ianthe. And tell Aggy to iron your pink satin."

"I will, Mama."

Lily, please be there, Ianthe prayed.

In the crowded townhouse, Ianthe wandered through the reception rooms searching for Lily. She had just given up when Lily entered dressed in an apple green crepe gown, her mother and stepfather beside her.

Forcing a smile, Ianthe went to greet them.

"Lily, Mr. and Mrs. Rowse, how nice to see you again."

Mr. Rowse's gaze rested on her. "And how delightful you look in pink, Lady Ianthe."

Mrs. Rowse wore an extravagant headdress decked out with feathers, which matched her purple gown. She did not look pleased. After an effusive conversation about how exciting London had become of late, Ianthe drew Lily away.

"What is it, Ianthe? You sound very unlike yourself," Lily said, alarmed.

"Your stepfather watches us. I must speak to Bret. Do you know where he lives?"

"He put up at an inn in Smithfield, but why…"

"Tate has disappeared. I am frantic. Bret might know something."

"My goodness. Here comes that horrid man," Lily said, as her stepfather moved through the crowd toward them. "Bret is at the Bull and Mouth coaching inn."

Ianthe squeezed Lily's arm. "Thank you."

Lily looked confused. "But surely you can't go there."

"I know, but if I don't hear by tomorrow, I'll send Bret a note."

"I hope nothing bad has befallen Tate," Lily whispered as her stepfather approached.

"What are you two lovely young ladies talking about?" he asked with false joviality. "So intense when you should be enjoying yourselves."

Nerves turning her stomach to knots, Ianthe made her excuses and left them. How long before she knew that Tate was safe? She couldn't bear it.

Chapter Twenty

TATE'S HEAD HURT. He gazed at the blurry vision before him. It cleared. Through the window, the early morning light rested on Bret, who sat in a chair, watching him with an anxious frown.

"Bret. What happened?"

"Donovan shot you."

"Have I been out for long?"

"We're into the third day," Bret said. "You woke a few times, but drifted off again, so I didn't disturb you. You were lucky Donovan's ball grazed your temple. When I brought you here, I called in a surgeon who said as well as the wound on your forehead, you'd bumped your head when you fell. I was relieved. I wouldn't know what to do if you'd died."

Tate laughed. "I appreciate how much you care," he said ironically while, with a wince, his fingers investigated the sore bump. He cautiously pulled himself up into a sitting position and put a hand to his forehead, his head aching. "Can't seem to remember what happened." He looked around at the small room. "Where are we?"

"My bedchamber at the Bull and Mouth. I thought it unwise to take you unconscious to Lindsey Court." He raised his eyebrows. "Might cause a ruckus, and the *ton* thrives on gossip." He nodded his head toward the door. "Your footman, John, is here, too. He's fetching food."

"What happened to Donovan?" Tate asked with an awful feeling.

"He's dead."

Tate stared at him. "Did I shoot him?" Dread tightened his chest.

"Your footman shot both of them," Bret said.

"What? John did?"

"Came charging around the corner and felled Donovan as if he was downing a wild boar." Bret chuckled. "Shot the other fellow, too, who was taking a swipe at me."

"Bloody hell." Tate studied the bandage on Bret's arm. "How bad is it?"

Bret shrugged. "A scratch. I'm more annoyed that he ruined my coat. I got a swift kick in, which drew his attention to his nether regions."

Tate chuckled then held his head when throbbing pain rocked through it. "I am ashamed to admit I underestimated you."

"Thought me the mild-mannered vicar's son and basically useless?" Bret raised an eyebrow. "I've learned a few skills along the way."

"So you have. And I'm grateful for it." Tate eased gingerly to the side of the bed and put his legs to the floor. His head swam alarmingly.

"What now, Tate?" Bret asked.

"I'll return to Lindsey Court tonight. We will meet soon and talk about getting you and Lily safely out of London."

"Best you lie low and recover. There'll be talk of Donovan's death, and because of the court case, people might link you to it."

"You make good sense. I have no intention of advising Bow Street. I refuse to have you and John drawn into this."

Tate urgently wanted to speak to Lord Granville. To assure him he was now able to offer for Ianthe. But Bret was right. He would have to wait until his appearance improved. It wouldn't do for her father to ask him some tricky questions. Time was not on

Bret's side either. "I'll meet you at the park on Sunday."

His footman entered with a servant in a mobcap. She carried a loaded tray, filling the air with delicious aromas as she placed plates of beef and kidney pies, bread and butter, and a bottle of ale on the table. Then, with a brisk bob, left the room.

"Ah, food." Tate discovered he was hungry. "John, I have you to thank for saving us. You exhibited quick thinking and remarkable skill, I'm told. I commend you."

John's fair skin reddened. "Thank you, Your Grace. Merely did what I could."

"Where did you learn to shoot so well?" Bret asked.

"I grew up on a farm." He went to the door. "We shot rabbits that got into the corn."

"But to shoot the two men who attacked us, that took a great deal of courage." Tate gestured to a chair. "There's plenty of food. Sit down and eat with us. We are all in this together. I value your discretion and may have further use for you soon."

John brightened. "Yes, Your Grace?"

"But not to shoot anyone," Tate hastened to add. He would have John deliver a message to Ianthe.

He took a bite of the pie, finding it filled with tasty chunks of meat in flavorsome gravy, and a crispy, buttery crust. Cloudhill remained in the family. He could hardly believe it was true. His uncle would have heard the news by now and would wait eagerly for a word from him. So much seemed to turn in their favor. Their investments were no longer at risk, and Clara was soon to marry Robert Manners.

Tate would be jubilant but for the nagging worry about Ianthe and that scoundrel, Ormond. Tate was remorseful not to have found anything to turn her father against the man. It might be too late. Once the engagement appeared in *The Morning Post*, Granville would refuse to listen to him. Tate washed down the pie with ale and wiped his hands and mouth with a napkin. Rising, he went to the small mirror hanging above the wash basin. A pale face greeted him with a bandage where the ball grazed him. Disheartened, he turned away. Another week of kicking his heels at Lindsey Court. But he must appear confident when he met Ianthe's father, whom his Uncle Clive considered a principled man with a fine intellect. Was he too late? He pushed the anguished thought away. "What about the horses, John?"

"Well tended, Your Grace. There's a large, well-run stables here."

Tate nodded. He would slip into his house under the cover of darkness. "We'll drive back to Lindsey Court tonight as soon as it's dark."

"I'll go down now, Your Grace, and see to it."

"Good man."

"You wish to stay here, Bret?" Tate asked, turning to him. "You are welcome to come home with me."

Bret shook his head with a chuckle. "I think your butler has had enough to contend with, without seeing us together." He leaned back in the chair. "I'll rest up. I'll need to be fresh for what I have in mind."

"Do you want to go over the plan with me now?"

Bret appraised him. "No. It can wait until Sunday."

Tate yawned and lay back on the pillows. "Forgive me for appropriating your bed."

"You're welcome." Bret propped his feet up on the occasional table and shut his eyes.

With some relief, Tate did the same. He didn't open his eyes again until John put a hand on his shoulder. It was dark. Time to go back to Mayfair.

When his long-suffering butler eyed him worriedly, Tate felt sorry for him. "In the wars again, Knox. I'll remain in my chambers or the library until I look presentable."

"You might wish to view the newspapers, Your Grace," Knox said. "They await your perusal in the library."

Tate nodded. "Thank you."

He sat in a leather armchair with a few fingers of Cognac in a balloon glass and thumbed through newspapers. His mood lifted.

There was no mention of Ianthe's engagement. But the *Times* had a piece about Donovan and his henchman found dead at the docks. It mentioned Donovan losing his court case to Tate. Ianthe's father must have read it. He took a few sips of the smooth, mellow liquid, which helped to ease the icy knot in his chest. Was Ianthe concerned about him? He hated the thought of it, but at this moment, there was little he could do. John was to pass a message to Ianthe through a footman he knew at the Granvilles' home.

Tate went back to the article. It was the reporter's opinion that Donovan's death resulted from a gangland dispute. Nothing written suggested Tate was in any way involved. Surely, if any unsubstantiated rumors arose, they would die down without fire to fan the flames. And his reappearance in London would soon relegate this distressing affair to the past. After all, who among society cared about a criminal like Donovan? How ironic that he harbored a burning desire to live like Tate's father, an honorable, decent gentleman, when Donovan could never be anything but an immoral and heartless thug.

Tate put the glass and the newspapers down, and rose to write a long letter to Uncle Clive. How pleased and relieved they all must be at Cloudhill.

⟫⟫⟩✦⟨⟪⟪

IANTHE HAD WHISKED Tate's message away from the footman before her father learned of it and hurried up to her bedchamber to read it. Tate assured her he was well. He and Bret were to meet in Hyde Park on Sunday to discuss his elopement. "And I will be there, too," Ianthe said defiantly as she sat curled up in her bedchamber's floral chair.

"Did you say something, Lady Ianthe?" Aggy asked as she tidied Ianthe's wardrobe.

"No. A dreadful habit, talking to oneself," Ianthe said, watching Aggy, intent on folding a nightgown. Her maid turned and smiled at her. Aggy had proved discreet when she'd accompanied Ianthe to the park on the previous occasions. She would come with her again on Sunday. Aggy didn't need to be bribed for her silence like Cecily's did when she was courting Gerald. Aggy was a loyal girl, but Ianthe would still give her that bracelet the maid so admired.

While relieved to know Tate was safe, troublesome thoughts still consumed her. Although Tate said he was well, he had not explained why he'd disappeared from sight after the triumphant result at court. Tate loved her. She was as sure of that as breathing. Did he believe she would marry Ormond? Ianthe couldn't wait to tell him about her grandmother's letter, which revealed the viscount's true nature. It made her lightheaded to consider she was free of him at last. She had to be patient until Sunday. She rose from the chair and went to the window. Outside, the rain drizzled down, dampening her spirits. "Please be fine on Sunday," she murmured. It was always dark on rainy mornings. With a deep sigh, she went downstairs for luncheon. Patience was something she had yet to master.

Soon, she and Tate would be together forever. Really together, like Cecily and Gerald. Her sister had told her a little about her wedding night, and Ianthe was eager to experience it herself with the man she loved.

Her mother looked pleased as Ianthe entered the dining room. "It is so good to see you smiling."

"I agree," Papa said. "Although, I've come to distrust it when my daughters have that look."

"Oh Papa, what a big, cross bear you are." Ianthe gave him a kiss on the cheek as she passed.

"Now I really am suspicious," he said, but his eyes twinkled.

Chapter Twenty-One

AFTER SEVERAL DAYS of rain, the sun finally emerged from gray clouds. The ground was still soggy underfoot and the air humid as Tate made his way to the oak tree where he and Bret always met. A crescendo greeted him from the bird life squabbling on the bank. A duck flew low across the lake, its trailing feet sending rivulets over the water.

Arriving early, he waited for Bret. Leaning against the oak, he removed his hat, enjoying the soft sun on his face and the smell of bark and wet leaves.

"Tate."

He straightened and turned around, his pulse leaping. She stood only a few feet away in a fetching yellow dress and blue spencer, gaily striped ribbons adorning her bonnet, a pretty parasol in her hand. He caught his breath. *"Ianthe."* His voice roughened with emotion. He opened his arms. She dropped the parasol and ran into his embrace.

"Sweetheart," he murmured, eyeing an angler beyond where they stood who watched them with interest. He eased her away with reluctance when two ladies came along the path.

Ianthe ignored them. Her blue eyes searched his face. She reached up to touch his cheek. "They hurt you."

He felt her shiver. "Just a slight graze."

"Was it Donovan?"

A lock of hair had escaped her bonnet, and he resisted the temptation to tuck it behind her ear. Did she now belong to Ormond? "It's over. He's dead, Ianthe."

"I know."

"You do?"

"Yes, Papa told me."

He saw relief in her eyes.

"I'm so glad to see you. I won't tease you by asking you to tell me all of it. Right now," she added, with a slight lift of her lips.

He chuckled. "I consider myself fortunate."

"I have so much to tell you," she said. "And so many questions."

Holding hands, they strolled a short way along the bank, the dank lake odors drifting on the breeze. A pair of noble swans sailed close to shore, arching their necks.

He had to know. He stopped and turned to her. "Tell me about Ormond."

"Ormond has withdrawn his suit."

He listened, struggling to take in what she told him. Her grandmother had achieved what he could not. "She is an indomitable woman."

"Grandmama saved me from what would have been a disastrous marriage. Papa was deeply shocked by Ormond's true character. When Ormond approached him at a soiree with his self-satisfied false smile, Papa drew him aside." She laughed. "I don't know what was said, but it was heartening to see Ormond slink away, Tate. Papa apologized and has become very reasonable. He will not deny me anything I ask of him right now!"

"I am delighted to hear it," Tate said with a laugh. "He saw the item in the newspapers about the court case?"

She nodded. "He is thrilled for you."

"I hope it will alter his view of my character."

"Nonsense. He likes you."

Tate shook his head. "His opinion of me has been sorely

tested over the past few months."

"Perhaps, but now he understands what you have had to deal with."

"Now that Cloudhill is safe, I am confident he will look upon me more favorably." With impatience, he watched another group pass them. What was everyone doing out this early? "But that must wait for a better time."

"When might be a better time?" She pulled back to stare up at him, a quizzical light in her eyes.

"Everything in its correct order, sweetheart." He smiled. "We must first help Bret and Lily on their way. I hope we can be inconspicuous. I still prefer you not to become involved in this." He frowned. "If your father got wind of it, it could cost us dearly."

Her brows drew together. "We shall have to be careful."

He feared that wouldn't deter her. "That may not be enough. It's a serious thing Bret undertakes. And it could go very wrong. And not just because of your father; the *ton* will heartily disapprove, not to mention Lily's family."

"Do you mean it would affect your standing in society?"

"That doesn't worry me. I want to marry you, Ianthe. But not under a cloud of disfavor. Should your father agree if he learned of this?"

Her gaze softened, and she reached up to stroke his chin. "You haven't asked me to marry you."

He smiled down at her. "First, I must speak to your father. Will you give up this idea? Leave it to Bret and me?"

She shook her head fiercely. "I know how Lily feels, because without my grandmother's intervention, I might have married Ormond. Lily needs me. And I have promised them. Without me helping Lily, they are doomed."

Tate sighed. "I won't attempt to stop you, my determined love. Their elopement is to take place during the last ball of the Season."

She nodded. "Lord and Lady Bellman. Mama has accepted an

invitation."

"Save the waltz for me."

Her eyes danced. "So you are finally to honor your promise and waltz with me?"

"I have long wanted to waltz with you," Tate said passionately. "I am determined to have you in my arms, and woe betides any gentleman who steps in my way!"

She giggled. "When Bret first entered the ballroom, I thought he was you coming to waltz with me, but I quickly realized it was not you. Imagine my shock!" She cast him a dark glance. "At first, I feared he'd killed you and taken your place!"

"I'm sorry. I might have known you'd guess he wasn't me. But wearing a mask, I thought Bret had a chance."

"Ha. As if he could! He hasn't your...grace and bearing, and his hair..."

Tate smiled. "I grabbed the chance to save Cloudhill. It was the only way to find out what had happened and offered a means to fight Donovan. Once I'd discovered that, I hoped to set the rest to rights."

"I have forgiven you."

He grinned. "So poor Bret didn't have a chance, eh?"

She shook her head and laughed. Then her eyes grew serious. "How brave you were, and how clever to get the better of that dangerous criminal."

"I couldn't have done it without Bret agreeing to undertake a demanding role."

"He certainly was convincing. No one but me suspected he wasn't you."

"Considering he knew little about London society. Only what I could teach him."

"You must share an ancestor."

"It appears so. I intend to make inquiries when I return to Cloudhill."

"Now, tell me about Clara! I was most upset when Papa sent me back to London. I very much wanted to wait for your return and see the baby. How is Rosamunde? Please tell me you brought her back to Clara?"

He smiled. "Clara is blissfully happy to have her baby with her again. I shall tell you all about it later. Suffice it to say, she and the baby are in Kennington with my Aunt Mary. And she will soon marry Dr. Manners. The doctor who took such wonderful care of her."

"Oh, my goodness! Does Clara like this doctor? Enough to marry him?"

"Yes. I believe he loves her. He's a good man. She always wanted a simple life and will make an excellent doctor's wife."

She sighed. "How absolutely perfect. I was worried about her." She looked wistful. "I would love to go to Kennington to see them."

Tate met her gaze, thinking of all those hours in the carriage as a married couple. "And we will, I promise you."

"Hey there."

Bret made his way across the grass to them.

"Bret, you must tell me what I am to do at the ball," Ianthe said. "But quickly, please. I have only a few minutes or they shall miss me at home."

"Lily and I are extremely grateful for your help." Bret drew a note from his pocket. "Please pass this message to her if you can. I cannot risk seeing her now. Read it, Ianthe. It will explain everything."

Ianthe tucked the paper into her reticule, which hung from her arm, and picked up her parasol. "I must go. I shall see you at the ball."

Tate walked up the road with Ianthe as far as he dared to see her home. The streets were busy with people on their way to church. When he returned to the park, he saw Bret waiting for him. Would the lovers succeed? It hinged on everything going according to plan that evening.

Happiness now seemed within all their grasps when, only a brief time ago, it seemed impossible. He knew hurdles remained, the biggest for him being Ianthe's father's agreement to their marriage, but he felt invincible now that Cloudhill was returned to them. As if anything was possible now. He smiled and bent to stroke a fat brown dog a lady led on a lead. "Good day to you, madam. A fine day."

"It is, and good day to you, sir."

He made his way over to Bret. Surely, Lord Granville wouldn't turn him down now. Ianthe was to be his wife, his dreams fulfilled.

⤜⤜⤜✕⤛⤛⤛

IANTHE AND HER maid entered through the kitchen door. She smiled at Cook and took two hot freshly-baked sweet rolls from the kitchen table. The cook shook her head, her laugh following them as they crept up the servants' stairs to Ianthe's bedchamber. She had only just shut the door with a sigh of relief and offered a roll to Aggy when her mother opened it.

"Where have you been, Ianthe?"

Ianthe hid the roll behind her back. "I took a short walk, as I needed fresh air, Mama."

Her mother held up her hand. "If you feel you must lie to me and treat me like a ninnyhammer, please say nothing at all."

Ianthe ducked her head, trying to hide her smile. She was at one with the world. Nothing could dampen her spirits. "I promise to tell you about it soon, Mama." Her mother looked worried. "I assure you, there is nothing at all to concern you. Everything is simply perfect."

"That is what I do worry about, my girl. You are a law unto yourself." She huffed. "And you can even get around your father! We are about to leave for church. You have missed breakfast. But send your maid down for hers. There's no reason she should go hungry."

"Yes, Mama," Ianthe said meekly. "And, Mama," she said as

her mother went to the door. "We are attending the Bellmans' ball, are we not?"

"We are. May I know the reason it has suddenly become so important?"

"Tate has asked me to keep the waltz for him."

"Tate? You have heard from him?" Mama sighed. "Never mind. I suspect you have, and I refuse to keep any more secrets from your father." She hesitated. "After that business your father read about in the newspaper, I am relieved nothing bad has befallen him." She hurried out.

Cecily and Gerald joined them at church. They had been away visiting his parents in the country. There was so much to tell Cecily, but Ianthe couldn't risk it now. After service, they lingered together in the street outside the church while their parents talked to the vicar.

Ianthe observed her sister. She knew that look. It was as though she had a special secret. "Cecily, you look positively radiant."

"I am going to have a baby," Cecily whispered, glancing over at their mother. "I haven't told Mama yet. It's early, and I don't want her to fuss."

Ianthe hugged her. "How exciting! I am to be an aunt!"

Cecily smiled. "But what about you, Ianthe? You were so miserable when Tate didn't propose. But you look happy now. Is it to be Ormond?"

Ianthe glanced over her shoulder. Mama left the vicar and walked in their direction. "No, it is not," she blurted. "I shall call at your home tomorrow. You are woefully behind the times."

"It seems I am." Cecily laughed. "And it all happened while I spent a tedious time in the country with Gerald's parents. He rode with his father every day to visit the tenants and the gamekeeper, not to mention a whole day's shooting while I was stuck indoors with his mother. She talked endlessly about his sister's grandchildren. Susan has six! It soon became clear to me that neither I nor any other woman would be good enough for his mother's darling boy until we have half a dozen children." She giggled. "And this might be the heir."

"It could be a girl."

"Do you know, I secretly hope it is? I would very much like a daughter. Girls are much more companionable. They stay close to home until they marry, and don't go off riding every day."

"She might," Ianthe said. "I did."

"We are not all like you, I'm thankful to say."

"What are you girls talking about?" Mama said. "Catching up on news?"

"Cecily's mama-in-law," Ianthe said blandly, aware that her mother wasn't overly fond of her.

Mama looked pained. "Well, come along. Your father is waiting."

The next afternoon, when Ianthe was shown into Cecily's morning room, her sister was appalled to hear the news. "Poor Tate! It is scarcely believable! And to have a perfect stranger try to claim Cloudhill as his own. This man Tate found must resemble him exceedingly well."

"He does. Except for me, no one suspected he wasn't Tate."

"Of course you knew." Cecily laughed. "You have made a close study of Tate since you were twelve. But this dreadful man, Donovan. I remember him from our visit to his gambling club. I found his attitude unctuous, but I did not know what he could do." She shuddered.

"He was ruthless," Ianthe said. She had never in her life wished anyone dead, but she was glad he could never return to blight their lives again.

"It must have been a troubling time for Tate." Cecily frowned. "But as to this other outrageous venture, Ianthe, you simply cannot help that couple elope. She is to marry a wealthy baron, and this man is a vicar's son. It will cause the most dreadful scandal. What if you're found out? Papa will never forgive you. And you can be sure he will never agree to your marriage."

A shaft of alarm caused Ianthe to draw in a breath. "I must, Cecily. I promised. And they need me. They have it carefully planned. I foresee nothing going wrong."

"Then you are beyond foolish! Mama always keeps an eagle eye on us at balls. She talks endlessly about rakes and fortune hunters, as if they're hovering about, ready to pounce." She raised her eyebrows. "I sometimes suspect one tried to compromise her when she first came out."

"Do you think so?" Ianthe asked, intrigued. "Mama was exceedingly pretty. Anyway, this is to take place after the supper dance. A gentleman will take me into supper, and Mama always sits with friends. I must make my excuses and leave him, but I intend to be quick. I'll be back before Mama misses me."

Cecily looked shocked. "Well, we will not be at the ball. Gerald is foolish. He insists I rest, although I am as healthy as a May hedge in bloom. But I must confess, I do tend to feel tired in the evenings, and balls always end so late. Anyway, I shall remain on tenterhooks until I hear what happened, though. Promise me you will send me a note *immediately* when it is over."

Cecily's reaction sent a wave of unease through her. "Of course. They must get away. It would be too sad if Lily had to marry that awful man." Ianthe tried not to show how nervous she was. Although Tate was unhappy about her involvement, she could not let Lily and Bret down.

Chapter Twenty-Two

T ATE ENTERED THE Bellmans' lively, smoke-filled ballroom at
ten o'clock. He searched for Ianthe and saw her dancing the
Roger de Cloverly with some gentleman whose rendition of a
hunted fox going in and out of cover was truly inspired.

Ianthe acknowledged him with a smile.

Lily danced with gray-haired, rotund Baron Bolton while her
parents watched from their seats. Tate groaned under his breath,
fearing for them all. The mission they undertook would be
difficult.

When the next dance was announced, Tate asked a debutante
for a country dance and smiled kindly at her when she blushed
rosily and stammered her acceptance.

At its conclusion, he spoke to an acquaintance, then slipped
from the ballroom. Outside, moonlight brightened the gardens,
creating deep purple shadows beneath the trees. The light would
aid their escape, but offered little cover. He could hear the river as
he reached the fence and located the gate opening onto the back
lane. Taking a sharp tool from his pocket, he inserted it, then
jiggled the padlock. It clicked open. He stepped into the lane
where his coach waited, the gray horses restive, the groom at
their heads. Tate approached the coachman, who sat on the box,
the lighted lanterns swinging gently in the faint breeze.

"Shouldn't be too long now, Milson."

"We're ready, Your Grace."

Bret opened the coach door and Tate climbed in beside him. "How are you bearing up?"

"Nervous as a bride on her wedding night," Bret said, his voice confirming it.

Tate laughed. "Stay calm. You'll be on your way out of London at first light."

"I am relieved to find you so confident." Bret put a hand on Tate's arm as he was about to get out of the coach. "Tate, Lily and I wish to thank you and Ianthe for giving us this chance of a life together."

If it is successful, Tate thought. "I owe you a lot, Bret." Tate smiled. "Ianthe is eager to help. We are determined to see you and Lily happy. Please let me know when you return from Scotland."

After wishing them a safe journey, he jumped down from the coach.

The garden gate closed behind him. Tate strolled through the gardens. On the terrace, he lit a cheroot from the brazier and leaned on the stone banister, adopting a relaxed pose, though he felt more like a runner waiting for the race to begin. What if the lovers' elopement was discovered before they got far away? Ianthe's parents would never forgive him for allowing her to become involved in this.

The French doors opened behind him.

"You and I are of like mind, Your Grace," said a man's voice.

The devil! Tate turned. Ormond withdrew a cigar case from his pocket.

Eager to get rid of him, Tate straightened. "We have never been that."

"Regarding Ianthe." Ormond drew deeply on his lit cigar and puffed out a trail of smoke into the air.

"I fail to see how." Tate waited, wondering what the man was about. "But don't trouble yourself to enlighten me."

Ormond ignored the jab. "I wondered if it was you who told

the Earl of Granville those lies concerning my marriage."

"Not I, but I certainly would have, should I have discovered it," Tate admitted.

Ormond's mouth stretched into a thin smile while his eyes remained cold. "Whoever it was has done a thorough job of convincing Granville it was true."

"If there's truth in it, I can only be grateful they did."

"Grateful? My reputation has been besmirched," Ormond snarled, losing the tight control he'd had over his emotions.

"You have only yourself to blame." Tate wouldn't spare him. "And nothing is served by discussing it with me."

He turned and went inside, leaving Ormond to his sour deliberations. Damn the man! Tate didn't trust him. Had Ormond seen him come from the garden? Not long now and Ianthe and Lily would make their escape. He must keep his wits about him.

⟫⟫⟩⟨⟨⟨

IANTHE DANCED IN the same set as Lily. When they stood side by side during the quadrille, Lily whispered, "My parents have altered their plans. I fear they are suspicious," she whispered, distress darkening her eyes. "We are to go home after the next dance, and shall leave for the country in the morning."

"Don't despair," Ianthe said, trying not to show her alarm. "We'll just have to leave sooner than we planned."

Her face strained, Lily nodded before the dance separated them.

Back at her seat after the dance, she twisted her gloved fingers together and searched the room. People moved about, some disappearing through the archway leading to the gaming room. There was no sign of Tate. He must be told. Had Bret arrived with the coach? It was two hours before they were to leave. It must be tonight. Once Lily's family left for the country, the couple would lose any chance.

"Why are you fidgeting, Ianthe?" Mama asked.

"I must visit the withdrawing room, Mama."

Her mother frowned. For a moment, Ianthe feared she would accompany her. Luckily, Lady Fortune, seated next to her, distracted her with a question concerning flower arrangements.

Mama turned back to Ianthe. "Don't be long."

Ianthe rose quickly, moving through the room before her mother focused on her again. Frustrated, she couldn't see Tate among the clusters of guests. She cautioned herself to walk slowly, fighting the desire to hurry, which would draw attention to herself.

There he was. Tate spotted her and, reading her expression, strolled her way. As he approached, she dropped her reticule.

He bent to pick it up. "What is it?" he asked, smiling at her as he returned it.

She quickly explained.

"Go now," he said, then bowed and walked away.

Lily waited in a back corridor a distance from the busy reception rooms, her face pale in the light from the wall sconces.

Ianthe drew in a relieved breath. They must not fail. She held Lily's arm, and they ran toward the servants' stairs.

She pulled Lily back as a footman came up carrying a tray of champagne flutes.

"May I help you ladies?" he inquired.

"We were looking for the ladies' withdrawing room," Ianthe said with a coy smile.

He flushed. "It is down that way." He gestured and scurried away.

They waited until he rounded a corner. "Quick," Ianthe said. They met no one on the narrow wooden stairs as they descended into the noise below. The staff entrance was next to the kitchen, which was filled with servants rushing about preparing supper. The chef barked orders, footmen hovered with trays, and kitchen maids worked hard at a long, scrubbed oak table covered with dishes. A delicious blend of aromas wafted from the room.

Ianthe and Lily edged along the narrow hallway. They passed the scullery where maids scrubbed plates and pots. The kitchen boy took little notice of them as he vanished into the pantry, obeying a command from the chef.

Ianthe eased open the door into the kitchen garden. The loud creak made her heart leap into her throat, but it failed to rise above the hubbub in the kitchen.

Then they were out in the cool evening air, the moonlight shining down on beds of vegetables. With relieved gasps, they hastened along the path past the drying areas and through a gate in the kitchen garden wall.

Clouds hid the moon, casting the scene in gray gloom. "Do you know the way?" Lily whispered, her voice shaking. "It has grown quite dark."

"Better it's dark." Ianthe almost welcomed the shadows. But it slowed them down.

As they moved cautiously along the path bordered by a high flowering hedge, a waft of smoke drifted in the air.

Ianthe grabbed Lily's sleeve and pointed. A man stood on the other side of the hedge. She put a finger to her lips.

He coughed.

Ianthe stopped, afraid to move for fear he'd see them. She carefully parted a leafy frond and peered through. A brazier lighted the area where he smoked a cigar. Her chest tightened. Ormond!

Ianthe clutched Lily's arm and shook her head. They could not go on. He hadn't seen them yet, but he would be sure to hear them and come to investigate. They waited in pained silence. Ianthe feared he could hear her heart beating. It was so loud in her ears. She struggled to find a sensible reason for them to be wandering about in the garden should he suddenly appear and ask her. But before she came up with anything, he dropped his cigar and ground it out with his heel, then turned to walk back to the house.

Ianthe took a long, deep breath. "He's left. Let's go on. We'll be all right now." She feared she failed to sound convincing, as she wasn't entirely sure where they were. The Bellmans' gardens seemed to stretch for miles. But they must hurry in case Ormond continued his nightly stroll and headed their way.

They emerged onto a lawn edged with flowering shrubs, their perfume overpowering in the night air. Another path seemed to lead away from the house in roughly the right direction. "It must be this way," Ianthe whispered.

They hurried on in taut silence.

"I can see a brick wall," Lily said a moment later. She pointed to a break in the shrubbery.

The Bellmans' estate was large, and the boundary wall would be long. Finding the gate might take a while. Already, her mother would wonder where she'd got to. At least Mama had become accustomed to Ianthe's tardiness.

As they left the shrubbery, Tate stepped out of the shadows. Lily squeaked. Ianthe ran over to him. "Tate! Thank goodness."

"I'll take Lily to the coach. Return to the house, Ianthe."

Lily threw her arms around Ianthe. "Bret and I shall be forever grateful to you both," she murmured.

"Promise to be happy," Ianthe said as tears sprung to her eyes.

"We will be."

Ianthe, her chest heaving with emotion, her eyesight blurred, ran lightly over the ground, retracing her steps to the house. At one point, she stopped, fearing she'd become lost. She wandered on. At last, the long hedge which had separated her from Ormond appeared. Might he still be about?

A rustling in the bushes stopped her again, and her pulse beat in her throat. When a ginger cat emerged stalking some prey, Ianthe stifled a giggle and went on.

She almost sank to her knees when she found the gate leading into the kitchen garden. Slipping through, she entered the staff door and darted up the servants' stairs, which again, were blessedly empty, the servants all upstairs laying out the supper dishes.

In the ladies' withdrawing room, Ianthe stood before the mirror. She brushed off her skirt and tidied her hair while waiting for her legs to stop shaking. The door opened and two women came in.

An older lady in delph blue smiled at Ianthe. "It's Lady Ianthe, isn't it? I'm Mrs. Wilson. Your mother and I met at a card party."

"How do you do? It's a lovely evening, isn't it?" Ianthe smiled, hoping her voice sounded normal while her head still whirled.

"Please give my regards to your mother."

"I shall, Mrs. Wilson."

She reached her mother just as couples moved toward the dance floor for the gavotte. Mama looked aggrieved. "You were gone so long. I feared you would miss the dance."

"I was chatting to Mrs. Wilson, who sends her regards," Ianthe said as her partner came toward them.

Her mother looked mollified. "Oh, yes. I remember her. How kind."

Tired before she began, the dance seemed to go on forever. Her flimsy silk dance slippers had suffered in the damp grass, and she must have stubbed her toe. She kept returning to the scene in the garden. Tate, in command of the situation, and Lily, struggling to believe that Bret waited for her beyond the wall. Lily said that once she stepped through the gate, her life would begin. Ianthe regretted she could not be there to see the lovers go off on their journey. Did they get away safely? Had Tate returned yet?

When she searched for him, she noticed Ormond, who watched her intently. Had he seen them in the garden? An icy chill passed through her. She gasped with relief when she saw Tate engaged in conversation with another gentleman. He looked her way with a slight nod.

Bret and Lily were on their way! Her emotions in knots, Ianthe had the urge to either laugh or cry and bit her lip. Her partner must think her very odd, so she lowered her head to hide her expression.

Exhilarated, she returned to her seat, glad to have time to compose herself. A footman presented a tray of lemonade. She took a glass and drank thirstily.

When the waltz was called, she was ready to dance the night away. "Mama, I am to dance with Tate." Ianthe put a hand on her hair. "After the gavotte, I must look a positive fright!"

Mama smiled and reached across to smooth the sleeve of Ianthe's white gown embellished with metal embroidery. "You look very pretty with that becoming flush on your cheeks."

Ianthe felt sure her cheeks were crimson when Tate came and bowed before them.

She felt so happy and safe in his strong arms as he swept her over the floor to the strains of a Haydn sonata. It was as if she floated, and even her sore foot and the dismal state of her slippers, which her mother would take her to task over tomorrow, were forgotten.

"Lord Ormond was in the garden," she whispered. "Smoking a cigar."

Tate frowned. "He didn't see you?"

"No, thank heavens. But I just saw him in the ballroom. He glowered at me."

"Nasty fellow, but I can't blame him for wanting you."

She met his intense gaze, and for a moment, they seemed alone on the ballroom floor.

Then, as they turned, Lily's mother and stepfather, the baron, and Lord Bellman came into view, all looking anxious.

Ianthe drew in a sharp breath, surprised that her euphoria at having saved Lily was now tinged with shame. "Was it wrong of me not to consider how distressed her mother would be to lose her daughter?" she whispered. "Were we right to help them?"

His hand tightened around hers. "Would you prefer Lily to marry a dangerously ill man? Condemn her to an untimely death or a life of torment?"

"No. Of course not." She sighed. "I wish I was sure…"

"Do you think her mother, or her stepfather truly care about her happiness?"

Ianthe shook her head, relieved Tate didn't remind her he hadn't wanted her to become involved. "I am thrilled for Bret and Lily," she admitted. "Lily will write to her mother once they are safely wed. But what will happen to them when they come back to London?"

"Parliament will soon be in recess for the summer. By the time they return, London will be all but deserted."

"Where will they live?"

He led her through the steps, his hand large and sure at her waist. "Bret wants to seek work somewhere away from London, and scandals fade as time passes, do they not?"

She had to admit it was true. When fresh scandals replaced old ones, which had engulfed the royal family, they were seldom mentioned now. Would Lily and Bret feature in the scandal pages? Neither she nor Bret came from a wealthy or titled family, but because of the baron, they might be considered persons of interest to the public.

Tate's eyes, dark with passionate yearning, searched hers. "I wanted our first waltz to be special, and here we are talking of Lily and Bret. If only I could draw you closer, Ianthe. I want so much to kiss you."

His male scent and lithe body moving with hers sent tingles through her. "I wish you could."

The music ended, and the dancers formed a line to leave the dance floor. "I have an appointment with your father at his club tomorrow."

"Oh, Tate," she whispered as love and desire for him warmed her to her toes.

Her hand resting on his arm, they left the dance floor.

He lowered his head close to hers. "I cannot live without you, Ianthe. I couldn't bear to think of you married to someone else. That was why I had decided to leave England if Cloudhill was lost."

"It almost broke my heart to think of it," she whispered as they crossed the floor to her mother.

"I will call on you in the afternoon after I've seen your father."

But something was wrong. Mama was on her feet, and she looked frightened. "A young woman has disappeared," she said, when they reached her. "There's talk that she has been abducted. Lord Bellman has contacted the Bow Street magistrate. It appears they have employed Bow Street Runners to find them. You must excuse us, Tate. I shall take Ianthe home. There might be a dangerous man roaming the grounds."

Would Bow Street find them before they were safely away? Horrified, Ianthe couldn't bear to think of them being caught.

"A wise decision, Lady Granville." Tate bowed. "Allow me to escort you to your coach."

Ianthe's worried gaze flew to Tate's as her mother urged her toward the front entry, where she sent a footman for their wraps and gave orders for their carriage to be brought around.

Tate saw them to the carriage. He nodded reassuringly at her as he closed the door.

Ianthe fell back against the squab as the carriage pulled away for the long ride back to Mayfair.

Would Bret and Lily escape? What if they were caught? Would Bret be thrown into jail and Lily be forced to marry that awful man? Ianthe felt like crying. Tate would speak in Bret's defense, of course. But her own father would withhold permission for them to marry. She sniffed and searched for her handkerchief.

Her mother glanced at her. "With Bow Street now involved, I'm sure this villain will be apprehended. They cannot have gone far."

"I imagine so. I think I'm coming down with a summer cold." Ianthe's voice was muffled by the handkerchief.

"Oh dear, I do hope not," her mother said as she arranged the evening wrap around Ianthe's shoulders.

Lying to Mama made her feel even worse.

Chapter Twenty-Three

TATE WATCHED IANTHE leave in the carriage with her mother. It had long been his plan to propose on bended knee on the terrace after their waltz, with her father's blessing. In the end, their first waltz together seemed rushed because of their fear for Bret and Lily.

He suspected that when he could finally propose, it would be without plan or fanfare, but be just as special.

It was a worrying turn of events for Bellman to be a good friend of the Bow Street Chief Magistrate. Stuck in Richmond past midnight, it was impossible for Tate to get a hackney, or even hire a horse. Unnerved, he waited for his coachman to return from driving the runaway lovers to the Bull and Mouth.

An hour later, the rising sun cast a pale glow over the landscape and Tate was on his way in the coach to the Bull and Mouth. Stagecoaches departed at daybreak. He drummed his fingers on the window ledge. The busy roads did nothing to ease his frustration. Bret and Lily would soon be on their way in the stagecoach for Scotland. He doubted he'd get there in time to warn them. Bellman must fear damage to his reputation as one of the best hosts of the Season, having acted so swiftly. Now, with Bow Street involved, their carefully thought-out plan crumbled. Constables would search all the stagecoaches leaving London. At the Chief Magistrate Sir Nathaniel Conant's instigation, Bow

Street Runners would ride after them on the Great North Road. Lily and Bret stopped before they reached the border.

It appeared increasingly likely Tate would have to follow them. He'd miss his appointment with Lord Granville. That was unlikely to impress the earl, but there was little Tate could do about it.

When they finally pulled up before the busy coaching inn, it was past eight o'clock, and the stage was long gone. Tate went to inquire if Bret and Lily were on it. Although their names were not on the waybill, a couple resembling them had boarded.

As Tate emerged from the inn, a wiry-looking gentleman in a yellow waistcoat, a Bow Street Runner by the look of him, nosed around asking questions.

"Lindsey Court, Milson," Tate ordered his coachman with gritty determination. Tate must reach them first. The toll booths would delay the stage as they traveled the Great North Road to Newcastle, and on to the Scottish border town where Bret and Lily could marry.

At home, he wrote a brief note of apology to postpone his eleven o'clock appointment with Lord Granville, aware it lacked a convincing explanation. While grooms put fresh horses in the traces, he changed his clothes, tossed down a cup of coffee, and eating a slice of toast, hurried outside. Within the hour, he was on the road again, traveling north. The London roads were jammed with laden wagons, drays, horseback riders, and curricles, and held up by an unwieldy coach, the passengers seated on the roof swaying precariously with each turn in the road.

Tate sat, arms folded, exasperated, wishing he was on horseback. But they would need the coach. Traveling in this vehicle would be safer and travel faster. No Bow Street Runner would have the nerve to stop a duke's coach and demand to search it.

But, depending on how events unfolded, it could be several days or even a week or more before Tate arrived back in London.

Out into the country at last, Milson cracked the whip and urged the horses on as dark clouds rolled across the sky. Tate cursed as he watched them through the window. Would a storm delay them? If the bad weather held off, they could catch up with the stagecoach at St. Albans.

Two hours later, the rain had eased off. Thankfully, the roads remained passable. His coach entered the busy cathedral town of St. Albans and progressed along the High Street of Tudor buildings.

The stagecoach, with the distinctive pouncing leopard painted on the side, traveled slowly ahead of them. At Tate's instruction, Milson drove up and pulled alongside. Tate signaled through the window for the driver to stop. The man stared mutinously at him. Stagecoaches stopped for no one, but with a glance at the Lindsey coat of arms on the door panel, he hauled his straining horses to a halt.

Tate leaped down and rounded the vehicle. "Won't keep you long. You have two passengers I must see." He pulled open the door. Bret and Lily were crammed in the corner. A black-suited parson sat beside Bret with a fat man eating a pie who took up enough space for two next to him. A woman with a piglet in her lap, and two children, sat on the opposite seats. The collective smells made Tate gesture to Bret and quickly retreat.

Bret helped Lily down from the coach. He looked bewildered as they stood on the road. "Tate! What's happened?"

"The Bow Street Runners have been called in. They will already be on their way."

Bret's eyes widened. "Good lord!"

Lily, her eyes round with fear, clutched Bret's arm.

They retreated to the footpath as their luggage was thrown down. Then the stagecoach lumbered off in a spray of dust. Tate urged them toward his coach.

Once inside, he explained. "Lord Bellman's a friend of the Bow Street Magistrate. He has half the officers in London searching for you. Should they catch you, you'll be taken off the stage and returned to London. I don't have to tell you what that means, Bret. Go on to Coldstream Bridge in my coach. You'll be safer."

"It was good of you to come all this way, Tate. But I can't allow you to do any more for us," Bret said, a stubborn cast to his jaw. "I appreciate the warning. We will hide away here until the mail coach comes along. By then, they will probably have given up on us."

Tate glanced at Lily. Looking small and scared in the fur-lined cape Bret must have purchased for her, she hadn't uttered a word as she sagged against Bret.

"Look at your bride-to-be, Bret. Lily is exhausted."

Several emotions flittered across Bret's face: concern, tenderness, and doubt.

Tate saw his friend faltering and continued to argue his point of view. "I've had a hand in your elopement, and I don't intend to see it fail. Think of the consequences, man. To Lily, if not yourself."

"But what about Ianthe's father? You cannot treat the earl in such a cavalier fashion," Bret said gruffly. "Your future is at stake, too."

Ianthe! Tate could not lose her now. He glanced over at the prosperous-looking stables across the road. "I'll hire a horse and ride back. Milson will take you on to the border."

Bret appeared to weaken. "If you're sure, Tate," he said finally.

"I'll make the appointment in time. It will be faster on horseback."

"I suppose that makes sense." Bret shook his hand and grinned. "You are indeed an excellent fellow."

"God bless you, Your Grace," Lily said.

Tate smiled. "Godspeed." He left the coach and returned to speak to Milson. Taking the letter of authority from his pocket, he handed it to his footman who sat on the box beside the coachman.

"You are familiar with the coaching inns where my father kept spare horses, Milson?"

"I am, Your Grace," his coachman replied.

"Take your time returning. Rest the chestnuts. Innkeepers will send accounts to Cloudhill."

Tate raised his hand in farewell and stood back as the coach rattled away down the street, Lily's handkerchief fluttering from the window. Then he crossed the street to the stables. He didn't want Bret to worry, but Tate didn't fool himself. There was no way he could keep his appointment, but he hoped to see Lord Granville later in the afternoon.

His decision to follow Bret proved a wise one when he passed a man riding hell for leather toward St. Albans and identified him as a Bow Street Runner. Tate's coach would be well ahead, the superior horses and well-sprung vehicle taking them faster over the miles.

Eight miles from London, the horse Tate hired went lame. Cursing, he dismounted. Hot and dusty and in need of a blacksmith, he led the animal along the road to the next village.

>>>><<<<

THE LAST OF the morning callers had just left when Ianthe's father arrived in high dudgeon, waving a piece of paper. "Your ardent beau has taken his time in claiming you, my girl. Tate has cancelled our appointment. I kicked my heels at my club for a good two hours before his message reached me."

Worried, Ianthe gazed at him. "He must have a good reason, Papa."

"If he has, he fails to mention it here. Perhaps another lady holds his attention?"

"Arthur!" her mother exclaimed. "There is no place for such talk."

He sank into a chair, massaging his brow. "I apologize. But what a frustrating business this has proved to be. After reading in the newspaper about his success in the court, I expected Tate to come knocking on my door weeks ago, begging for your hand, Ianthe." He shook his head. "I had high hopes for you. You are a pretty lass, much like your mother. Sweet-natured, for the most part." He raised an eyebrow as if to refute this. "I have resisted many a fellow who showed an interest in you since you came to London because I hoped...well, it doesn't matter now what I hoped. And then, when things looked grim for Tate, I considered Lord Ormond; well, enough said about that." He nodded thoughtfully. "Lord Charmers tells me his son seeks a bride. An excellent family."

"No, Papa, we must wait for Tate," Ianthe said, alarmed. "He intends to ask for my hand. I know it!"

"Does he? Funny way of showing it. And worse." He glowered fiercely at her mother, "Your delightful son, Colin, madam, has been sent down for doing something at university I cannot mention in the company of ladies!"

Mama looked horrified. "Oh no, not Colin. It must be a mistake."

"Angelic Colin." He sighed heavily. "Progeny. They can be the bane of a fellow's existence."

"Ianthe, please leave us," Mama said.

"I shall deal with Colin when we arrive in the country," her father said as Ianthe went to the door. "No point in waiting until the heat makes travel unendurable. Order the luggage to be packed," he said to her mother. "We will leave in the morning."

"But Arthur, the staff have had no notice," her mother said.

"I'll send a footman to advise the butler of our changed plans."

Where was Tate? Ianthe plodded upstairs, struggling with questions which were unlikely to be answered for some time. She wasn't sure she could bear the wait.

"We are going home to Ashford, Aggy," she said miserably when the maid came into her bedchamber.

Aggy looked disappointed. She would have expected better news. "So soon, my lady?"

"It's not so terrible," Ianthe said, her lips trembling. "The weather is more agreeable, and I can ride Freckles. I do miss her."

"And it's a splendid rider you are, my lady," Aggy said bracingly as she hurried over to the wardrobe.

Ianthe couldn't think about packing. Surely when Tate learned her family had left London, he would come to Cloudhill. But when? What could be more important than asking Papa for her hand? It must concern Bret and Lily. Had their attempt to elope fallen foul of the law? Ianthe slumped into a chair while footmen brought in her trunk from the attic and Aggy bustled about with her clothes.

Chapter Twenty-Four

T HE TOWN CLOCK chimed eleven o'clock when Tate wearily dismounted at the stables in the mews behind his house. He'd had a long wait while the blacksmith attended his daughter's wedding. After a light supper, he retired to bed, where he lay unable to sleep. His mind steadfastly remained on the following day, when he would see Ianthe's father, unsure of his reception. If news of their involvement in the elopement hadn't reached his ears, Tate was confident it would go well, but he wished he could give a better explanation for his reason for postponing their meeting.

In the afternoon, Tate rode to the Granville house, a handsome mansion several blocks from Lindsey Court. When no footman appeared to assist him, he tied the reins to the iron fence and mounted the steps. The shutters were closed over the windows and the butler was removing the knocker from the door.

"You've missed the family, Your Grace," he said. "They left for Kent first thing this morning to spend the summer there."

Tate's first thought was that Granville had learned of their roles in the elopement. "I expected the family to remain in London for a sennight or more."

"That was their intention, Your Grace."

Uneasy, Tate thanked him and rode home. It had certainly

seemed impromptu. Ianthe had not spoken of it. He must return to Cloudhill.

Tate told his butler and housekeeper he would leave on the day after tomorrow. Then, restless, he looked for a distraction. Hart always had an ear to the current gossip doing the rounds. If anything was mentioned about Bret and Lily, he would know of it. His friend might be available for an evening at Whites. He sent a footman around with a note.

In the billiard room at White's club, where loud conversation and cigar smoke flowed in from the cardroom, Tate brought Hart up to speed on all that had happened since they last spoke.

Hart remarked that talking to Tate was always entertaining, although rather alarming.

"Heard anything about the runaway lovers?" Tate asked.

"Questions are still being asked. How did they manage it under the noses of the *ton*? But Lord Bellman seems to have lost interest, and the girl's family is not well-liked. Unless they bring the lovers back in disgrace, I expect the whole thing will die down."

Tate's cue sent the red ball rolling into a pocket. "I intend to marry Ianthe within a matter of weeks. God willing."

His friend raised his glass of whiskey. "Well! Congratulations, Tate. So she wasn't to marry Ormond."

Tate scowled. "Over my dead body."

"I've heard the Marquess of Lyle, Ormond's father, threatened to alter his will in favor of a cousin if his son hadn't married and produced an heir by next year." Hart shook his head. "Bad blood between them. I almost feel sorry for the fellow. He'll be marquess when the old man dies, but would lose a large part of his unentailed fortune if he ignores the threat."

"Ormond is a nasty fellow. Perhaps his father has the same opinion."

"Where is your wedding to be held?" Hart asked. "St. George's?"

Tate hoped not. He didn't want a long-winded affair. It would take far too long to organize, but Ianthe might wish for all the trimmings. "It hasn't been decided. After I purchase a special license, I'll ride to Kent and propose. We'll discuss it then."

Hart laughed and shook his head. "Indeed, you must!"

Tate grinned briefly when he considered what lay ahead. He expected his suit to be accepted, but he wasn't sure of the reception he'd receive after creating that embarrassing scene at the victory ball. Then disappearing from London, leaving Granville no wiser. He wanted them to be on good terms. He'd known Ianthe's father for most of his life and respected him. Although, he'd found Granville surprisingly indifferent to Ianthe's wishes regarding Ormond. But it had occurred to Tate that Granville might have troubling financial problems of his own, which skewed his thinking. He'd always been a loving father, and Ianthe, a favorite. Tate shook his head, bemused.

"It's your turn," Hart said, raising his dark eyebrows. "Or would you rather stop and share a bottle of wine in the library?"

"An excellent suggestion," Tate said, putting away his cue.

The next day, Tate consulted his solicitor and visited his bank, where he extracted items of jewelry from the family collection. Then he rode to Doctor's Commons and purchased a special license for twenty guineas from a representative of the Archbishop of Canterbury.

The following day, Tate left instructions with his butler to send word to him when the coach returned from Scotland, and departed for Cloudhill in the curricle after breakfast.

Early in the afternoon, when he'd brushed off the dust, he entered the morning room where his mother and Emily warmly greeted him. Even the family cat, Blossom, came to rub herself against his legs.

"Tate, sit beside me." His mother smiled and patted the sofa. "Clara's letter arrived today. She and Manners were married on Saturday. They have taken up residence in the doctor's house and she plans to refurbish the parlor."

Relieved, Tate took a cup of coffee from the footman. "That

is good news." It appeared his decision had been the right one.

"Clive wishes to see you. There are matters to discuss. He is as eager to put this dreadful time behind us as we are."

Tate smiled at his sad mother, pale in her dark clothing. "Indeed, we are, Mama."

Emily sweetly smiled. "Does this mean I shall make my debut next year, Tate?"

"You will, Emm," he said fondly. Might Ianthe agree to be her chaperone? He cautioned himself not to put his chickens before they were hatched, tossed down the coffee, and rose. "Bayard will need exercise." He bent to kiss his mother's cheek.

"But you should eat first," his mother protested.

He couldn't eat. Not until he was sure. "I will later, Mama."

Tate rode over to the Granville estate. In a paddock beside the stables, he encountered a vision. Ianthe, in a celestial blue habit and black hat, led her horse, Freckles, across the grass.

Tate leaped down from Bayard and vaulted the fence.

"Tate!" Ianthe dropped the rein and ran into his arms.

"Sweetheart." Their first kiss was long, passionate, and deep. Pressed against each other, they murmured incoherent words of love. His passion for her roused, he reveled in her sweet scent and the warmth of her body. "I want you with all of my heart and soul, my love. I can't live without you. Will you marry me?"

"Oh Tate, yes. Yes, I will." She gazed lovingly into his eyes, her fingers stroking the hair at his nape.

He kissed her. When he finally released her, his breath came hard and fast as if he'd run all the way here. "I must see your father," he said, impatient to have the matter settled.

Ianthe's head whirled. She could scarce believe it. At long last, Tate would speak to her father.

"I hope to find him pleased to see me," Tate said wryly.

"He was in a better mood this morning. Papa never stays angry for long." She frowned. "But I am so worried about Bret and Lily. Have you heard from them?" They led the horses to the stables. "Will they have reached Scotland safely?"

"I haven't yet. But they had a good chance continuing their journey in my coach from St. Albans."

She widened her eyes. "You met them at St. Albans? That was why you didn't keep your appointment with my father."

Tate nodded. "I rode back to London and hoped to see him, but the horse I hired cast a shoe. I went to see him the following day and found you had gone. Was he angry with me?"

"He has another matter to deal with."

"Nothing to do with the elopement?"

She gazed at him anxiously. "Papa has made no mention of it."

"He must be annoyed with me, and rightly so." Relieved, Tate picked up a currying brush and stroked it over Bayard's satiny neck.

Ianthe shook her head as she attended to Freckles. "Perhaps a little, but he was delighted to hear Cloudhill remains in your family." She hung up Freckles' nose bag. "I wish it were possible for Papa to know what a good friend you are to Bret, rushing to his aid. Otherwise, they would have been caught before they went very far." She closed the stall door.

"Can we go somewhere more fragrant, sweetheart?" Tate asked.

They walked across the lawns to the fountain, where lilac bushes scented the air.

Tate gazed down at her lovely face and enticing mouth. He wanted to draw her soft body against his and kiss her endlessly. But out of a corner of his eye, he saw a gardener slip behind a hedge with his clippers while another bent low over a garden bed. Perhaps not.

"It is Colin who has Papa in a rage," Ianthe said. "He's been sent down from Oxford. I overheard my parents discussing it. They found a woman in Colin's rooms." She giggled. "In *flagrante delicto*, Papa said."

Tate laughed. "Colin? I didn't know he had it in him. We used to tease him for being so serious."

"Papa says he isn't made of money. He complains about the cost of Colin's education and says his sons are a burden. He loves them, of course, and doesn't really mean it. They are good boys. Stephen will make a fine earl one day, although he's keen to continue in academia. Papa believes he should devote himself to the estate. Frederick wants to join the church, and William has expressed an interest in the navy."

"Does Bertie still want to be an artist?"

"Yes. It would horrify Papa, but he does paint exceedingly well." She sighed. "The expense of my come-out is a thorn in Papa's side," she said ruefully. "He considers that to be also a waste of money."

"I hope he greets my proposal favorably."

Her blue eyes danced. "Oh yes, darling. Papa will be pleased. He was angry when you punched Ormond, but not anymore. Now he knows what a horrid man Ormond is."

Tate slipped his arms around her waist and bent his head to kiss her. *Too bad if this gets back to her father*, he thought, delighting in her soft lips and sweet breath. Kissing Ianthe was entirely worth it, and after all, he was about to beard the lion in his den.

"Would you prefer a wedding in London like your sister's?" he asked as they continued their walk, her hand clasped in his.

"Do you want that?"

"St. George's must be booked, and it's always busy."

"Cecily's wedding caused such a fuss. All those trips to the dressmaker for fittings. The organizing Mama had to do exhausted her. And Papa always objecting to the cost." She gazed up at him. "Why don't we elope? It would be very romantic."

He grinned as they approached the house. "I refuse to involve myself in anymore clandestine arrangements."

"Papa will prefer a smaller wedding," Ianthe said as they stepped up onto the porch. "A grand affair like Cecily's would take an age to organize. He has invested money in a new venture, Mama tells me, which makes him short-tempered. He will complain endlessly about the cost."

"A small, intimate one then? What about the church at Cloudhill?"

She sighed. "Oh yes, that's a lovely idea."

"We'll put it to your parents. Do you think they'll consider it?"

"They must." She rose on her toes to kiss him, startling the footman who had opened the door.

⟫⟫⟫⟪⟪⟪

IANTHE HURRIED UPSTAIRS to find her mother and share the news. "Tate is with Papa now."

"Oh, my dear." Mama rose from the desk in her sitting room to hug her. "I have long prayed it would be Tate."

"Papa will agree, won't he?" Ianthe said, still a little anxious.

"I'm sure he will. Or he'll have me to deal with, as well as your grandmother."

Ianthe laughed. "Shall we go down?" she asked. She was too nervous to sit. "We've decided on a small wedding, Mama," Ianthe said as they descended the staircase. "Do you mind very much?"

Her mother shook her head, but Ianthe didn't miss her regretful sigh. "I shall be content to see you both happy and beginning your lives together."

As they approached the library, the door opened, and her father emerged, smiling, with Tate behind him. "Ah, there you are. I've sent for champagne."

"Oh Arthur," her mother murmured, going to kiss him.

It was all Ianthe could do not to run and throw her arms around Tate, whose green eyes mirrored her delight.

Chapter Twenty-Five

A STAND OF ancient rowan trees grew beside the small stone church. The news had spread. Those from the village and surrounding areas gathered outside the church door for a sight of the bridal couple and greeted Tate as he entered with Hart. Throughout the church, tenant farmers and families from the area filled the pews. It was a modest gathering with no time for those who lived far afield to attend. Ianthe had expressed disappointment that Cecily could not come, but her husband, Gerald, and her doctor forbade her to travel.

His best man, Hart, stood beside him at the altar. Tate turned as the vicar's wife played the organ. Ianthe, beautiful in pale pink with roses on her bonnet, walked slowly down the aisle, her hand on her father's arm. In white muslin with a small posy of spring flowers, Emily followed with a serious expression.

"You're a lucky fellow," Hart murmured to Tate.

"I am." Tate breathed deeply as Ianthe handed Emily her bouquet and, with a smile, took her place beside him before the altar.

The vicar cleared his throat and began... "Who giveth this woman to be married to this man?"

Lord Granville placed Ianthe's gloved hand over Tate's and stepped away.

"Will you love, honor, and obey His Grace, Tarleton, Duke

of Lindsey?" the vicar began.

Ianthe answered in her soft voice. She bent her head, her fair hair curling on her swanlike neck. Tate felt an overwhelming desire to protect her from a world that wasn't always fair and kind. But he did not expect Ianthe to always obey him. He very much doubted she would in some matters. He was not foolish enough to think they would agree on everything and foresaw some stimulating exchanges ahead. Impassioned arguments, too. And when they made up, that too would be passionate. She might look like a delicate flower, but she was adventurous and strong-willed. He admired that about her, that and her humor, her kindness, and her passion. He was, as his best man had observed, a very lucky man.

His breath hitched when he realized he might have lost her.

Tate said his vows.

The vicar intoned, "Should anyone present know of any reason that this couple should not be joined in holy matrimony, speak now or forever hold your peace."

There was a long silence. Then someone in the church coughed. Tate turned to search the pews. Ridiculous to fear Ormond might yet take his revenge. But, of course, he wasn't there.

⇥⟫⟪⇤

"YOU MAKE A very beautiful bride, Your Grace," Tate said, his eyes soft as they bowled along the lanes in Tate's curricle to Ianthe's parents' house for the wedding breakfast.

Ianthe nestled close to him. "It was a perfectly lovely wedding."

"It was. The vicar was nervous." He grinned. "He kept clearing his throat."

She sighed. "Poor man. Marrying a duke on such short notice."

Pulling up before her parents' house, Tate tossed the reins to a footman and helped her down. He took her hand. "Come, sweetheart, I am impatient for our waltz. I intend to enjoy every minute of it."

Some hours later, everyone gathered in the hall to see them off. Ianthe turned and tossed her bouquet over her shoulder to Emily. Emily caught it with a cry of delight. Ianthe did not miss Tate's sister turning eagerly to look Hart's way. But the viscount failed to witness it. His head bent, he talked to Sir Henry Green's attractive widow. Poor Emily, Ianthe hoped she wasn't smitten. She liked Hart immensely, but he was a man who enjoyed the company of women too much to settle down with one. It would be difficult for any woman to entice him to the altar, let alone a girl just out of the schoolroom.

Tate's curricle waited in the driveway, a groom at the horses' heads. Ianthe hugged her parents and her brothers, whispering to Colin to buck up. She was sure that Papa would see the dean and get him reinstated. "Try not to do anything like that again," she said.

"A man shouldn't discuss such things with his sister," Colin protested, pushing back his fair hair, shame in his blue eyes.

"Nonsense, I'm a married woman," she said briskly.

Hart wished them well.

"Thank you for coming down at such short notice," Tate said.

"I was happy to. Especially when assured it wasn't catching," Hartley said with a wink.

"One day, soon perhaps, a woman will capture your heart," Ianthe warned him.

Hart grinned. "When I am a hair's-breadth from my dotage."

Seated in the curricle, Ianthe looked back to wave and take a last look at the home she had known all her life. Cloudhill wasn't far, but it seemed as if she was moving so much farther, perhaps because her life was about to change forever? Tate returned her smile, his hand loose on the reins while she leaned against his shoulder.

At Cloudhill, the butler, Knox, welcomed her into the great hall adorned with statuary and massive paintings. He handed a letter to Tate. "You asked me to give this to you as soon as it arrived, Your Grace."

In the lofty library, books spanned from the floor to the ceiling. Seated on a sofa, she watched Tate open and read the letter. He handed it to her with a relieved smile. "From Bret. He and Lily are married and plan to spend a month touring Scotland."

᛫ She read the letter with a deep sigh. How worried she'd been for them. "It was all worthwhile then, wasn't it?"

"Indeed it was. And it's my hope that Bret will agree to work for me as my secretary."

Ianthe admired her new husband. "You are very generous, Tate."

"I have the interests of Cloudhill in mind. I'm in desperate need of a capable secretary I can trust, and who better than Bret? There's one other matter I should mention to Knox. I have engaged a housemaid."

"A housemaid? Who is she?"

"I've yet to tell you about Annie. She saved my life after Donovan's thugs attacked me in Covent Garden. I will have to go up to London to fetch her. She is in a difficult situation."

"You must! I remember those awful bruises. Tate, you have kept so much from me. I want to know everything."

"I will tell you, sweetheart. Eventually. There's no rush, is there?"

"No." She suspected there were some things about that scoundrel Tate would never tell her.

Tate poured her a glass of Madeira. "Hungry?" He carried it over to her. "Shall I ring for supper?"

She shook her head. She couldn't eat. Their first night together was uppermost in her mind. Would she please him? Despite his casual denial, she was sure Tate would be an experienced lover.

He joined her on the sofa, cradling a brandy balloon. "My

mother has removed to the dower house with Emily."

Ianthe was glad to have Tate to herself. "It was unnecessary, but good of your mother," she said. "We'll visit them tomorrow before we leave for London."

"My uncle will be there. He wishes to discuss a few things with me," he said with a thoughtful frown. "Estate matters have languished too long."

He was eager to take on the responsibility of this vast estate. She must find something useful to do herself. She refused to be one of those wives forever waiting for their husband to pay attention to them.

"I should like to breed horses," she said as they walked up the staircase. She waited for Tate's reaction.

His eyes widened. Then he laughed. "I don't know why I'm surprised. You will excel at it, my love."

Tate kissed her outside the duchess' suite and left her.

Ianthe stepped inside and glanced around the elegant room. The maids had turned the silk coverlet down and lit the candles, bathing the room in a soft glow. Vases of flowers scented the air. The walls papered in a subtle flower pattern, an enormous swathe of pale gray silk damask hung from the gold coronet above the four-poster bed and over the long windows. It was so romantic. She tingled all over as her imagination took hold.

She was glad of the distraction when a pair of footmen carried a hip bath and pails of hot water into the adjoining dressing room.

Aggy arrived with her arms full of fluffy towels and scented soap. She managed a wobbly curtsey. "Your Grace."

A small fire had been lit in the dressing room, the hip bath placed before it. It looked very inviting. Ianthe began to undress.

"It's such an enormous house, Your Grace," Aggy said, tying up Ianthe's hair. "I fear I'll get lost."

Ianthe listened to Aggy prattle on as she slipped blissfully into the warm water. She closed her eyes. An image of Tate striding naked across the carpet caused her eyelids to fly open. She grabbed the sponge and ran it over her breasts while imagining his hands on them.

"But I knew where everything was at the other house," Aggy was saying. "I'm not sure I can even find my chamber."

"It will soon become familiar to you." Ianthe sponged her shoulders, admitting that the advice should apply to herself.

"I met Mr. Knox, the butler, and Mrs. Burton, the housekeeper, and a footman, Jerry, who showed me the kitchen and the staff hall," Aggy said at the wardrobe door. "A maid, Cathy, was nice to me. We are to share a room."

Aggy would have noticed the handsome footmen in their splendid livery. Ianthe leaned back in the scented steam. Would Tate come soon? At that thought, she stood abruptly, spilling water onto the tiles as she reached for the towel Aggy held out to her.

Dried and powdered, Ianthe dressed in a pale pink nightgown with a matching negligee while wondering if it was a wise choice. She'd purchased it in London at Cecily's urging, hoping one day to wear it for Tate. And now that day had come, and she wasn't sure.

Before the mirror, her hair loose over her shoulders, she was vexed to find the steam had turned her locks into a riot of curls. While she attempted to order it with her hairbrush, she gasped. Her nipples showed clearly through the material. Would it shock Tate? Would he expect her to be more modest in white lawn? No, she smoothed her hands over the silky fabric, as anticipation tightened her stomach. She was sure he would not.

Chapter Twenty-Six

T ATE'S BREATH CAUGHT as he entered Ianthe's bedchamber in his dressing gown. Glowing light from the candelabra on the table behind her outlined her slim legs and her body's curves through a filmy peignoir so sheer she looked naked. Her long fair tresses fell almost to her waist.

"Is anything wrong?" She sounded nervous.

"*Au contraire*, sweetheart," he said, his voice hoarse. How was he to keep his passion in check when his bride was so gorgeous? "Everything is perfect at last."

With a gasp, she ran barefoot across the bedroom to him, and he caught her, hugging her tightly. This siren was his Ianthe. The woman he loved.

"Darling." Feeling her tremble, he eased aside a silky lock and kissed the tender spot beneath her ear, her soft, fragrant body cleaving to his. He pressed kisses along her jaw, and settling her close into his arms, took her soft lips in a deep, open-mouthed kiss. Heat slammed through him as the kiss lengthened, their tongues intermingling. Murmuring, Ianthe coiled her arms around his neck. He'd wanted her for so long. Thought about this so much. Aware of her heart thudding against his chest in tune with his, Tate rested his hands on her shoulders and eased her away. Despite his body demanding release, he must not rush their union. "Shall we drink some champagne?"

Her blue eyes widened. "Don't you want me?" She swept her hand over her breasts, making him groan. "Should I not have worn this?"

His lips on her neck, he breathed in the sweet scent of her silky skin. "Want you? Ianthe, I want you so much. I fear I'm about to explode."

She giggled, a sound of delicious abandon. "Then take me to bed."

Tate wrapped his arms around her, lifted her up, and carried her over to the bed. He gently eased her down. A knee resting on the bed, he leaned over his bride, tenderly gazing at her. "Have I mentioned that I love you?" he asked, his voice tight with emotion.

"I love you, madly, and forever, darling." Ianthe slid her hands up to his nape and pulled him down onto the bed with her. His hands cupped her sweetly rounded bottom, pulling her provocatively against his arousal as they kissed. Her lips parted beneath his and her full breasts and taut nipples pushed against his chest. Ianthe's kisses were a blend of innocence and brazen sensuality that surprised and delighted him.

As her fingers tangled in his hair, he nuzzled her neck, breathing in her skin's warm fragrance. His hands slipped inside the low neckline of her nightgown. Her skin was incredibly soft. Shaping her breast in his hand, he thumbed a pebbled nipple.

"*Mm,*" Ianthe murmured.

With a deep intake of breath to keep his rioting emotions under control, he drew the fabric over her slender thighs, exposing the curls covering her sex, edging higher to reveal her delicate hipbones and the curve of her waist. She helped him unfasten the peignoir, and when it fell away, pulled her nightgown over her head. He tossed them onto the chaise longue at the foot of the bed and turned back to her.

Immediately, Ianthe hid her private part with her hands. Biting her bottom lip, swollen with his kisses, she removed her hands and boldly lifted her gaze to his, a telltale flush spreading over her cheeks. Her skin was like freshly churned cream, her nipples like delectable strawberries.

"Your beauty has exceeded my imagination," he breathed, as he lay beside her and drew her close. Lovelier than when he'd conjured her up, lying sad and alone in his bed, while wondering if this could ever be.

His breath shortened, his cock demanded release. Tate rolled off the bed and stripped off his dressing gown.

IANTHE WATCHED HIM disrobe, marveling at the strength of his body, muscles playing beneath his smooth skin. The breadth of his chest and the small nest of dark hair edging down over his ridged stomach down to his rampant manhood thrilled her and made her burning hot. She was restless with desire, impatient and hesitant at the same time.

Tate joined her on the bed and held her against his hard male body. She twined her fingers up through his hair. His scent teased her senses as she breathed in clean skin, woody soap and the brandy he'd drunk earlier. Then all thoughts fled as he claimed her mouth in kiss after kiss, which had them gasping with need.

He gently traced her ribs, her waist, and her hips. She gasped as his hand slipped between her thighs while he bent to nuzzle her breasts and draw a nipple into his mouth, causing a surge of pleasure.

Moving down, Tate's fingers teased her sex, drawing ripples, waves, then shudders from her body. She murmured and moaned and succumbed to the relentless, seductive ravishment of his mouth and hands. A restless sensual need engulfed her as she trembled on the brink of something indefinable, which shattered with waves of exquisite pleasure.

With a cry, she floated mindlessly as Tate kissed her mouth, rousing her body to an instant desire for more. To have him inside her.

His knee nudged hers apart, then his warm body settled over hers. Skin to skin, it felt so good, so right, that with a moan, which was almost a sob, she widened her legs to welcome him.

His eyes sought hers, his hands on her hips; his blunt erection slid inside her, slowly, but when her body tensed, he stilled. "Am I hurting you?"

Ianthe shook her head and raised her hips in invitation. With a jolt of pleasure and pain, he pressed deeper.

Smooth thrusts carried her away in the dance of love. With a loud groan, a gush of warmth inside her, he stilled, his body heavy on hers, their panting breaths filling the room.

She closed her eyes, her body languid and sated.

Tate moved aside and stroked a hand over her hip. "Sleepy, my love?"

She smiled dreamily. But she didn't want to end this wonderful night. She propped her head on her elbow and gazed at her handsome lover. "I'm hungry."

He laughed. "We missed supper. I'll send for a cold collation. You ate very little at the wedding breakfast."

"Please." Ianthe sat up, covering her chest with the sheet. She watched Tate walk naked to pull the bell, her gaze running over his strong, lithe body, her thoughts filled with their passionate lovemaking. Were men always so comfortable to be seen naked? She gathered the sheet around her and struggled from the bed.

"Don't trip," Tate warned, laughter in his voice.

Running into the dressing room, Ianthe washed and hovered there to hide from the footman.

When the door closed on the servant, she returned wearing her dressing gown. On the table was a plate of cold chicken, cheese, bread rolls, and a chocolate pudding. Tate, in his silk robe, poured champagne into flutes.

Sitting on the bed, Ianthe ate the chicken with her fingers, a napkin in her lap, while Tate, a chicken leg in his hand, talked about the last few months, filling her in on all that had happened.

Or most of it. She sensed he left those things out he considered not suitable for her ears. When she prodded him to tell her more about Donovan, he stubbornly remained vague, only to say that he was indebted to his footman for his life. She shuddered and grew silent.

They drank their champagne then Tate took away the plates. He returned to join her in the bed. "Sleepy now?"

"Mm, a little." A contented drowsiness made her deliciously languid.

He snuffed out the candles. Breathing him in, safe in his strong arms, she closed her eyes.

Ianthe wakened to morning light filtering through a break in the curtains. She had heard some gentlemen returned to their own suites at night, but Tate was asleep beside her.

Ianthe gazed tenderly at his ruffled dark hair. Lying half on his stomach, he had thrown off the covers. She couldn't get enough of his body, his powerful legs and muscled bottom, a warm living replica of a marble statue, although more generous in some areas. Blushing, she hoped they would make love again before breakfast. She put a hand to her hair, which must look a fright. She slipped carefully from the bed so as not to wake him and sat at the dressing table, untangling the unruly curls with her brush.

Tate called from the bed, an arm over his eyes. "Where are you, Ianthe? Come back here."

With a laugh, she ran and climbed onto the bed and into his arms. His hand on her bottom, he pulled her against him, and she marveled again at his intoxicatingly hard, strong masculinity.

She toyed with the dark curls on his chest. "When did you first fall in love with me? Was it at that house party? I hoped you would kiss me that night. Why didn't you?"

Obviously amused, he shook his head. "I wish I'd known it. I wanted to kiss you very much, darling. I'd suddenly realized you had changed from a minx into a ravishing young woman. One I very much desired."

Her look half-gleeful, half-condemning, she said, "I was never a minx!"

He cocked an eyebrow. "No? What about that time when you pushed Colin into the pond because he wouldn't let you play coits? And Stephen?" He rolled his eyes. "How you nagged the poor fellow to let you ride with us."

She poked him in the chest. "You, sir, are a dreadful tease."

"I admit it. I love to see your beautiful eyes flash and your very kissable lips pout at me." His hands framed her face, and he pressed his mouth to hers, his tongue tracing over her lips.

She sighed and put a hand on her stomach. "Perhaps we made a baby last night."

He raised his eyebrows. "Or today?"

At the intent in his eyes, a throb of needy desire made her gasp. She slid her hands through his hair and nipped his lower lip with her teeth.

Tate groaned. He ran his fingers lightly over her collarbone and bent his head to ravish her body with his mouth, nibbling, licking, finding places like the back of her knee she had no idea could be so arousing. She giggled when he kissed her toes, then taking hold of her other foot, proceeded upward.

"*Oh, Tate.*" She wriggled, then sighed then moaned.

Epilogue

Cloudhill, four months later

B RET AND LILY arrived in the early afternoon. They looked blissfully happy as they took tea in the drawing room.

"We saw no sign of Bow Street Runners on the way to the border towns," Bret said. "Your coachman put us down in Coldstream Bridge. We were married the following day. That afternoon, a surly Runner approached us. He looked frustrated when I showed him our marriage license. Almost felt sorry for the fellow. He knew he could do nothing but report back. Fearing Lily's parents might try for an annulment, we remained in Scotland, lying low until we read in a newspaper that Baron Barton had chosen another bride. Lily knows the lady, a girl of seventeen in her first Season.

"Lily wrote to beg her parents' forgiveness and explain her reasons, didn't you, sweetheart?"

"As soon as we were married," Lily said. "I expected nothing from my stepfather, but I thought Mama might have forgiven me." She sighed. "If she'd really cared about me, she would never have wanted me to marry Bolton."

"We hoped that once they heard about the baron's health, they might forgive Lily, but as time passes, it seems unlikely."

"I don't care," Lily said. "All that matters is Bret and I are together."

Bret smiled. "We are thrilled with your generous offer, Tate."

"I am in dire need of an efficient secretary," Tate said. "Someone I can trust. Especially after the experience I had with Lynch."

"We shall have to find accommodation in the village," Bret said, rubbing his hands. "I can't wait to begin."

"There's a pile of correspondence awaiting your expertise," Tate said, his grin tinged with relief. "I want to show you more of Cloudhill. When the ladies have changed into their habits, shall we ride to the village?"

The air was crisp. The trees were breathtaking in their autumn splendor. A damp, pungent smell rose from the carpet of fallen leaves stirred up by the horse's hooves. Some trees were stripped of their leaves, skeletal, heralding the onset of winter.

Riding Freckles, Ianthe reined in beside him and they shared an intimate smile, which made him recall their earlier lovemaking with a surge of pleasure.

On the outskirts of the village, they reined in beside a thatched roof, whitewashed cottage surrounded by a picket fence.

"How charming. Who lives here?" Lily asked.

Ianthe shook her head and smiled. She had been thrilled when Tate had told her of his intention.

They dismounted and Tate opened the gate, stepping up to the door.

The others followed, glancing at each other when, without knocking, Tate opened it. He stood aside for Bret and Lily to enter through the door. "Welcome to your new home. A gift from us."

Lily squealed and hurried inside followed by Ianthe.

As the women rushed about, commenting on each room, and climbing the narrow stairs to the two bedchambers above, Bret remained beside Tate on the small porch. "I cannot allow you to do this."

"Of course you can." Tate shrugged. "Should I leave the

cottage empty because of your foolish pride?"

Bret shook his head. "You have me at a loss."

"And, after all, there's a good chance we share ancestors in the past."

"Then I suspect mine came from the wrong side of the blanket," Bret said with a laugh.

"We should investigate that further in the future." Tate grinned as another cry of joy emerged from the interior. "So, do you agree?"

His throat working, Bret nodded. Deep emotion darkened his eyes, but he merely slapped Tate on the back before he went to join Lily.

Ianthe emerged and came over to him. On tiptoe, she stroked Tate's cheek and pressed a kiss onto his lips. "I've married a wonderful man. You will be an excellent father."

Tate drew her away, his eyes asking questions he couldn't bring himself to voice.

She smiled. "I didn't plan to tell you until I was sure."

"Sweetheart!" Tate gathered her into his embrace and held her, his hand on her hair. "Should you be riding?"

She pulled away and frowned at him. "You couldn't order me not to, Tate, when I was twelve, and certainly cannot now."

He laughed. "I enjoy a good argument."

"You just like the making up part." There was amusement in her gaze, but caution too.

"I do. But beware, before much longer, I am determined to win this one."

She shook her head at him.

Tate grinned and bent to kiss her cheek. "A baby. Imagine our mothers' delight at the chance to offer sage advice."

She laughed. "I foresee some disagreements between them."

As THEY RODE home, Ianthe smiled over at her handsome husband riding Bayard. Except in the bedchamber when he was just the gentle, passionate man she dearly loved, Tate had a commanding presence. He had taken his place in the House of Lords when parliament reconvened, and their portraits in their robes hung in the great hall at Cloudhill.

Their family was enlarging. They'd heard Clara was increasing again. And Cecily had given Gerald his heir. The viscount was apparently over the moon. Cecily believed she was now in a splendid position to insist they didn't spend the shooting season with his parents. *Choose your moment to make your demands, Ianthe,* her sister had written in one of her frequent letters. *When you know you have a good chance of winning.*

Ianthe doubted she'd have the patience. She was always too impulsive. She thought about the advice her mother had given her; how a man liked a peaceful home, and it was a woman's job to keep it so. But Grandmama's advice differed. In her last letter, she mentioned her own marriage, which had been a love match. A good husband, she wrote, whether or not he admitted it, preferred his wife to have a mind of her own, and to take part in important decisions. Even to take him to task when necessary. Grandmama was very modern in her thinking. Ianthe was confident she and Tate would have such a marriage.

Bret and Lily rode side by side, their conversation ranging from the color they would paint the parlor to acquiring a cow, a goat, ducks, and chickens.

"It's time for afternoon tea," Ianthe called, impatient to get home. She was always hungry these days. "Shall we gallop?"

"No, we shall not," came her husband's stern reply.

"I will give you the last word this time, Your Grace. But don't take that as a precedent."

Ianthe smiled as they cantered toward home.

ABOUT THE AUTHOR

A USA TODAY bestselling author of Regency romances, with over 35 books published, Maggi's Regency series are International bestsellers. Stay tuned for Maggi's latest Regency series out next year. Her novels include Victorian mysteries, contemporary romantic suspense and young adult. Maggi holds a BA in English and Master of Arts Degree in Creative Writing. She supports the RSPCA and animals often feature in her books.

Like to keep abreast of my latest news? Join my newsletter.
http://bit.ly/1m70lJJ

Blog: http://bit.ly/1t7B5dx
Find excerpts and reviews on my website: http://bit.ly/1m70lJJ
Twitter: @maggiandersen: http://bit.ly/1Aq8eHg
Facebook: Maggi Andersen Author: http://on.fb.me/1KiyP9g
Goodreads: http://bit.ly/1TApe0A
Pinterest: https://www.pinterest.com.au/maggiandersen

Maggi's Amazon page for her books with Dragonblade Publishing.
https://tinyurl.com/y34dmquj

CPSIA information can be obtained
at www.ICGtesting.com
Printed in the USA
BVHW051417050523
663655BV00011B/838